ALSO BY SHAWN K. STOUT

Penelope Crumb

Penelope Crumb Never Forgets

Penelope Crumb Finds Her Luck

Penelope Crumb Is Mad at the Moon

Shawn K. Stout

a tiny piece of sky

PHILOMEL BOOKS

PHILOMEL BOOKS
an imprint of Penguin Random House LLC
375 Hudson Street, New York, NY 10014

Copyright © 2016 by Shawn K. Stout.
Penguin supports copyright. Copyright fuels creativity, encourages diverse
voices, promotes free speech, and creates a vibrant culture. Thank you for
buying an authorized edition of this book and for complying with copyright laws
by not reproducing, scanning, or distributing any part of it in any form without
permission. You are supporting writers and allowing Penguin to continue to
publish books for every reader.
Philomel Books is a registered trademark of Penguin Random House LLC.
Library of Congress Cataloging-in-Publication Data is available upon request.
Library of Congress Cataloging-in-Publication Data
Stout, Shawn K.
A tiny piece of sky / Shawn K. Stout.
pages cm   Summary: In 1939 Hagerstown, Maryland, eleven-year-old Frankie
faces suspicion that her German-born father is a Nazi spy.
[1. Family life—Maryland—Fiction. 2. Fathers and daughters—Fiction.
3. German Americans—Fiction. 4. Prejudices—Fiction. 5. Hagerstown (Md.)—
History—20th century—Fiction.] I. Title. PZ7.S88838Ti 2016
[Fic]—dc23 2015008567 Printed in the United States of America.
ISBN 978-0-399-17343-1
1 3 5 7 9 10 8 6 4 2
Edited by Jill Santopolo.   Design by Semadar Megged.
Text set in 11/17-point Electra LT.

For the three Beck girls

"It is a long journey, through a country that is sometimes pleasant and sometimes dark and terrible."

—The Witch of the North,
from *The Wonderful Wizard of Oz* by L. Frank Baum

Some Words, First

A summer spent without a favorite sister could not be called a *summer at all.* This was a firm belief held dear to the two Baum sisters. Well, that's not exactly true. It was a firm belief held dear to *one* Baum sister: Frankie Baum. As Joan, the just-barely-older of the two, was about to spend the summer months with their aunt Dottie by the lake in rural Pennsylvania, Frankie would be left behind in their small apartment in Hagerstown with nothing to do but add to her scab collection. And honestly, what good was collecting scabs if you didn't have anyone around to admire them?

And speaking of being honest, Joan was not very. Not really and truly. Sure, Joan was unhappy about going away from her favorite sister for these many months, but just because the two would be separated didn't mean she was going to declare that it was going to be no summer at all. Heavens, no. There was a lake at Aunt Dottie's, let us not forget. Besides, Joan would have her own room at Aunt Dottie's, in particular her own bed, and that excited her even more than the lake. But Joan, who was quite sensitive to others' feelings and who could call up a fresh batch of tears just as easily as her favorite actress, Shirley Temple, made a point of adding some gloom to her appearance so as not to cause her beloved younger sister any further distress.

There was enough distress in the world these days, anyway. Trouble was brewing overseas, a continent away. The kind of trouble that Frankie and Joan didn't really understand, but from Mother and Daddy's whisperings of war, of the Germans, and, yes, of death, they felt something awful was coming, like a shadow that was going to one day, perhaps soon, reach across the ocean and block out the sun.

Are you frightened? You should be. War is a terrible thing. But let's not get ahead of ourselves. The war has not yet begun, not officially. There are other troubles to speak of first, serious ones that lay heavy on the heart. And so, our story begins with a good-bye.

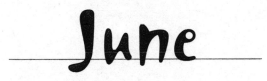

June

1

ACCORDING TO FRANKIE MARIE Baum, being Number Three in the family was a lot like Mr. Wexler's fried pork and sauerkraut sandwiches. They both left an awful taste in her mouth.

Oh, pardon the interruption, and right at the start of the story, too. You now must be wondering how Frankie Baum is Number Three when only *two* sisters have been mentioned thus far, Frankie and Joan. There was indeed another sister, the eldest one, Elizabeth. She was often called Princess by Mother and Daddy and was practically without a fault, at least to their eyes, which may help you to understand why she was not mentioned before now. There, that's taken care of. Those were the *three* Baum girls: Elizabeth, Joan, and Frankie, in that order. Now back to the story.

"Number Threes aren't so bad," Joan told Frankie. The two were sitting together on the side porch of the Baums' first-floor apartment.

"Prove it," said Frankie, folding her arms across her chest. Joan was a Number Two, after all, and there was a mighty big difference between a Number Two and a Number Three. You might not have known it to look at them, but Frankie swore there was.

Joan thought for a moment while Frankie waited, poking her in the ribs every now and then, until she came up with some examples—three, actually—to serve as proof: "Okay, I've got it," said Joan, pointing her finger up at the tiny piece of sky that was visible above the alleyway between their building and the one next door. "Third time's the charm."

Frankie shook her head. "That's one of Mother's." She wasn't a believer in Mother's superstitions and she had never seen herself as charmed. She fingered her skate key around her neck. "What else?"

"The Holy Trinity," said Joan, matter-of-factly.

Frankie nodded. There was no debating that one.

"And," said Joan, giving her sister a gentle nudge with her elbow, "there's Judy Garland. She's the youngest of the three Gumm sisters, you know. Just like you."

Frankie knew what she was doing. Joan always tried to make her feel better, usually by bringing up Judy Garland, the singer and actress Frankie most admired. Much of the time it worked. But not today. Frankie didn't look at her. She just ran her fingernail along the chipped paint of the iron porch railing and watched the specks fall like black pepper to the concrete below.

Joan tried again. "I'm only going to be gone until August, Frankie. Just like Elizabeth was last time. And next year, it'll be your turn to spend the summer with Aunt Dottie."

Frankie shrugged. Always the last to do everything. For once, she wanted to have a go at being first. That's Just Not How the World Works was what Mother said whenever Frankie asked why she couldn't do something before Elizabeth and Joan. Not fair was what she said in return, which wasn't much of an answer, but who was she to change the world?

"Anyway," Joan said, "you'll be having so much fun right here that I'd bet you ten cents you won't even miss me."

Frankie rolled her eyes and muttered, "I swear."

"Don't you let Mother hear you say *swear* while I'm away," Joan said, giving Frankie's arm a pinch. Joan was twelve. Only one year, three months, and five days older than Frankie, but Frankie swore sometimes she acted more and more like Elizabeth. That was a Number Two for you, always ready to take over the Number One spot.

Frankie looked right at her. "But you're leaving me alone with Mother and Daddy and boring old Elizabeth, who'd rather have her nose in a book than race me down to Wexler's Five and Dime on skates. What fun will there be?"

Joan gazed up at the sky, way above the chimney tops, as if the answers of the summer, and maybe of the world, might be floating around somewhere up there. While she was looking, she couldn't help but let her mind drift to wide open spaces, and Aunt Dottie's lake, and about how soon she might hoist herself upon a raft and float on it. Float and float and float away.

She floated for quite a while, too. Or her thoughts did, anyway. Right up there with the clouds. Joan was really good at thinking about what could be and forgetting about what *was*. Frankie was just the opposite. "Joanie!" Frankie said, knocking her own knee against her sister's.

"What?" It took Joan a few moments to realize she was still there, sitting under the roof of their side porch, lakeless. It took her a few moments more to realize she was smiling. (The confused look on Frankie's face, followed by disappointment, gave it away.) And it took her only a few moments after that to quickly pinch the skin on her calf, just under the hem of her cotton dress, hard enough to make her eyes full. Shirley Temple certainly would've been proud.

"Never mind." Frankie wanted to tell Joan that she hated her for leaving. She wanted to. But she didn't. Joan's big green eyes, same as Grandma Engel's, cooled Frankie's fiery mood like a bed of grass under hot bare feet. So Frankie spit on her hand and stuck it out. "You're betting ten cents that I won't miss you?"

Joan eyed Frankie's hand. She nodded. "Ten cents." Then she spit on her own hand and they shook.

Frankie knew darn well that she would win it, Joan wouldn't pay it, and Frankie wouldn't take it even if she did. Joan grinned and then wiped her hand on her dress. She knew it, too.

Daddy's car growled to a start in the garage behind the apartment and Frankie knew he'd be out front to fetch Joan any minute. Frankie's stomach felt like she'd eaten a pound of raw potatoes.

"I better go get my suitcase. Daddy wants to be back before supper." Joan sprang to her feet and pulled open the screen door. Before ducking into the kitchen, she asked, "You're gonna see me off, aren't you, Frankie?"

Frankie looked away, squeezing her skate key tight in her hand, and then nodded.

The door slammed shut and Frankie wiped her eyes on her dress sleeve. Inside, she could hear their two cousins, Ava and Martha. "Where's Frankie?" they asked Mother, then Grandma Engel, then Elizabeth. Frankie didn't know why, but right then she didn't want to be found. So she crawled into her secret hiding spot between Mother's wringer washer and a stack of milk crates. And just listened.

Ava and Martha called her name over and over again until Frankie could hear Mother tell them that they were wearing at her nerves and to take their search party outdoors. The screen door creaked open and slammed shut. Footsteps wandered around the porch and then stopped real close by. Frankie peered through a crack in a milk crate stacked three high, but it was as dark as a can of Daddy's Shinola shoe polish.

Frankie stayed real quiet, and she could hear whispers and giggles and heavy breathing. Frankie wished she could see who was with them. Only Joan and Bismarck knew about her hiding spot, and Joan wouldn't dare tell.

Something nudged the crates and whimpered. And then Frankie knew the identity of the fink who had betrayed her. "Shh, Bismarck," Frankie whispered. "Shoo."

But that only made him more excited, and he started barking and whining. So Frankie had to give up before everybody came complaining about the noise and found her secret place. She slid the milk crates away until there was enough room for her to crawl out. When Bismarck saw Frankie, he barked and licked her face like he'd just dug up the moon after years of forgetting where he had buried it.

"Good dog," said Ava, scratching behind his ears. She pulled a piece of bologna from her dress pocket, tore off a chunk, and gave it to him. Ava was just a year younger than Frankie but a good deal shorter and more stout. She was bossy, to the point of rudeness, and spent most of the time in some sort of punishment or another. The only outcome of these punishments, which were intended for reformation and rehabilitation, was that Ava emerged even more of a conniver, fiendishly plotting her next offense to top the one that came before. Don't let the mop of curls on her head fool you; Ava was well on her way to becoming a criminal mastermind.

"Traitor," Frankie said, giving Bismarck a sideways glare. "I should have known you could be swayed to the other side by cold cuts."

"Let me have a bite," said Martha, who was wearing this morning's breakfast on her chin and dress: some type of red jam and a dribbling of soft-boiled eggs. Martha was seven, an accomplice-in-training.

Ava raised her eyebrows and said, "Only if you do a trick first."

"Like what?"

Ava winked at Frankie and then said, "Martha, go find Joanie."

"All right," said Martha, looking as eager as Bismarck. She raced back into the apartment. But before the screen door smacked closed, Ava tossed the rest of the bologna into Bismarck's open mouth.

"Don't worry," Ava told Frankie. "Your secret hiding place is safe with me."

"What about Martha?"

"Oh, don't worry about her," she said. "That's what's good about having a little sister. They do whatever you tell them."

Daddy's car horn tooted twice, and Frankie left Ava and took off up the alley. Bismarck passed Frankie before she got to the corner of the building.

When Frankie reached the street, Daddy was opening the door to his blue Studebaker. Bismarck jumped in the back. "Not this time, boy," said Daddy. He snapped his fingers and Bismarck leaped out. That shepherd dog was smarter than most people you came across in an average day, Daddy always said. And it was true. He had found Bismarck in a ditch alongside a Texas road, on one of his business trips. The pup had been no more than a few weeks old, and there was something about his eyes, Daddy had said, how they looked closer to human than animal, and how they watched Daddy as he spoke, intent on every word, as if Bismarck seemed not only to hear but *understand*.

Unable to leave him behind, Daddy stowed the pup in his carrying case and brought him home for Mother. Daddy was always doing things like that, hoping that one day Mother would learn to like surprises.

"Joan, let's get this show on the road," said Daddy, leaning his hand against the back window of the car.

"Patience now, Hermann," said Mother. She, Joan, Grandma Engel, and Elizabeth were in a huddle on the front stoop, and although Frankie couldn't hear what Mother was saying, she'd bet a nickel that Mother was reminding Joan for the umpteenth time to mind Aunt Dottie and be polite and help with chores and, most of all, not get into trouble.

When they finished, Daddy took the suitcase from Joan. She jumped off the stoop and then hurried over to Frankie. "Don't let Bismarck get too used to my side of the bed," Joan said. "And don't let Ava use my skates. She'll break them."

"All right."

"And remember the right way to hook up Dixie to the cart if you take her out."

Frankie nodded. "I know, I know, she's my pony, too."

Joan went on. "And give her enough hay and fresh water. Not too many oats. It makes her lazy. And don't forget to practice your skin-the-cats on the—"

"Stop bossing me so," Frankie told her.

Joan pinched Frankie's arm and grinned. Frankie pinched her back.

When Daddy pulled away from the curb, Frankie waved once. Then she looked away so she didn't have to watch Joan disappear down Antietam Street.

2

JOAN WAS STILL THINKING of lakes and floating bubbles and other fanciful, up-in-the-air things while Daddy steered the 1937 Studebaker Dictator through town. They passed Wexler's Five and Dime on Locust Street and Inkletter's Drug Store on Franklin Street, and then turned left onto North Potomac. Daddy held up his hand to his good friend Mr. Mueller, who was sweeping the sidewalk in front of his spirit shop.

"I need to make one stop before we head out of town," said Daddy, slowing to the curb. "I'll only be a minute."

Daddy set the brake and got out of the car, leaving the engine running. He shook hands with Mr. Mueller, who was known by the Baums and to a few others simply as Fritz. Why? No one knows; that's just what people called him, so that's all the explanation you are bound to receive.

Daddy patted him on the back. Daddy was a good bit shorter, the top of his dark hair coming up only to Fritz's shoulder, and Fritz was not what anyone would describe as tall. At least not anyone who had a proper sense of height, or good vision. Besides, at the top of any list describing Fritz would have been his balding head and double chin. After exchanging a few quiet words, Daddy gave a nod at Joan, and the two men disappeared inside the store.

Joan rested her head on her arms on the open window and waited. As the sun warmed her face, she let her eyelids fall closed. She took in the sounds of the street—the clunking of the occasional car that motored by, the quiet whir of a passerby on a steel-frame bicycle, the *sproing* of pogo sticks. She opened her eyes when she heard the latter. Two girls she knew from school, Mary and Agnes Mills, bounced in unison down the block. And then, for a reason she couldn't quite explain, Joan thought of Frankie and felt a pull in the pit of her stomach to go back home.

All that was familiar to her, the people and the places, everything that she had always known, Joan was just now realizing, would be away from her for three long months and replaced by things Strange and Unfamiliar, and quite possibly Frightening. How well did she know Aunt Dottie, anyhow? Not very well, if you wanted to know the truth. Aunt Dottie was Daddy's older sister, and Joan hadn't spent much time with her outside of Christmas and Thanksgiving and Easter suppers, to which Aunt Dottie always brought a dish of egg custard. Sure, the egg custard was deliciously sweet, but there was a lot more to a person, Joan believed, than just creamy desserts.

And what about that lake? People drowned in lakes often enough, didn't they? Although Joan knew how to swim—she and her sisters had all had private lessons at the Alfred M. Bunkling Municipal Swimming Pool—she had never swum in a lake before, and now that she thought about it, didn't fish live in lakes? Hungry ones with razor-sharp teeth? Oh me, oh my, oh dear.

Just as a feeling started to come over her, such a feeling that involved a dizzy head and a good deal of sweat in her armpits, a feeling that could be called Terror by those who were familiar with the sensation, she saw Leroy Price and his younger brother Marty standing in front of Daddy's car.

"Look at that," said Leroy, rapping his knuckles over the metal bird-in-flight ornament that crowned the Studebaker's long, sloping hood. "Pretty fancy." He elbowed his brother in the gut, prompting him to say "Uuf," because of the elbow, and then "Yeah, fancy," afterward.

"Probably costs a pretty penny, too," said Leroy. "A Studebaker Dictator. My father says he would never buy a Studebaker Dictator, not unless he was a supporter of Hitler."

Hitler! Joan gritted her teeth and then craned her neck out of the car window. "My daddy is going to be out here any minute now, so you better get going, Leroy."

"Come on," said Marty, in a quiet voice. He pulled at Leroy's shirtsleeve.

"Naw," said Leroy, shaking Marty loose. "I bet it's got a radio, too." He walked around to the driver's side of the car and pressed his face up to the window. "Heck, I told you. Look, there it is, right there."

Joan felt her face flush at all the fuss Leroy Price was making over Daddy's car. Modesty was impressed upon the Baum girls with as equal weight as reading and good penmanship, and it made Joan feel uncomfortable to be singled out for something she had that others didn't. Although there was some admiration in Leroy's voice for the car and the radio, there was something else, too, an accusation perhaps, that Joan didn't recognize. But she knew she didn't like it. "Go on," she said, swatting the window from her seat. "I don't think my daddy would appreciate you pawing all over his car. Don't you have something better to do?"

Marty pulled again at Leroy's arm. "Let's go."

Leroy slipped out of his grasp and puffed up his chest. Then he grinned, showing his crooked teeth, and said, "I'm not afraid of that *German*."

Joan gasped. "What did you say?"

"Your daddy is a German," he said slowly, letting each word sink in.

The last word made Joan wince. She brought her hand to her mouth.

Leroy Price watched her and waited. Boys like Leroy wanted nothing more than to see you cry. But Leroy Price did not get to see Joan cry that day, no sir, he absolutely did not. Why? Because at that precise moment, Daddy and Fritz came out of the shop. Daddy smiled at the boys and called them by name, for he knew of the Price boys, in particular their father, Sullen Waterford Price, Esquire, who was president of the Hagerstown Chamber of Commerce. Mr. Price had recently announced his bid for mayor in the upcoming city-wide election, and had papered the town's storefronts with campaign signs and banners bearing the slogan THE PRICE IS RIGHT WITH SULLY W. PRICE! There was even one hanging in the window of Fritz's spirit shop, just above Daddy's shoulder.

Upon Daddy's greeting and steady gaze, all Leroy Price could do was back away from the car and shrug. And when he did, his shoulders stayed up by his ears for some reason, like they were frozen in place, which made his neck sort of shrink. And when Daddy raised his hand and yelled, "So long, boys!" Leroy turned and ran, with Marty lumbering behind.

"Strange," said Daddy as he climbed into the car. He placed a square package wrapped in brown paper on the backseat. "What was that all about?"

"I don't know," Joan said quietly. She kept her eyes on her bare knees peeking out from under her dress hem. Joan knew that Daddy's parents, Otto and Beate Baum, whom she'd never met, were from Bavaria. But Daddy, Aunt Dottie, and Uncle Reinhart were raised right here in America. So that didn't make him a *real* German, did it? Not the kind that she'd heard people talking about, anyway. Right?

"Well," said Daddy, "are we ready?"

Joan cleared her throat and tried to sweep Leroy Price from her thoughts. What did Leroy Price know, anyway? She nodded and said that yes, she was ready. As ready as she ever would be.

Daddy released the brake and off they motored, heading north to Pennsylvania. He pressed the buttons on the Motorola radio until they heard singing voices on the advertisement of Continental Baking's Wonder Bread: *Yo-Ho! Yo-Ho! Yo-Ho! We are the bakers who mix the dough and make the bread in an oven slow!*

"Can we listen to *Pretty Kitty Kelly?*" asked Joan, hoping that the drama of her favorite soap opera would help make the trip seem shorter.

"Pretty Kitty who?" said Daddy.

"You know, Pretty Kitty Kelly. She's the Irish girl who comes to America but has amnesia and doesn't know that she's really the Countess of Glennannan."

"Amnesia?"

"Yes, Daddy," said Joan. "That means she can't remember that she's sort of royalty and doesn't know she's not supposed to pal around with regular people."

"Of course it does," said Daddy, smiling.

"Last week, Kyron Welby, that's her cousin, tracked her down. She was engaged to him before she lost her memory, you know. I'm not sure what the police inspector thinks of that. She's gotten quite friendly with him lately."

"Has she, now?" said Daddy.

Joan nodded. "Yes, and he's so much better for her than that Welby person. Did people really used to marry their cousins? Elizabeth says that people who marry their cousins have babies with eleven fingers or no tongues. Is that true?"

Daddy gave Joan a sideways glance and told her that he didn't think he could stomach this conversation or a soap opera for the length of the trip, unless the latter starred John Wayne. And so he came up with a compromise: the Arrow News Show broadcast from Baltimore for the first thirty minutes, and then any music program of Joan's choosing for the remainder of the drive. Joan agreed, and although normally she would have blocked out the news events of the world with daydreams or the passing scenery, this time, after what Leroy had said, she couldn't help but listen with a keen ear.

3

SUNDAY MORNINGS MEANT TWO things for Frankie Baum: *Flash Gordon* and church. One she couldn't wait for, and the other, to be honest, she couldn't wait for to be over. It wasn't that she minded the idea of church so much, but she could have done without all the fuss Mother made about getting gussied up with hair ribbons and petticoats. And then there was all the sitting and thinking about all the bad things you've done over the course of the week before. For goodness' sakes, an hour was a long time to try to remember those kinds of things. Frankie could usually remember eight or nine at most, but after she said sorry to God for those, she often spent the rest of the hour inventing some more, you know, just to fill the time. Boy oh boy, could she make up some doozies.

"You two get yourselves cleaned up for church," Mother said to Frankie and Elizabeth as she cleared away the breakfast dishes. "Since you're singing today, your white eyelet dresses with the pink sashes would do nice."

Frankie was deep in the Sunday funnies with Flash, Dale, and Dr. Zarkov on their latest adventure with Fria, the Snow Queen of Frigia. It was only a matter of time till Flash Gordon would go up against Ming the Merciless once again. And when you're that deep in the planet Mongo, you don't hear your mother talking about singing at church.

"The famous Baum girls," said Daddy, smiling at Elizabeth and Frankie over his newspaper. "Well, two-thirds of them."

"Mother, aren't I too old to be dressing like her?" asked Elizabeth. She kicked Frankie under the table. "I'm nearly fourteen, you know."

"Ow!" Frankie dropped her newspaper. "What did you do that for?"

"You better come in at the right time," said Elizabeth. "Last time you were two beats late."

"Wait, we're singing?" said Frankie. "How can we sing without Joan?"

"Same as you do with her, I'd gather," said Mother. She had her back to the kitchen table as she poured from the box of powdered soap into the porcelain sink and turned on the hot spigot.

"But Joan's got the voice," Frankie said. "She always sings the main parts; we just fill in the rest behind her. Who's going to sing the main part, I want to know, because without Joan we stink."

"Speak for yourself," said Elizabeth. "Robbie McIntyre thinks I sing like Judy Garland."

"Robbie McIntyre has a brain like a—"

"Frances Marie," said Daddy, laying the newspaper on the table. "You and Princess have fine voices. And besides, the Good Lord does not care what your voices sound like, or for that matter the size of your brain, as long as you put your heart into it." He winked at Frankie. "And the Baum girls have got stout hearts."

Well, the Good Lord may not care if they sounded like a couple of sick crows, Frankie thought, but she happened to know that the people sitting in the pews at St. John's Lutheran would think different.

Frankie knew she'd been right about that after she saw the look on Reverend Martin's face when he greeted the Baums at the church door and asked Mother and Daddy of Joan's whereabouts. "She's spending the summer with her Aunt Dottie in Pennsylvania," Mother explained. "Been gone four days now." Mother poked Frankie in the back to stop tugging at her petticoat, which was tickling her bare legs.

"Oh, I see," said the reverend. "How nice." He looked at Elizabeth and then at Frankie and then at Daddy. "So, just Elizabeth and Frances will be singing for us today?"

Frankie wished right then and there that she could bottle the look on the reverend's face and mail it to Joan so she could see. He might as well have swallowed a spoonful of castor oil. Daddy put his arms around Elizabeth's and Frankie's shoulders. "That's right," he said.

"How nice," said Reverend Martin again, clearing his throat. "And they'll be singing . . ." He paged through the printed program he had tucked inside his Bible.

"'How Great Thou Art,'" said Mother. It was one of her most favorite hymns. Frankie couldn't think of a worse hymn to sing without Joan, because this one had a mess of high notes. Frankie hated the high notes and most of the time just skipped over them and let Joan take them on. Mother poked Frankie again and she stopped scratching at the back of her legs.

Reverend Martin nodded and smiled, but Frankie noticed that he was blinking an awful lot. Which Frankie knew was something people did when they were nervous or weren't telling the truth. Like the time Reverend Martin found a Toby Wing pinup stuck in the altar book in the middle of Sunday service. He had held it up in front of the entire congregation and asked the owner to come forward to claim it and beg the Lord for forgiveness, but no one budged an inch in their pews. The reverend barely held the picture by its very corner so as to not have his fingers touch any part of Miss Wing, who was wearing nothing but sparkly shorts and a bathing suit top made from a single piece of Christmas ribbon.

Reverend Martin's eyelids fluttered like butterfly wings the whole time. And as he waved the picture around, the temperature in the sanctuary seemed to go up ten degrees. Frankie, along with Joan, Ava, and Martha, could tell that every boy in the entire place was sweating. "That's the hellfire, most likely," Ava whispered to Martha, who then assumed they were all about to burn and immediately began to bawl.

In the middle of all that heat, Robbie McIntyre's eyelids were blinking rapid-fire. Everybody between eleven and fifteen years of age knew the pinup belonged to Robbie, had seen him the night before at choir practice bragging about it and offering a peek for a penny. He'd nearly been caught by Miss Fisk, the church organist, and so he hid it in the altar book and forgot to get it afterward. But he would never admit to it. Never in a hundred years.

That blinking, though, sure as the sun will rise, spelled G-U-I-L-T-Y.

Now Mother and Daddy ushered the girls to the sanctuary, and they sat in their regular pew in the first row. Daddy always said that on Sunday mornings he wanted to get as close to God as he could without crossing Heaven's gates. But Frankie and Joan knew that it was because he only had one good eye—the other being made of glass—and he wanted to sit up front so he didn't miss anything. You see, when Hermann Baum was a boy, he and his friend Charlie Lohman were playing with pocketknives, as young boys back in those days often did. They practiced throwing the knives at tree trunks to see whose blade would stick fast in the bark. They sharpened their blades on fieldstones and tried to see whose knife could saw through the most black locust saplings in ten seconds. Hermann's record was eight saplings, but he knew he had it in him to cut through eleven or twelve.

One afternoon, after they'd cut through a handful of saplings from Charlie Lohman's backyard and whittled them into spears for throwing at each other, young Hermann thought of a new game. "Toss your knife in the air and try to catch it one-handed," he told Charlie. Hermann flipped his pocketknife a few inches into the air and as the blade fell, he pulled his hand out of the way before it nicked his skin. He tried it again, this time catching the knife rather clumsily by the smooth, wooden inlay handle.

Charlie, not the sort of boy to be outdone, grinned and tossed his knife up higher, so that the blade surpassed the top of his head by at least a foot. He grabbed the handle with ease on its way down. "Beat that," he told Hermann.

Hermann sucked in air through his teeth and dried his palms on his pants. Then, after counting to three, he let go of the knife with enough force to send it high above his head. As he tilted his head back to gauge the blade's trajectory, the sun came into his eyes for a few unfortunate moments.

Remember this, boys and girls: it only takes a few seconds to lose something.

Hermann wore an eye patch for a couple of months after and then was fitted for a glass eye the color of an emerald, which was close, but not an exact match, to his real eye. His glass eye wasn't immediately noticeable to others if they didn't know to look for it— but because the iris didn't move in concert with the *good* eye and could "look" only straight ahead, never up or down or side to side, it became obvious soon enough.

While Elizabeth had her eyes on the program during the opening hymn, Frankie shifted in her seat to relieve herself from the increasing irritation caused by her petticoat. "When do we go on?"

Elizabeth pointed to the place in the program where it said "The Baum Girls." Right after Reverend Martin's homily and just before the offering. "Not until then?" Frankie said, because she really wanted to get this over with.

"Shh," said Elizabeth, and then she nodded at the hymnal to let Frankie know she should be singing and not talking. If they weren't in church right then, Frankie would've given her an earful about how Elizabeth wasn't the boss and should stop acting like she was. But instead, Frankie just stared at the paintings on the arched ceiling.

Reverend Martin's homily was about the troubles overseas and the Golden Rule. And he asked God to bless the people in Europe, in particular the Jewish people who were on a ship called the *St. Louis*, who were trying to get away from the Germans but were turned away from Cuba and then weren't permitted to come here. Reverend Martin also blessed President Roosevelt. And it made Frankie wonder why the president wasn't doing something more to help those people.

The reverend finally said "Amen," and that was Elizabeth and

Frankie's cue to take their places at the altar. Miss Fisk looked over the organ at them with raised eyebrows, and Elizabeth nodded at her. She started playing, and Frankie glanced nervously at all the people she knew. There was Mother and Daddy right there, smiling. Well, Daddy was smiling. Mother was watching with intense scrutiny. There was Mr. Wexler, a few pews back, nodding off. Behind him, Inky and Fritz, Daddy's best friends, all done up in vests and bow ties. Also Aunt Edith, Uncle Hal, Ava, and Martha. Ava was crossing her eyes and sticking fingers up both nostrils like a lunatic, trying to make Frankie laugh. And all the way to the right in the second row was Robbie McIntyre, staring absolutely bug-eyed at Elizabeth.

When Miss Fisk came to the end of the introduction, she looked up at Frankie and Elizabeth and started to mouth the first word, which happened to be "Oh," so they knew when to come in. *They knew when to come in.* That wasn't the problem. The problem was that when they did come in, they came in on notes that together produced a sound that was, well, *unnatural.* And the thing about singing is that when you started off in that sort of place, it was really hard to go anyplace else.

Still, it was nearly impossible to tell what people in church were really feeling, because you were not allowed to clap or holler. That was a rule that wasn't written down anywhere, but it was a rule that everybody knew and was expected to mind. You were also not allowed to wish you were someplace else or think about how much you'd like to kick Leroy Price in the shins for pulling your chair out from under you in the lunchroom. You had to be quiet and still and proper and for a whole hour think about God and about all the bad things you'd done, and sometimes even longer if there was communion.

Mother had her own set of rules about acting proper in church. She didn't even like her girls to sneeze or cough. Crying was permitted. As long as it was the quiet sort without sobs or mucus. Mother said that the Baum girls should always act like ladies—something Frankie didn't give a fig about.

Which is why it was particularly bad when, near the end of "How Great Thou Art," Frankie started to get an especially itchy feeling in her backside from the bunching of her petticoat. She shifted her feet and wiggled a little to shake it loose. When that made no difference, Frankie inched backward until she could feel the corner of the mahogany altar behind her. On a few trips through the countryside, you see, Frankie had watched cows use fence posts for scratching, which she thought looked to be quite effective. And so she positioned herself to give that a try. But as she did, Elizabeth turned around and shot Apache arrows from her eyes until she returned to her side.

Frankie made it three-quarters of the way through the next stanza before the itching was about to send her into madness. There was only one thing left to be done. Frankie looked at Mother as she sang "And take me home, what joy shall fill my heart," trying to tell her with her eyes how sorry she was for what she was about to do. Also, she said sorry to God just in case what she was about to do was a sin. Most things seemed to be.

Then with quiet desperation she promptly reached both hands up the back of her dress and grabbed at the miserable petticoat that was plaguing her rear end. She began to scratch at it furiously until she felt the most wonderful relief. So wonderful, in fact, that Frankie finished the last lines of the hymn—still scratching, mind you—with renewed vigor.

By the last chord, Miss Fisk was staring at Frankie with an open mouth and still holding down the organ keys with enough firmness that her fingertips had lost their color. Finally she released the organ keys, and when the very last note faded away into the high, arched ceiling, Ava, all red-faced from laughing, hollered, "Great snakes, Frankie!"

Then Mother fainted.

And Frankie thought, *Too bad Joan is in Pennsylvania, because she would have loved to see this.*

Dearly departed Joanie Baloney,

You've only been gone for four whole days and look what happens. Mother fainted at church. It was right at the end of "How Great Thou Art," which Elizabeth and me sang without dearly-departed-you. Daddy's reflexes are getting better because this time he caught her before she hit the floor. Reverend Martin splashed some holy water in her face. And that seemed to rouse her fine. Honest to goodness, I've never seen Elizabeth so red-faced!

Lo and behold, it wasn't because I scratched my behind while singing at God's altar. Mother said she didn't even see that! She said she fainted because she was full of worries on account of a big announcement that Daddy had to make. So right away I thought maybe we were going to have a new baby brother or sister because of how Eddie Milnick's mother fainted that time at the cinema, do you remember that? And sure enough a couple of weeks later Mrs. Milnick's stomach swelled up like a watermelon. Anyway, this is what I was thinking was wrong with Mother, and then how I wouldn't be stuck in the last spot anymore.

But then Mother told me to go round up Grandma Engel and Aunt Edith and everybody, and when we were all there in the kitchen waiting for Daddy to say we have to make room for little Shirley or Groucho, Daddy said, "We're going into the restaurant business." That's the big announcement. Daddy bought a restaurant across town and we're all going to have to work there, they said, until it's up and running. Except not you, because you're not here! It's no surprise that Elizabeth thinks it's a wonderful idea. She would never disagree with Mother or Daddy about anything, even if it means working at a restaurant all summer long and not having any amusement.

Do you see what happens when you go away? Bad things. Bad things happen, I'm telling you.

How are you getting along at Aunt Dottie's? Don't say a word if you're having a lot of fun because I don't want to know about that.

Your sister (who you've dearly departed) in Hagerstown who has to work in a restaurant and who misses you more-than-tongue-can-tell,

Frankie

4

"EVERYBODY PILE IN," said Daddy, holding open the door of the Studebaker.

Mother adjusted Grandma Engel's shift dress over her knees as she eased her fragile bones into the front seat. Mother, Elizabeth, and Frankie climbed into the back.

"We've got to be back by three," said Grandma Engel, smoothing her long white braid. "I've got a date with the Senators on the radio."

"We'll be back in time for the game, don't worry," Daddy assured her. "I just want you all to see the place." He barely turned the key before they were off down Antietam Street. As they made a sharp turn onto Locust Street, Mother and Frankie slid into Elizabeth and caused her to drop *Black Beauty*.

"Frankie, you made me lose my place," Elizabeth said.

"You've only read it a thousand times," Frankie told her, holding on to the top of the seat in front. She didn't understand how Elizabeth could read the same book over and over. The only book that Frankie ever read more than once was *The Wonderful Wizard of Oz*. It was a favorite of hers, not only because she shared the name of its author, but because Dorothy, a girl not so different from her, got to travel to a magical place and live there for a time. Only, Frankie never understood why Dorothy wanted to go back to gray old Kansas when Oz was so much more exciting. Every single solitary time, Frankie would have stayed with the Winkies.

"Hermann!" squealed Mother. "Slow down!"

"Let her rip!" shouted Grandma Engel, who was always looking for a thrill.

Daddy laughed and hit a bump in the road. Mother, Elizabeth, and Frankie bounced in their seats so high that Mother's head swept the roof of the car. "Hermann!"

"Thattaboy!" said Grandma Engel.

Daddy turned left down Jonathan Street and came to a stop in front of a building covered in dark brown shingles and wooden beams that made a crisscross pattern. "Here we are," he said, turning off the car.

Elizabeth, fumbling around with her book, was taking forever to open the door on her side, so Frankie climbed over her and did it herself. "Honestly, Frankie!" Elizabeth yelled, but Frankie was out the door and on the sidewalk before she could say anything else.

Frankie had seen this place before—she and Joan had been by it on their pony, Dixie, more than a few times on the way to the municipal pool—but it was the sort of place you noticed once, for its strange, dark exterior and its paper-covered windows, then forgot about thereafter. The building had been empty as long as Frankie could remember, but she knew that at some point in its lifetime it had been a restaurant, for black metal letters spelling, simply, RESTAURANT stretched from one end of the slate roof to the other.

"What do you think?" asked Daddy, pulling Grandma Engel to her feet onto the curb.

"Well," said Grandma, "at least it don't say 'Shoe Repair.' That would confuse people."

"It's brown," Frankie said. "Really brown."

"It's called *alpine-style*," Daddy said. "Just like in Bavaria."

"Don't you know anything, Frankie?" said Elizabeth, turning her back on Frankie and following Daddy to the front door.

Frankie extended her foot to give Elizabeth a push on her behind, but Mother promptly interfered, with a particularly strong grip of Frankie's arm that stopped her cold.

"It's been empty for a couple of years, so don't expect too much," said Daddy as he pulled a silver key from his vest pocket to unlock the door. He paused before turning the key and leaned his shoulder against the door.

"Are you all right?" asked Mother.

Daddy cleared his throat. "Of course. Just eager for you to see the place."

Frankie did wonder why the place had been empty for so long, but it was on the edge of the colored part of town, the last cross street before you got to the place where all the colored people had to live, and whether that had something to do with it, she didn't know. All she knew was that she and Joan and Elizabeth weren't permitted to go down Jonathan Street. And they never did.

As soon as Daddy turned the doorknob, Frankie pushed in front of Elizabeth so she could get inside first. While Daddy held open the door, Frankie squeezed by and caught a glimpse of the wide room, which she presumed was the dining room, before he let the door swing closed, leaving them all in the dark. She had seen a few wooden tables and overturned chairs scattered about, and a long wooden bar with a brass railing, and round metal stools with green cushions on the far left of the room. There was a musty smell, too. And dust, which was as thick as cotton and collected in her nose, making her sneeze.

"Gesundheit," said Daddy, clearing his throat. "Just a little polishing is needed here and there."

"More than a little, I'd wager," said Grandma Engel, coughing.

"Now," said Daddy, "nobody move until I get the lights."

Frankie took a step forward in the dark but ran directly into something solid. She rubbed her bare knee to soothe the ache and smiled when she felt a wet spot. She would soon have a new scab for her collection.

"Frances Marie," said Mother, sighing. "Be careful."

"Didn't you hear Daddy say not to move?" scolded Elizabeth.

Frankie stuck out her tongue, knowing full well that no one could see.

Moments later, two of the three chandeliers hanging from the white tin ceiling illuminated the room. "There we are," said Daddy. "A little light on the subject makes all the difference."

Indeed, it did. Mother gasped at the sight, covering her mouth with the back of her hand. Elizabeth put her arm around Mother's shoulders to steady her in case she went down again.

Grandma Engel said flatly, "What an enormous dump."

But Daddy's enthusiasm could not be dampened. "This will be the main dining area, but there's another, smaller dining area," he said, pointing to the back of the room, "through those doors. I was thinking we could rent out that room for private parties and such."

The room fell quiet, aside from the sizzling sort of hum that came from one of the miswired chandeliers, as everyone took in the room and its dilapidated state. All Frankie could think about was that this place—what did Grandma Engel call it?—this *enormous dump* was going to rob her of the whole summer. Lucky Joan, to have escaped just in time.

Mother still had Elizabeth holding tight to her arm when she finally found her voice. "Hermann," she said, "don't you think it's a bit too . . . you know . . . much?"

Daddy shook his head. "This room can seat seventy-five, but don't worry, we're not going to fill up the whole place with tables." He strode over to the corner at the end of the bar. "We've got to have room for the orchestra."

"An orchestra?" said Mother. "In a restaurant?"

"It would be just on weekends," said Daddy. Then he pointed to the balcony upstairs that overlooked the room. "And we'll have an organ up there so that during the week, customers can listen to music while they dine."

"An organ!" said Mother.

"I know 'Chopsticks,'" offered Frankie, who had already started thinking about which jobs in the restaurant were the best to have, and wanted to beat Elizabeth to them. Number Threes had to think a lot faster than Number Ones or they'd never get to do anything good. "Oh," she said, "and also 'When the Saints Go Marching In.'"

"We don't want to drive away the customers, Frankie," said Elizabeth, smirking.

"Sorry, Frankie," said Daddy with a wink, "I've already got somebody in mind for that job." He rapped the bar with his knuckles. "Anybody thirsty?"

"I'll have a Schmidt's," said Grandma Engel.

"Soon," Daddy said, "we'll have the biggest selection of beer in town."

Grandma Engel hoisted herself upon a bar stool and leaned her back against the bar. She swung her legs like a schoolgirl and pretended to open an invisible long-necked bottle. "Ahh!" she said after she took an imaginary swig. Then she wiped her mouth with the back of her thick, wrinkled arm.

Grandma Engel was Mother's mother, but the two couldn't have been more different. Grandma Engel was tall and stocky. She wore men's shoes, drank beer from the bottle, swore when it suited, and played penny poker on Sundays. Mother, simply, did not. Do not misunderstand, Mother had her share of fun. She played pinochle, went to the horse races, and listened to soap operas on the radio, but Mother didn't have Grandma Engel's flair for adventure. Adventure made Mother nervous. One could get injured in an adventure.

Frankie raced behind the bar and said, in her most grown-up voice, "Can I interest you in something else? Perhaps some eggs or corned beef hash?"

Grandma Engel replied, "Two eggs, over easy, if you please."

"Coming right up, ma'am," said Frankie, nodding. She grabbed a dusty tray from a shelf behind the bar and, gripping it with both hands, walked around the dining room delivering invisible plates to imaginary customers.

"That's not how you do it, Frankie," said Elizabeth. Only Elizabeth could find fault in pretending. She snatched the tray from Frankie's hands and positioned it higher up, using her shoulder as a pedestal. "Like this."

While the two sisters debated the proper way to waitress, the color in Mother's face was fading. "Hermann," she said, shaking her head.

Daddy was examining the unlit chandelier from directly below it and was preoccupied with the puzzle of its malfunction. He did not notice Mother calling for him, or her paleness.

"Hermann," she said again, louder and slightly more frantic.

Daddy stopped examining the chandelier and went to Mother's side. "I know it's not much to look at now," he said, pulling her close. "But just give me a couple of weeks and you won't recognize the place." She nodded, after a moment, and smiled. Daddy's arms could melt troubles away like nothing else. "Come, now," he said, giving her a squeeze. "Wait until you see the kitchen."

Frankie, Grandma Engel, Mother, and Elizabeth followed Daddy through a swinging door that squeaked like a lame mouse. And speaking of rodents, they would've felt quite at home there. Daddy switched on the lights. The kitchen, to be frank, was in worse shape than the dining room. Paint was hanging from the plaster walls in long peels, and the windows were missing glass. The gray tiled floor was dull and had a dark stain that covered a great deal of it and stuck to the soles of Frankie's leather sandals.

Butcher-block countertops filled most of the kitchen, and cushioned in the middle was a wide silver stove with a griddle longer than Frankie was tall. On the far wall were two white Frigidaires side by side, and next to them a row of gray cupboards, which—if they had doors on them—would be a perfect hiding spot.

"Well?" said Daddy. "Aside from a couple of small rooms upstairs for offices, and the lavatories, this is it." He looked from Mother to

Elizabeth to Grandma Engel to gauge a reaction. Then he wrung his hands and looked at Elizabeth and Frankie. "What do you say, Princess?"

Elizabeth hesitated. "Well, I mean . . ." She had always been characteristically agreeable to Mother and Daddy's intentions, but at that moment, amid the filth and threadbare conditions, she was caught between the two of them and wasn't sure what should be said.

Frankie, on the other hand, was beginning to feel sorry for her father, not to mention uncomfortable in the silence. *Was that the tiny paw steps of a rat she just heard?* So she gave her biggest grin and lied. "It's really keen."

Daddy's smile was full of relief. "It is, isn't it?" He pulled Frankie close and gave her a squeeze.

Elizabeth quickly recovered and inserted herself. "What are you going to name it?"

"Well," said Daddy, taking in a deep breath, "I was thinking of Baum's Restaurant."

"It don't matter what you call it as long as you've got a good cook and a bartender who knows how to make a rickey," said Grandma Engel, opening the door to one of the Frigidaires.

"Baum's," said Mother. "Really?"

Daddy nodded. "A family restaurant run by the Baum family. It will be a lot of hard work, Mildred, but I know we can turn this into something, together."

"Our own family restaurant," whispered Mother, as if for the first time she were trying the idea on for size. Before Daddy, Mother owned nothing except for a few housedresses and one pair of secondhand T-bar heels. She had quit school in the sixth grade so she could wash dishes at Mr. McGruder's restaurant and help out her family, who were, like a lot of families, quite underprivileged. Young Mildred Engel had hidden behind garbage cans on the way to Mr. McGruder's so the truant officer wouldn't catch her and force her to attend school. She earned twenty cents a day washing dishes and had to stand on a wooden crate to reach the sink. Keeping a nickel of each day's wages for herself, she gave the rest to Grandma Engel. In a few years, she worked her way up to waitstaff and even tended bar, but never did she imagine she would one day have a place of her own.

Daddy appraised the room. "I know that we can make this a place of wide renown."

Mother nodded and smiled, the color returning to her face.

There was something about Hermann's confidence, in everything that he did and dreamed of doing, that made others believe in him, no matter how strange his ideas. Just the year before, he had convinced Inky and Fritz to go in on a peanut farm in east Texas *and* a pineapple orchard in Missouri. This was during the Great Depression, remember, when money was scarce and finding and keeping work nearly impossible. Very few had extra money lying around in banks or stuffed under mattresses, and if they did, they were much too afraid to spend it. Especially on peanut farms and pineapple orchards. But Hermann was different. Not even President Roosevelt's Agricultural Adjustment Act of 1938, which called for a cut in farm production to increase farming prices, could deter him. In those troubled times, he still had hope—and Inky and Fritz, you could say, found his hope contagious.

5

MOTHER LIKED TO TEASE Daddy that his glass eye made him see the world in nothing but green. And perhaps he did.

6

AND SPEAKING OF SEEING the world in green, that's just how Sullen Waterford Price, Esquire, preferred to view it. As president of the Hagerstown Chamber of Commerce, a job which he undertook with immense conviction, Mr. Price made it a point to get to know all of the upstanding businessmen in town and inspire—though some might say *persuade*—them to become paid members of the chamber. Over his four-year term, he had collected more money from the memberships of local businesses than any of his last three predecessors combined. A record for which Mr. Price was very, very proud.

But amid his successful membership campaign, Mr. Price also had the reputation of determining whether the businesses in town met his own personal criteria of what it meant to be "upstanding." The word can mean different things to different people, you know, but to Sullen Price, it meant something very specific. What that was, only he knew for certain, and the rest of us could only guess.

But here's one thing you should know: The businessmen who had the misfortune of falling short of Mr. Price's criteria, let's just say, weren't businessmen for much longer.

A few years before, for example, a young man named George Robertson had opened a music shop on Potomac Avenue. It was a small, quaint store, on a single floor, the kind of shop where you could spend a day browsing sheet music if you could spend an hour. Mr. Robertson, a native of Chicago, had hopes of creating a Tin Pan Alley in town, a place where local musicians and performers could be discovered. After the shop opened for business, Mr. Robertson completed an application to become a member of the Chamber of Commerce, and promptly turned over his membership dues. But upon an interview with Mr. Price, who thought it his business to ask a number of things about Mr. Robertson's personal life—such things that had nothing at all to do with his music business, by the way—Mr. Price's opinion started to sour. Like spoiled cream.

Mr. Robertson endeavored to answer the questions truthfully, but even so, Mr. Price must not have liked what he heard, because two weeks later, his application to become a member of the Chamber of Commerce was denied. Three months after that, Mr. Robertson's music shop was out of business. Out of business!

How, you might ask, can one person in town have that much power? Well—Mr. Price might have asked, *How can one person get even* more *power?* In fact, that's exactly what he did ask. And now that his four-year term as president of the chamber was coming to an end just as the current mayor of Hagerstown, Lloyd Mitchell, announced plans to retire, he had his answer.

But it wasn't going to be as easy as all get-out. Because little did he know that George Robertson—yes, *that* George Robertson— would decide to oppose him in the race for mayor.

Oh, to have seen Mr. Price's face on that day. What a sight!

7

AFTER MORE THAN A week without Joan, Frankie was a sight to see as well. She felt her sister's absence in every room of their apartment. Everywhere she looked there were things that belonged to Joan, proof that she had lived there and was part of Frankie's life—her skate key, her Patsy doll with eyes that blinked, her jump rope—but no one to claim them as her own or to tell Frankie to be careful when she went to play with them. Joan was there, but she wasn't. To Frankie, it was like living with just the shadow of her sister.

And not hearing a word from Joan since she'd left certainly wasn't helping.

Frankie missed Joan no more so than in the evenings when they would huddle in front of the Philco radio in the living room and listen to their favorite program. This evening, though, while Elizabeth was reading on the porch and Mother and Daddy were in the kitchen, Grandma Engel joined Frankie just as the set was warming up. Frankie turned the dial until the familiar voice of the announcer crackled through the speakers, advertising Blue Coal. *"Ask for Blue Coal by name,"* he declared. *"It's the solid fuel for solid comfort."*

Indeed, solid comfort. It was eighty-nine degrees outside. Comfort would be swimming in an ice pond.

"The Shadow, a mysterious character who aids those in distress and helps the forces of law and order, is in reality Lamont Cranston, a wealthy young man about town. Cranston's friend and companion, the lovely Margo Lane, is the only person who knows to whom the unseen voice belongs. The only one who knows the true identity of that master of other people's minds—The Shadow. Today's story, 'Guest of Death.'"

"'Guest of Death,'" said Grandma Engel from her easy chair. "This sounds like a good one."

Frankie grinned and they both listened as the organ music began: *dum-da-da-di-dum-dum-doe-da-di-dum-DUM!*

"Does Aunt Dottie have a radio?" asked Frankie.

"I believe so."

"Good." Frankie closed her eyes and laid her hand on the rug beside her. "Then it's like she's here with us."

"Don't worry," said Grandma Engel. "I'm sure you'll hear from Joan soon. She just needs some time to settle in, is all."

"*Shh,*" said Frankie. She turned up the volume dial. "We're missing it."

"*Shh* yourself," said Grandma Engel.

Frankie smiled. That's just what Joan would've said.

8

ABOUT HALFWAY THROUGH THE program, just as the Shadow was about to cloud the mind of someone and find out what evil lurked in his heart, there was a knock at the Baums' door. Frankie at first thought it was coming from the Philco, and paid no attention. Grandma Engel was asleep in the chair and heard nothing.

But the knock came again, and this time louder. Frankie didn't want to miss her program, not when the guest of death had yet to be revealed, so she hollered, "Someone's at the door!"

"Who died?" said Grandma Engel, awaking from a dream with a spark. She looked around the room, trying to get her bearings, until she laid her eyes on Frankie, who could only shake her head and laugh. "Wait until you get old," said Grandma Engel. "Mark my words, you won't think it so funny."

Daddy appeared then, followed by Mother, on their way to the door. "My goodness," said Daddy, "that must be a gripping episode, seeing how the door is only—what would you say, Mildred? Five feet away?"

"Really, Frances," said Mother.

Daddy winked at Frankie and then opened the door just as the Shadow's ominous laugh seeped out from the radio—*heh-heh-heh-*

heh-heh. Frankie rubbed her bare arms, which had turned to goose-flesh.

In the open doorway stood Mr. Price, puffing on a fat cigar.

"Good evening," said Mr. Price, first removing his derby and then his cigar. "I'm sorry to bother you at home, but I stopped by your new place of business and must have just missed you." He peered into the living room. "I hope I'm not intruding, but I'd like to speak with you, Mr. Baum." He smiled at Mother. "About Chamber of Commerce matters."

Puff.

Puff.

"Do come in," said Daddy, ushering him through the living room and offering him a seat at the dining table.

"Would you like some coffee or tea?" asked Mother.

"How about something with ice?" said Mr. Price, setting his derby on the table. He retrieved a handkerchief from his linen jacket pocket and mopped the sweat from his forehead.

"Will do," said Mother. On the way to the icebox, she circled back into the living room, reached in front of Frankie, and turned down the volume on the radio.

"I can't hear it now," complained Frankie. "And neither can Grandma." She looked over at Grandma Engel, but her head was set deep into the chair cushion. She had nodded off once again.

Before heading into the kitchen, Mother raised her eyebrows at Frankie as if daring her to touch the volume dial, a dare Frankie knew better than to accept. So Frankie pressed her ear against the speaker and tried to listen as best she could.

Meanwhile, Mr. Price pulled out a piece of paper from his

breast pocket and laid it in front of Daddy at the table. Then he retrieved a small black notebook and pen from inside his jacket. "Let me first congratulate you on your new business. I've heard it's a restaurant?"

Puff.

Puff.

Puff.

"That's right," said Daddy, getting a small glass dish that he used as a paperweight from atop his desk and setting it before Mr. Price. "A family restaurant."

Mr. Price smiled and cradled his cigar in the dish. Then he jotted that down in his notebook. "Family businesses are generally quite acceptable."

"Acceptable?" said Daddy. "To whom?"

"The chamber, of course," said Mr. Price. "Now, I'm sure you are aware that as president, it is my duty to encourage all businessmen in town to become members. I noticed that you haven't yet submitted an application or made it down to my office to discuss membership, which is the reason for my visit this evening. Certainly, it is in your best interest to become a member, as we can provide numerous benefits for your business, which I'm sure you already know."

Mother returned then with a glass of iced tea, which she placed on the table in front of Mr. Price. The glass was sweating already, almost as much as Mr. Price.

"Thank you," Mr. Price said, and he knocked back the entire thing. When he returned the glass to the table, the slivers of ice clinked against the bottom like pennies into an empty money box.

"I am aware of the benefits being a member of the chamber

provides," said Daddy, clearing his throat. "But our doors aren't opening for a few weeks. In truth, we've been so busy with the new restaurant construction that I haven't gotten around to thinking about, well, much else."

Mr. Price tapped the cigar to shed ashes into the dish and then stuck it in the corner of his mouth. He pushed the piece of paper closer to Daddy. "Well, there's no time like the present." He held out his pen.

Puff.

Daddy looked at the application and the pen and smiled. "I'll think it over, and I'll be sure to get back to you about our decision."

"Your decision?" said Mr. Price.

Daddy nodded and stood up.

Mr. Price did not. He wasn't quite sure what was happening, as something like this had never happened to him before. In his mind, there was much more to discuss, and so on he pressed. "There are some questions I always like to ask prospective members, if you don't mind. First, I see that you are married and have at least one child. Is that right?" He looked in Frankie's direction.

"We've got two others," said Mother. "Both girls."

Mr. Price nodded and shook off more ashes into the dish, the bottom of which was now black with tar. "And you've lived here in Maryland for how long?"

"More than twenty years," said Daddy, who was beginning to lose patience and started tapping his fingernails on the edge of the table.

"And you were born here, Mr. Baum?" said Mr. Price. "In this country, I mean?"

"I beg your pardon," said Daddy. "But what does all this have to do with being a member of the chamber?"

Mr. Price shifted in his chair. "Purely a formality, Mr. Baum. But the way I see it, I mean, the way *we* at the chamber see it, is that the business owners are the backbone of our town. That being so, as president, it is my business, shall we say, to make sure we have the right sort. A town with a weak backbone, should a crisis occur of an economic or moral nature, will collapse on its feet. Now, where did you say you were born?"

Puff.

Puff.

"I understand completely," said Daddy, pushing his chair in to the table. "Why don't you come by the restaurant anytime."

"Pardon?"

Daddy put his arm around Mother's shoulders. "We are going to have quite a menu."

At that moment, Mr. Price was, among many things, confused. Somehow, the evening had taken a turn and had not gone according to plan. And for Mr. Price, things always went according to his plan. They had to, otherwise what was the confounded use of having a plan? He had money to collect and questions to be answered, but there he was with no money and no answers. And he hadn't even had the chance to mention the upcoming election or his bid for mayor.

Meanwhile, Mother and Daddy stood there at the table, staring at Mr. Price and patiently waiting for him to get up, but he did not. It was as though Mr. Price's behind was stuck fast in cement. "Thank you for stopping by," said Daddy, trying to dislodge him.

Mother did her part to help. "I hope you enjoyed the tea."

Mr. Price took a long puff on his cigar and blew a cloud of smoke that hung in front of Daddy until he coughed and fanned it away from his face. Finally, Mr. Price managed to break loose of the chair. "I see," he said as he tucked the notebook and pen back into his pocket. Alas, he did see what was going on, and he didn't care for it at all. Even more, he couldn't quite believe it was happening. This was, after all, the first time in the history of his term as president of Hagerstown's chamber of commerce that Sullen Waterford Price, Esquire, was being turned away.

As Daddy walked him to the door, Mr. Price worried that perhaps he was losing his touch. Perhaps he was getting too soft. He turned to face Daddy, to try to take hold of the situation and force his plan back on the right track. "Now, look here, Baum," he started to say.

By this time, Frankie, who had missed most of her radio program and was going to continue to miss it as long as Mr. Price was there talking, had been working her fingers up to the volume dial. She glanced over at Mother, ever so innocently, and to Frankie's surprise, Mother was looking right at her with half of her mouth turned up in a smile. Then, Mother gave the tiniest of nods.

Frankie did not hesitate. She turned up the volume. Oh boy, did she ever.

"You see, it's useless, Keezy," said the Shadow. *"You can't destroy what you can't see."*

"Why have you come here?"

"To end your criminal career . . ."

"I've committed no crime," said Keezy.

"What'd I miss?" said Grandma Engel, awakened by the sudden loud voices.

Mr. Price lingered in the doorway. "What was it you were about to say, Mr. Price?" asked Daddy, shouting over the radio.

Mr. Price took out his cigar as if he were going to make a speech, but decided better of it. *Another time,* he thought, *another time.* "Good evening to you, Mr. Baum." He sucked on his cigar and slipped on his derby.

"And to you," said Daddy.

"I'll be seeing you," said Mr. Price under this breath as he stepped out into the night air.

9

THERE WAS NO NIGHT air coming through Frankie and Elizabeth's bedroom window, not even as much as a whisper to waft the curtains. Frankie lifted her head from the pillow and kicked off the cotton sheet to cool her bare feet. She rolled over in her bed and found Bismarck next to her, stretched out in Joan's spot. His head was only a few inches away, his mouth open and panting from the closeness of the June heat. Frankie turned back over to get away from his hot breath, which incidentally had the scent of rotted beans. The thin mattress squeaked on the metal frame when she turned, and Elizabeth stirred in her bed across the room.

Frankie didn't know what time it was, or how long she'd been asleep, or for that matter why she had awakened. But the sun had not yet made itself known, so she figured it was either very late or very early. No matter, she decided; she was awake, and so she got out of bed. As her feet touched the wood floor, Bismarck lifted his head and whined. Frankie whispered to him that he shouldn't be bothered with what she was up to and to go back to sleep, which he promptly did. That dog.

Frankie slipped out of her room and down the hall toward the kitchen for a glass of water. The apartment was dark, and she stepped lightly on the floorboards so as to not awaken anyone. Guiding herself using her hands along the walls, she felt for the walnut dresser that stuck out a good bit in the hallway, the one that she had tripped over more than once even with the lights on. The dresser belonged to Grandma Engel, passed down from her mother, but was too big to fit in Grandma Engel's apartment, too big to fit in the Baums' apartment either, to be honest, but there it sat in the hall serving as a catchall for extra bed linens, holiday candles, and anything else that no one knew where to put.

Daddy cursed the thing on more than one occasion because it sat just outside his and Mother's bedroom, on the left side of the hall, which happened to be in his blind spot. Coming out of his bedroom, he must've knocked his knee on the side of it a thousand times, and after each swore, "Mark my words. One of these days, you will meet your fate with an axe!" Daddy didn't own an axe, so far as Frankie knew, but still, she wouldn't have been surprised if one day she came home and there was nothing left in the hall but a pile of splinters.

Frankie filled a water glass and sipped from it on the way back to her room. She was thinking of Joan and feeling lonelier than she remembered—*do you ever notice how things always seem worse at nighttime?*—when she heard something. She stopped and listened quietly for a moment, not sure what she'd heard or if she'd really heard something at all, for sometimes, as it was in her experience, the ears could play clever tricks. She waited, still listening, until just about the time she would have given up, when she heard another something that was, she was sure, an *actual* something. And it came from the living room.

She tiptoed through the dining room without giving a thought about what could have made the actual-something noise, which, in truth, was a careless thing to do, for who knows what terrible things lurk in the dark? But still, on she went into the living room, where she promptly tripped over an outstretched leg. A leg! She screamed, understandably, and dropped her water glass, which shattered against the floor.

Daddy yelled then, for he was as startled as Frankie, perhaps more so, as it turned out that the leg she tripped over belonged to him.

"Daddy!" said Frankie after he switched on the lamp. "What are you doing?"

He quickly picked up the handset of the telephone, which he had dropped moments before, then mumbled something into it and returned it to the base. "Quiet," he whispered to Frankie, looking toward the hall as if he expected to see Mother or at least Bismarck coming to see what was going on. "And I should ask you the same."

"I was just getting a drink and heard a noise." Frankie knelt down and started gathering the pieces of broken glass from the braided rug. She glanced up at Daddy still sitting in the upholstered chair and then at the telephone on the side table next to him.

"It was dark and I didn't think anyone was . . . It must've been you I heard, on the telephone. What time of night is it?"

"Close to three, I believe. Now go get yourself a towel," said Daddy. "I'll take care of the glass."

Frankie hurried to the kitchen and grabbed a tea towel from the drawer. By the time she returned to the rug, Daddy was on his knees picking up the shards of glass. Frankie pressed the towel into the braids to soak up the spill.

"There, now," said Daddy, holding the shards in his cupped hand. "I think that should do it. I don't think we need to worry Mother about this, do you?"

Frankie shook her head. Frankie and Joan, and even Elizabeth, went out of their way to keep Mother from worrying. Mother worried about everything, and made a big to-do about the littlest things, which, to be honest, was embarrassing. If it weren't for Daddy, none of the Baum girls would've learned to roller-skate or swim or ride a horse. Mother would've been too nervous to allow it. So Frankie was happy to keep the secret with Daddy, although she wondered if there were other reasons besides the broken glass that he didn't want Mother to know.

Daddy took the damp towel from her and carefully emptied the broken glass into it. He started to get up but fell back to his knees.

"Daddy?"

"Give me a hand, would you, Frankie?"

She gripped his arm and helped him upright. "Are you all right?"

"Fit as a fiddle," he said, taking some deep breaths. "Now, back to bed." He kissed her forehead.

"Good night." Slowly, Frankie padded out of the room, but then turned in wonder. "Aren't you going to sleep, too?" she whispered.

"Soon," he answered.

Frankie continued on, and looked back once more as Daddy sat back down in the chair and switched off the lamp. She climbed back into bed beside Bismarck, who was moving his paws in a dream chase. There Frankie lay for quite a while, listening to Bismarck's occasional whimper and wishing more than anything that Joan were there. It wasn't like Daddy to be up in the middle of the night, and whom was he talking to at this hour?

"Elizabeth," whispered Frankie. "Psst, Elizabeth!"

"Go to sleep," murmured Elizabeth as she turned over in her bed with her back toward Frankie. This was just as well, because telling Elizabeth anything would ensure it got back to Mother eventually.

Frankie hugged her pillow tight, but it wasn't until she heard Daddy knock into the walnut dresser a while later, on the way to his bedroom, and then curse at it, that she was able to fall asleep.

June 18, 1939

Dearly Departed Joan,

    I'm so sorry that each and every one of your fingers was broken in a tractor accident at Aunt Dottie's. The pain must be just awful. It's been painful here, too, you know, not receiving a letter from you since you've been gone. Which is why I can only figure that your fingers are all bandaged up on account of some sort of a farming mishap and are preventing you from holding a pen properly. Certainly, if your fingers were working, you would have written me by now.

    But, my fingerless Baloney, I do have to wonder why you haven't asked Aunt Dottie to write on your behalf. Maybe because you feel so foolish about the tractor and your clumsiness, or you don't want Aunt Dottie to know how miserable you are in her company? I bet the food is terrible there, isn't it? Egg custards all day long, I'm guessing.

    If you can manage to scribble something on a slip of paper, a napkin even, maybe by holding a pen between your teeth, just to let me know that you have received my letters and actually read them, it would come as a great relief.

                Your sister, IF YOU REMEMBER ME AT ALL,

                           Frankie

10

FIRST THING IN THE morning, Frankie dropped the letter to Joan at the post office. On the walk back to the apartment, she was feeling a good bit alone and sorry for herself, which are quite frankly terrible feelings to feel, and so with her mind occupied on such things, she didn't see Ava and Martha coming out of the alleyway. They were both in bathing suits and swim caps with towels hung around their necks. Seeing that Frankie didn't notice them, and always up for a good scare, Ava and Martha jumped out at her as she passed. Frankie hollered and stumbled backward, nearly landing on her behind. "What a dirty trick!" she said, after regaining her balance.

"Gotcha!" Ava twisted up her towel and snapped its tail end at Frankie.

What a snap it was, too. It produced a sting on Frankie's arm that made her screech like a gobble-pipe. Ava bent over in a fit of giggles, while Martha continued chewing on a chunk of buttered bread with her mouth open.

"Cut it out!" Frankie yelled, examining the red mark on her arm. "That smarts."

"You should've seen your face," said Ava, slapping her knee. Then she instructed Martha to help her reenact the whole scene so

Frankie could witness firsthand the general hilarity of it all. "Martha, you be me," said Ava, positioning her in the alley. "Okay, now, I'll be Frankie." Ava backed up about ten steps. Then she slumped her shoulders and put on the most sullen face, as if she'd just been handed a life sentence without parole.

"That doesn't look like me," protested Frankie.

"It certainly does," said Ava. "Try looking in the mirror sometime." She turned to her sister. "Ready, Martha?"

Martha popped the last chunk of crusty bread into her mouth and nodded. Then she adjusted her swim cap and put her hands on her bare knees, readying for the jump. Ava began walking slowly, in the same way that Frankie had, and when she got to the opening of the alleyway, nodded at Martha to do her thing. Right on cue, Martha leaped forward like a jumping frog. Then Ava launched herself into the air, squealing ridiculously and waving her arms around like she was one of Prince John's cronies from *The Adventures of Robin Hood* who had just been stabbed through the heart.

Frankie rolled her eyes at the overdone performance and started past Ava, who was now nearly seizing with laughter.

"Where you going, Frankie?" asked Martha.

Frankie climbed the stairs to the front door of the apartment building. "Inside," she said flatly.

"Aw, come on," said Ava. "I was only kidding around. Come swimming with us."

"Yeah, come on," said Martha. "Ava is gonna try and sink me. And she's gonna need some help because she told me just this morning that I was so full of hot air."

"Ain't that the truth," said Ava.

"I don't think that's what she meant, Martha," said Frankie.

"Anyway, come on," said Ava. "I've been on punishment for five whole days, since Mary Jacobs told her mother that I ripped the eyes off her teddy." She gritted her teeth and said under her breath, "No-good Mary Jacobs." Then Ava wiped a bead of sweat that was finding its way down her nose. "And I've been itching for a swim."

"Did you?" Frankie wondered.

"Did I what?"

"Did you pull the eyeballs off that teddy?"

"Of course I did it," said Ava. "*You* knew I did it. Everybody in the whole school knew I did it. But I gave them back to her the next day, and she *still* told on me." Ava looked down the street and narrowed her eyes. She stared intently at nothing, her face calm and almost peaceful as she plotted heinous revenge. Poor Mary Jacobs. It would not end well for her. Then, after a long, eerie moment, Ava returned from wherever she was, her mouth tightening at the corners. "So are you coming or not?"

Frankie shrugged.

"Great snakes," said Ava. "What else is there to do?"

Frankie knew she had a point. It was either swimming with her cousins—which would be sort of fun, although not as much fun without Joan—or hanging upside down on the jungle gym out back until her head filled up with enough blood that she got a headache. "Okay," Frankie said, after giving both options a good deal of thought. "Let me get my suit."

Frankie pulled open the door and ran into their apartment. She called into the kitchen on the way down the hall to her room, "I'm going swimming with Ava and Martha!"

Mother, who was pouring coffee grounds into the percolator, called back, "I don't think so, young lady."

Frankie stopped halfway down the hall, turned around, and marched back to the kitchen. "Why not?"

"Because you're going to the restaurant this morning to help your father," Mother said. "That's why not." She put a plate of buttered white toast on the kitchen table and licked a dollop of butter from her thumb. "We're leaving right after breakfast."

"But why do I have to help?" said Frankie.

Mother raised her eyebrows and cocked her head to the side as if she didn't understand the question. Frankie repeated the question, which turned out to be a mistake. Mother's eyes grew bigger, magnified behind her thick, horn-rimmed eyeglasses. There was indignation swirling inside them, plain as day. "Because you do," she said, as if that answered everything.

"What about Elizabeth?" said Frankie.

"You don't worry yourself about your sister," said Mother, grabbing a handful of silverware from the drawer. "She'll be along later, after her riding lessons."

Frankie shook her head. "No fair."

"I don't want to hear it," said Mother. "No one ever said life was fair." She set the silverware on the table, and as she did, a butter knife slipped out of her hand and landed on the floor. Mother stood over the knife, looking down on it as if she were trying to decide whether to pick it up. "Well, you know what that means."

"What?" said Frankie. There were so many superstitions that Mother knew of and believed in with the whole of her heart that Frankie couldn't keep them all straight in her head.

"A man's going to visit," said Mother. Then she picked up the knife, wiped it on the apron of her skirt, and set it back on the table. "I wonder who it will be."

Frankie trudged into the living room, the dread of the day to come pressing down on her shoulders and slowing her steps. She managed to open the front window that looked onto the street and stick her head out. Ava and Martha were just where she had left them, on the sidewalk playing a clapping game and belting out:

> *Alice stepped into the bathtub*
> *She pulled out the plug.*
> *Oh my goodness*
> *Oh my soul*
> *There goes Alice down the HOLE . . .*

Frankie felt a pang of jealousy seeing the two of them, and now more than before wanted to join them for a swim. She whistled at them to get their attention and then said, "Go on without me. I can't go."

"Why on earth not?" said Ava.

Frankie just shook her head. "I have to help at the restaurant."

"Too bad for you," said Ava. "See you around." She grabbed Martha's hand, and they skipped away down the block as Frankie closed the window.

11

WHILE MOTHER WAS CLEANING up the breakfast dishes in the kitchen, Frankie sat quietly under the dining room table examining her newest scab. It was small, and certainly not her best, but it had already formed a nice, dark crust on her knee and was ripe for the picking. She played with the loop of the drawstring on her tiny blue silk bag, the one with an embroidered star on the front that Daddy had brought back from a business trip to Texas. Carefully, she shook out its contents and admired the seven scabs in her collection, lying like thin wafers in her palm. Frankie's very best, the one for which she was most proud, came off of her elbow more than a year and a half ago, soon after she'd gotten the idea to start a collection.

She and Joan had hooked up Dixie to the cart one morning and taken her out on Antietam Street to stretch her legs. About halfway up the block, they had gotten Dixie into a steady trot when Mr. Canard, as he fumbled the key to the door of his shoe repair shop, dropped a box of cast iron cobbler form molds. They made a terrible clang when they spilled out onto the brick sidewalk, causing the girls to jump and Dixie to take off at full gallop. Joan lost her grip of the reins as Dixie tore down the street. The girls held tight to each other as their spooked pony ran wild. Joan was in tears, begging

Dixie between sobs to stop, and bribing her with promises of carrots and lumps of sugar. However, it seemed as though Dixie had other things on her mind. What are carrots and sugar lumps compared to freedom?

On they sped over the cobblestone streets. On and on. This pony did not tire easily. In her younger years, before she came to live with the Baums, Dixie was a rodeo pony whose job was to warm up the crowd by doing "ONE-OF-A-KIND, AMAZING TRICKS YOU'LL NEVER SEE ANYWHERE ELSE." She was billed as "The Pony With the Human Brain," not because she could wave good-bye with her hoof, say her prayers, and count to ten. She could do all of those things, but so could most of the other horses in the rodeo. There were even some potbellied pigs in the show that had those tricks in their repertoire. Yes, that's right, I said *pigs*. But Dixie, she was a horse of a different color, you could say.

Rodeo Stan, who owned the traveling rodeo, would bring Dixie into the center of the arena before the main performance—barrel racing and brahma bull riding—and ask the crowd to shout out numbers. "Any number between one and fifty!" he'd say. "Don't be shy! Let's hear 'em!" Then, after he had two numbers from the audience, he'd ask them if they wanted Dixie to add, subtract, multiply, or divide. "Divide!" the crowd would often yell, because division was the hardest, and those rodeo-goers, well, they loved a challenge. Then, Rodeo Stan would tell Dixie, loud enough so everyone could hear, "All right, Dixie girl, let's see if you can handle this one. How many times does two go into eight?"

After a few seconds, Dixie would nod her head enthusiastically. "I think she's got it!" Rodeo Stan would say, cheering her on. "Oh boy, oh boy, she does think she knows this one! What do you say, folks?" Then, after fervent applause, Dixie would tap her hoof on the ground four times, giving, of course, the correct answer. "She did it! Amazing! Incredible! The Pony With the Human Brain has done it once again, ladies and gentlemen. Let's hear it for her! And tell your friends, because you won't see her anywhere else but here, at Rodeo Stan's Wild Rodeo!" Dixie would then bow and wave, and perhaps add a spinning waltz or two, if it pleased her, sending the audience into a complete frenzy.

The point is, Dixie was a performer. She could work five shows a day, sometimes six. Even years later, after she had left show business and settled down to a quiet retirement, she still—every once in a while—yearned for applause. And this ride around town with Joan and Frankie? Well, she saw it as her chance to take center stage once again.

Certainly, there was no question she was gaining a significant audience in the streets. Shop owners rushed out of their stores and gaped helplessly as the trio raced by. The few cars on the road swerved to miss them, and some pulled over to watch. One tried to block the road in an effort to stop Dixie, but that human-brained equine easily maneuvered around the car by cutting over to the sidewalk.

She had no plans to stop anytime soon. None. In fact, the farther she ran, the more people lined up to watch her, and it seemed to Frankie that their wild ride would never end, or end badly, she wasn't sure which. At this rate, they would be in Virginia by suppertime. Dixie rounded the next street corner with such speed that the cart tilted up on one wheel, and Frankie thought for sure the cart would upset and she and Joan would spill out on somebody's door-step. The worst part being that there would be no keeping something like that from Mother.

So, when Dixie hit a straightaway on East Avenue, Frankie wriggled out of Joan's grip and made a grab for the reins. She missed and nearly slipped off her seat, and she would have—would've fallen on her head and been run over by the cart—if Joan hadn't grabbed her by the dress sleeve in time. "Close one," said Frankie. "Now hold on and don't let go." She stretched her arm and reached for the reins once more while Joan anchored her to the cart. Frankie hooked the reins with her fingertips, even as Dixie flicked her tail in Frankie's face, and she managed to grab enough of them to slow Dixie a little. Once Frankie had a better grip, she yelled for Joan to pull her back to the seat. Joan did, but she pulled on Frankie at the same time that Dixie, having felt the pull on her bridle, came to the conclusion that her fun was over. And as Dixie abruptly halted, right in front of Barnard's Pharmacy, Frankie flew out of the cart and landed on her backside in the street, scraping the skin clear off her elbow.

The scab that formed a week or two later was in the shape of a Hercules beetle, and it was the pride of Frankie's collection.

Anyway, back under the dining room table, Frankie had just gotten her fingernail under the edge of her newest scab, which was quite small by comparison, when Mother called for her. "Where has that child gone now?"

Frankie remained hidden and still. If you didn't know Mother, you'd have thought she had a special talent for knowing when any of the girls were up to something they shouldn't be. But the truth was, she always thought they were up to something, because often enough she was up to many somethings when she was their age. The worry switch in her brain, or her heart, wherever it was housed, was permanently set to the ON position.

"Katie," said Mother, "have you seen Frances?"

"No, ma'am," said Katie from the kitchen. "But I just come in from the side porch. You the first person I seen." She took out a handkerchief from the pocketbook slung over her forearm and wiped the sweat from her neck. "Hot as all get-out today." Katie Resden was employed by Mother as a housekeeper, and had been for a few years' time. She came every Thursday to help with the laundry and the ironing and the other household chores, while Mother helped Daddy with his business affairs and tended to her social obligations in town.

"Don't I know it," said Mother, pulling at the waist of her cotton dress to give her skin a chance to breathe.

"Headed to your Eagles meetin', Mrs. Baum?" asked Katie. "Ain't you supposed to be gone already?"

"Not today, Katie," said Mother. Then she said under her breath, "And thank the good Lord for that."

Mildred Baum was a member of the Women's Club of Hagerstown and the Ladies' Auxiliary, as well as the Lioness Club and Eagle Club. She didn't particularly enjoy the obligatory monthly meetings and social events sponsored by these women's organizations, although she believed in their causes for the most part. Mildred only joined them at the request of Hermann. "When you're a part of a community, it's important to act as part of the community," he had told her.

Although Mildred liked many of the women in these clubs,

some—like Ann Margaret Price, wife of Sullen Waterford Price, Esquire, and mother to those Price boys—she could do without. But still, she would do anything for Hermann. Even if it meant luncheons with well-to-do women with a penchant for gossip.

"Miss Elizabeth done gone to her riding lessons?" said Katie.

"Hermann dropped her off on the way to the restaurant," said Mother. "Hal is going to give us a ride in his taxi as soon as I find Frances."

"I'll check the basement," offered Katie. "That wee pet. Sometime I catch her down there doing I don't know what."

Frankie watched Katie's thick dark legs pass by the table toward the front door of their apartment. She had a generous figure with a slow, swinging gait that was as much side-to-side as it was forward motion. When the door closed behind her, Mother jetted past the table and down the hall toward the bedrooms. "Frances Marie!" she hollered. "Your uncle will be here in five minutes to take us to the restaurant, so you'd better produce yourself right now or I'll get out the cake turner!"

Mother was known on occasion to chase the girls—well, Joan and Frankie, never Elizabeth—around the apartment with a metal cake turner, something that resembled a spatula. Although she promised to use it on their behinds for doing something they shouldn't have, Mother never made good on those promises, much to the relief of Joan and Frankie—not to mention their behinds.

Frankie eased her scab collection back into the bag and cinched the drawstring. She didn't want to go to the restaurant to help. She wanted to swim with Ava and Martha, or do nothing at all, except for maybe lie in front of the fan in the living room and listen to her radio programs or hang upside down on the jungle gym out back and stare up at the gray sky. It was much too hot to do anything else, especially when she didn't have a choice in the matter. She tucked the bag into her dress pocket and started picking again at her knee. She straightened her leg so she could loosen one side, and as she did, her foot knocked into the chair leg closest to her, sending the chair back a few inches.

Mother's footsteps stopped. "Rats!" Frankie said under her breath. She grabbed hold of the chair legs, quickly returning the chair to its original spot. A few moments later, Mother stood at the table just a couple of feet from Frankie. Katie returned then, too, out of breath. "She ain't downstairs," she said. "Maybe she run off somewhere."

"I don't think so," said Mother.

Frankie held her breath. But it made no difference, because the next thing she knew, Mother yanked at the top of the chair. Frankie grabbed for the chair legs and held on tight. Although petite, Mother was deceptively strong—all those years washing dishes— and she lifted the chair off the floor, dragging Frankie out partway from under the table. "I don't have time for these games, Frances," said Mother.

"I want to stay here," said Frankie, getting to her feet and knocking her head on the table on the way up.

"Not by yourself, you're not."

Frankie rubbed the top of her head. "But I won't be by myself. Katie's here." She sidled up next to Katie and looked at her with pleading eyes.

"No indeed," said Katie, shaking her head and reaching into

her dress pocket for a lemon drop. She unwrapped the candy and popped it into her mouth. "There's a lot of work to be done round here. Last time I was supposed to watch you and Miss Joan, you snuck out on that horse. Got yourself in a bad way. No, ma'am. Now I got to do my work." She crinkled the candy wrapper between her fingers and then ambled down the hall, leaving Frankie to face Mother alone.

Mother bent over and looked at the empty space under the table. "What were you doing under there?"

"Nothing."

"Frances Marie, what have I told you about picking at yourself?"

Frankie glanced at her leg and sighed.

"That leg of yours is going to turn green and they will have to cut it off. Then you'll know something."

"Will not," said Frankie. But the truth was, she wasn't so sure.

"Oh no? Just last week Mrs. Vanner told me that her cousin's little boy had a hangnail on his finger that he wouldn't let alone, and his finger swelled up the size of a banana. Marshall, his name was, I think." Mother raised her eyebrows. "Do you know him?"

Frankie shook her head. And then for a second she swore she almost saw the corner of Mother's mouth turn up into a smile. "Oh, well then, it was an awful thing. Worse than a snakebite, Mrs. Vanner said, you know, the pain. That boy's screams were heard all the way on Mulberry. Which is a long way from Cannon Avenue."

"Cannon Avenue?"

Mother nodded. "That's where the poor boy lives. The agony he must've been in. Just think on it. His mother told him over and over to quit picking at the thing, but that boy just couldn't let it be. You know how boys are. He was a nose-picker, too, no doubt about it." Mother took a step closer to Frankie and leaned down so she could look at her straight on, the space between the tips of their noses only wide enough to pass a dime. This was Mother's technique, to get as close to you as possible so that the words coming out of her mouth, along with every single ounce of their meaning, wouldn't have far to travel and couldn't hop on a breeze and take a detour. She did not trust regular talking distance when it came to matters as serious as amputation. "An infection came next," said Mother. "They had to bus a doctor in from Pennsylvania to work on it. A specialist."

"For hangnails?" asked Frankie.

"That's right," said Mother, with conviction. "A hangnail specialist. Doctors here never saw anything like it."

Frankie swallowed.

Mother straightened her back and took off her glasses. She polished the lenses with the hem of her skirt, then held them up to the light and, once satisfied, slid them back on. "A couple of days later," she continued, "his whole finger turned a lovely shade of green. They tried to save it, but . . ."

"But what?" said Frankie.

"WHACK!" Mother brought the side of her hand down on the table.

Frankie flinched and tucked her fingers into tight fists.

"Poor boy had to learn the hard way," said Mother. "Now, doesn't that make you think twice about it?"

Frankie nodded. It certainly did make her think twice—about hiding under the dining room table again, where she could be discovered so easily.

"Now, then." Mother smoothed her hair in the mirror as if they had just finished talking about the weather and not about some poor boy's chopped-off finger. "Your father's waiting for us."

"What about Elizabeth?" asked Frankie again.

"Don't you worry so much about your sister. That's my job." She picked up her pocketbook from the table and made it to the door in five efficient strides, her square heels clicking on the hardwood floor. "Come on, now."

"Forever a Number Three," Frankie said under her breath.

Mother turned her head. "What was that?"

"Nothing," said Frankie. "I'm coming."

12

THIS WAS ONLY THE second time Frankie had been inside the restaurant, and she didn't think it possible for the place to look any worse for wear than the first time she'd laid eyes on it. But man oh day, was she entirely wrong. For one thing, the walls by the bar and dining room were very much gone. Knotted wooden beams stood there instead, like the bare bones of the old place that hadn't seen the light of day for a hundred years and were wondering why all of a sudden they were indecent. Mercy! Buckets of plaster sat in the middle of the floor, where the tables and chairs were just a few days earlier, and men in blue overalls milled about, looking intent on fixing something but not sure where to start.

At the sight of it all, Mother grasped Frankie's shoulder and squeezed. The edge of her gold wedding band dug into Frankie's skin, and thankfully, just as Frankie managed to slip out of her grip, Daddy appeared.

"Come in, come in," he said, taking Mother by the hand. "And watch your step." Then Daddy turned to Frankie and said, "Just in time. I think you're just what we need in the kitchen."

"The kitchen?" said Frankie. She felt that making sure the organ was in proper tune—not working in the kitchen—was the sort of job best suited for her talents. "To do what?" She guessed that she could see herself wearing one of those tall white hats and nibbling on loaves of warm, crusty bread right from the oven. "Like be a chef or a baker?"

"I was thinking along the lines of a more junior position," said Daddy.

"Junior?" Frankie didn't like where this was going at all.

"Just to start out, Frankie. The kitchen is the heart and soul of a restaurant, the lifeblood. And you'll be in the center of it. You know, peeling potatoes, snapping beans, washing dishes—"

"Washing dishes!" Frankie yelled, sickened by the notion.

"Frances Marie," warned Mother. "Mind your tone."

"You're just not old enough yet for some of the other responsibilities around here," Daddy explained. "It's not as bad as you think. You'll see."

Frankie could not see anything past dirty dishes.

"Go on," said Daddy, nodding toward the kitchen. "Mr. Stannum, the kitchen manager, is in there, and he'll show you what to do." Then he and Mother headed to the offices upstairs.

Frankie sat down on a bucket of plaster and stared at the kitchen door. She hadn't been sitting very long when there was some commotion coming from the kitchen. She could hear voices, loud ones. Right then she thought about sneaking back home, grabbing her bathing suit, and making her way to the municipal pool. She would be punished, for certain, but she honestly could not imagine a punishment worse than what waited for her in that kitchen.

So, up she stood and quickly got herself to the front door. She would have made it there, too—would have made it outside to the street, even—if not for the colored woman who ran out of the kitchen then. "I done told you," the woman said, "I never did work a cookstove like that one before." She was short and round, with cheeks as plump and friendly as warm apple dumplings. She pulled off a white apron from around her neck, folded it carefully into a neat pile, and laid it on a stepladder.

Then she walked toward Frankie, who stood there dumbfounded, blocking the front door. "Which way you headed?" she asked.

"Me?" said Frankie.

"You the only one here, ain't you?"

Frankie nodded.

"So, you staying or going?"

Frankie wasn't sure. She had momentarily forgotten her plan.

"Amy!" A man's voice shouted from the kitchen.

"If you please," she said to Frankie, taking a step forward. The woman, who looked to be much younger close up, gave a nervous smile and looked as eager to disappear as Frankie did. And so Frankie nodded, for there was little she understood better than the desire to skedaddle, and she stepped out of the way.

The woman reached for the doorknob and started to turn it, but the kitchen doors swung open and the man attached to the voice was there calling her name once more—this time with less severity, after laying eyes on Frankie. He was tall and skinny as a rail, with a full silver mustache that hung low over his lip. He shifted his gaze from Amy to Frankie, and then, for Frankie's benefit, put on a smile. When he did, the mustache covered his entire top row of teeth, and Frankie wondered how he could live with such a nuisance of a thing, which would surely get in the way of eating an ice cream cone. "Ah," he said, "you must be Frances. Mr. Baum said you'd be helping out today."

"Frankie," she said.

"All right, Frankie," he said, nodding. "The name's Mr. Stannum. So, I understand you're going to be working in the kitchen?"

Frankie looked at Amy, who was for some reason still standing beside her, and then said, "Well, I guess so, but I'm not sure I know how to work the cookstove, either."

Mr. Stannum blew air out of his mouth that came out sounding like *ppffffffftttt*, and the fringe on his lip parted like a curtain. "There's plenty to do, plenty to do." He put his hand on Frankie's shoulder and gave her a shove toward the kitchen. "You can start by unpacking the boxes of pots and pans. Amy here will show you where they are." He turned then to Amy and waved his fingers at her to follow. His fingernails were long and caked with grease. "Come on. If you think you can handle pots and pans." There was more exasperation than malice in his voice this time, and perhaps Amy heard that, too, as she did come along, but only after mumbling something that Frankie couldn't quite make out.

Frankie was surprised to find the kitchen in better shape than the rest of the place. Rats no more! The lights worked, for one thing, and the walls, which she was relieved to see were not missing, were freshly painted white. The cupboards, though still gray, were clean, and most of them now had doors on them. This was particularly pleasing to Frankie, for hiding places with doors were much preferred to those without. A round fan mounted to the wall above the stove was spinning at full speed, but only moved hot air around the room and provided no real relief. Stacks of boxes covered the butcher-block countertop and blocked the back entrance.

Speaking of the back entrance— *When did that door get there?* Frankie wondered. Because she hadn't noticed it before. She made a plan to start with the boxes there, rather than on the counter, so she could clear the way to the door and slip out when nobody was looking.

Besides Mr. Stannum and Amy, there were three others working in the kitchen. Mr. Stannum introduced Frankie to the group as Mr. Baum's youngest daughter, the third one—*he did indeed*—who would be helping for the time being while staying out of the way. He also warned them to watch their language around her and to step up the work, because the restaurant would open in a few weeks' time and there was about two months' worth of work yet to be done. He's seen circus elephants work faster, he told them.

Julie Bulgar, an older lady with her light brown hair pulled into a tidy bun on the top of her head, was the baker. Her dimples were deep and pronounced when she smiled, like someone had poked her pale, doughy cheeks with two fingers just because. "How do you do, young lady?" she said.

Leon Washington, the line cook, nodded in Frankie's direction but didn't speak to her. He was as tall and slender as Mr. Stannum, but colored, and without any facial hair. He had a jagged scar under his right eye about the size of a key and Frankie noticed that he kept his head lowered when he talked, like he was afraid of what he might see in others, or afraid of what others might see in him.

Next to him was Seaweed Turner, a young boy no more than fifteen, the prep cook for Mr. Washington. He was tossing up a washrag by the grill, snatching it out of the air before it hit the ground, balling it up in his fist, and then tossing it again.

"I've got to check on the potato shipment," said Mr. Stannum. He nodded at Amy and Frankie. "Get to work. No time to waste."

After Mr. Stannum left, Seaweed grabbed two ends of the washrag and wound it around itself until the rag was the likeness of a rope. Then he unwound the thing and tossed it from one hand to the other.

"That's for cleaning with, boy, not for doing no tricks," said Mr. Washington. But Seaweed didn't pay him any mind, and instead flashed a wide smile at Frankie and then spun around quick while the rag flew into the air. "Frankie?" he said to himself, loud enough that she could hear. "Thought that was a boy's name."

This time, Mr. Washington grabbed for the washrag but missed. "Boy, if you don't start working like you playing, you going to be out of a job right quick."

"Easy, boss," said Seaweed, waving the rag above his head like he had just dropped his weapon and was surrendering to the other side. "I got you covered." He flashed another smile at Frankie before dropping the rag onto the soiled grill top and leaning into it with both hands, back and forth.

"I'm not sure a boy called Seaweed has a right to make a remark about anybody else's name," said Frankie, her hands balled up into fists by her side. She was surprised at how quickly this came out of her mouth, but she was already riled up from having to be there in the first place, and she wasn't going to let a smart-mouthed boy get one up on her.

Seaweed blinked and then his eyes got wide. He stopped scrubbing. Frankie stood firm and readied herself for a comeback, but he just looked at her, and eventually his mouth turned up in a grin.

"She's got you there, Seaweed," said Julie.

Seaweed went back to cleaning, and after a quiet minute or so,

Mr. Washington whistled and said, "Oh man oh man, see here, see here. The boy's been stumped. That's the first time he's shut up all day." He hung his apron on one of the wall hooks behind him. "I'm going to the toilet," he said to Seaweed, "and when I get back, you and me are gonna scrape clean the inside of this here oven." The lavatory for kitchen help was in the far corner of the room, and as Mr. Washington passed by Amy and Frankie, he said, "Yep, this girl gonna be good, I say."

"Shoot," said Seaweed, shaking his head.

Frankie felt her cheeks burn. Amy took her arm and led her to the stack of boxes by the back door. "Don't pay him any mind," she whispered. "Seaweed just playing. He don't mean nothing by it."

Frankie didn't know if Amy was worried about Frankie's feelings getting hurt or if she thought Frankie would tell Daddy and get Seaweed in trouble. But Frankie wasn't much bothered about the remark itself—after all, it wasn't the first time somebody had made fun of her nickname, and in truth, it *was* a boy's name. And one thing was for sure: Frankie Baum was no snitch. "I'm not going to tell," she said to Amy.

Then the doors swung open, and there stood Mr. Stannum, appraising the room and any progress that had not occurred in his absence. He came to a stop in the center of the kitchen, and as he looked around, he began tapping each finger to his thumb on his right hand like he was trying to follow the beat to a drum. "Where is Leon?"

"Toilet," said Seaweed.

Mr. Stannum craned his neck in the direction of the lavatory. He set his jaw and stared, while his fingers found a steady rhythm.

Beat, beat, beat, beat. Finally, Mr. Washington emerged from the lavatory and returned to work without fail and without noticing Mr. Stannum watching him intently. But Seaweed noticed. He most certainly did. "Mr. Stannum," he said, "you all right?"

That seemed to knock Mr. Stannum off his cadence. His fingers slowed and then came to a stop. "What?"

"You just standing there staring," said Seaweed. "My grandma's got sugar and does that sometime, you know, goes off staring at nothing for no good reason. Most of the time when she been into the cookie jar. You got sugar?"

Sugar was one problem Mr. Stannum didn't have. But he had others. "Why are those boxes still unpacked?" he yelled. "Amy, I suppose you find boxes as hard as cookstoves?" He bit at each word as he spoke them, and his mouth began to produce enough froth so that by the time he got to the word "cookstoves," a glob of spittle the size of a shirt button flew out of his mouth and clung to his mustache.

"No, sir," said Amy. She quickly set about opening the box closest to her and pulled out a stack of aluminum jelly roll pans. She kept her eyes on her work and would not allow herself to look at Mr. Stannum, lest she see the thing that was now hanging past his lips. Amy had barely put the jelly roll pans on the counter before she dove into the next box.

Mr. Stannum shook his head—*Do you know that glob of spittle hung on?*—and eyeballed the grill top. "Didn't I tell you that a steel brush is what you need for that?" he growled at Seaweed. "You've got to be hard on it. It's the only way you'll get anywhere, for Pete's sake." Only he didn't say "for Pete's sake." He said something worse and seemed to forget that Frankie was standing right there. His fingers were really moving now, as if he was still trying to follow that drum and keep time to it, but he could barely hear its beat, beat, beat.

"Don't you worry none, Mr. Stannum," said Mr. Washington. "We'll be ready."

"We'll be ready," mocked Mr. Stannum. "We'll be ready. Look around you! Do you know how much there is to do before this is a working kitchen? A couple of weeks. We've got a measly couple of weeks and I've got . . . I've got"—he looked around and threw up his arms—"*this*." The spittle couldn't hang on any longer. It fell, first stretching into a thin line and then finally letting go of those silver hairs and splattering on the toe of his shoe. Whether he noticed or not was uncertain, but he muttered a few words to himself about colored people, and having to do everything around here himself, and then he left the kitchen once more.

"Why is he so upset?" said Frankie.

"He ain't upset," whispered Amy. "He just ain't got no heart."

13

THE DAY CREPT ALONG in the tiniest of increments. After the remark about Frankie's name and the period of silence that had followed, it didn't take too long for Seaweed to start up his tricks again. Mr. Washington tried several times to cut him down to size, but Seaweed had the sort of personality, it seemed, that could not be easily cut down or contained, at least not within the four white walls of a reasonably small kitchen.

Frankie concentrated on clearing the stack of boxes by the door. Finally, after every pot and pan was properly shelved, she gathered up the empty boxes to take outside. She pushed open the door, but could only open it partway, as the brick building next to the restaurant was so close, it hindered the door's full potential. The space between the buildings was wide enough that Frankie could squeeze through the door, but not with all of the boxes filling her arms. She looked back inside the kitchen. Everyone was tending to their own tasks. Everyone, that is, except for Seaweed. But as soon as Frankie noticed him watching, he turned his back and emptied the dirtied wash bucket into the deep porcelain sink.

Frankie let the boxes fall to her feet and then slipped through the door. She stepped out into a very narrow alleyway, if you could even call it that, because it was so thin, she could fit only if she kept her arms by her side. Once outside, even as she was so confined, she found she could breathe. She looked up at the narrow strip of sky that lit the small space around her, and with stiff soldier arms followed the alley all the way to the street.

The alley emptied out at Potomac Street, and she stood for a minute trying to decide which direction would be the quickest route home. Before she could make up her mind, Leroy Price came up behind her and kicked the backs of her knees so that her legs buckled and she fell to the brick sidewalk. "Smell that?" said Leroy to Marty, who was standing a few feet behind him. Leroy got close to Frankie and sniffed her hair. "Stinks like sauerkraut."

Frankie got to her feet and charged at Leroy, swinging. He put his hand on her forehead and kept her at such a distance that her arms couldn't connect. And he laughed. Oh brother, did he laugh.

Marty Price came forward then, just as casual as could be. "So, Frankie," he said, "have you been swimming yet this summer?" He said this as if it were the most normal thing in the world to have a conversation with someone while she's in the act of trying, albeit unsuccessfully, to knock their big brother's head off. "Me and Leroy's been twice," he went on, "and I can do a backflip off the side. Just learned how."

Frankie was still swinging at Leroy and grunting like a trapped pig. "That's nice, Marty," she managed to say.

"Think you might be going sometime soon?" he asked. "You can watch me."

Finally, Frankie's flailing arms got tired and she quit fighting. "I don't think so," she said, catching her breath and turning her head under Leroy's grip so she could eyeball him.

"How come?" said Marty.

She grabbed Leroy's wrist with both hands and tried to pry his hand loose. "Because I guess I have to be here, most days."

Leroy maintained his hold. "What kind of a restaurant is this, anyway?" He reached down with his thumb and pushed against the tip of Frankie's nose. "What do Germans like to eat?"

A fire ignited inside Frankie. "What did you say?" she yelled.

Then Seaweed stepped out of the alley holding a wire brush. He cleared his throat and it sounded like a low warning growl of a dog. "Heard a lot of racket out here. Thought maybe one of the pigs from the butcher down the street done got loose. And here it was just you, Frankie."

Frankie gritted her teeth at him.

Leroy let go of Frankie's head, finally. "What business is it of yours?" he said.

Seaweed looked right past Leroy and said to Frankie, "Your daddy come huntin' for you in the kitchen."

Leroy kept his eyes on Seaweed, and while he did, Frankie kept hers on Leroy and thought of at least two clever things she wanted to say about him being so stupid, but since he wasn't paying attention, she decided instead to kick him in the kneecaps. As she brought her leg back, though, Seaweed warned, "Now, Frankie. I know you don't want to keep your daddy waiting."

Frankie dropped her leg mid-kick and nearly lost her balance. Leroy looked right at her. "Yeah, Frankie," he said, laughing. "Better do what you're told."

Frankie was burnt up about the both of them: Leroy, for being . . . well, Leroy, and Seaweed, for treating her like a Number Three.

What she didn't need was another keeper. She made her way back to the alley and kept going past Seaweed without even putting eyes on him.

"See you, Frankie," said Marty, before Leroy smacked him on the back of his head.

Frankie didn't reply, but marched stiff-armed down the alley back toward the kitchen. Only then did she notice the wooden, painted sign on the door: COLORED ENTRANCE.

"There you are," said Daddy, who, along with Mother and Elizabeth, was standing next to Mr. Stannum. Daddy smiled when he saw Frankie and held out his arm to fold her in, but she pretended not to notice and instead kept her eyes on the floor. The fire inside her was still burning. Daddy dropped his arm and gave Mr. Stannum a pat on the shoulder. "The kitchen is certainly shaping up. But are we on track to open on the fifth?"

Mr. Stannum swallowed. "Yes, Mr. Baum." He glanced around at Mr. Washington, Amy, and Julie, and then his eyes narrowed on Seaweed, who had just come in from the alley. "Come hell or high water." Then he looked at Frankie, and Mother and Elizabeth, and cleared his throat. "Pardon me."

Mother gave a polite smile, but Frankie had other things on her mind. She didn't know where Leroy Price was getting his information, but she was not about to let his remark go unanswered. She took a step forward so that she was in front of Daddy's good eye and asked, "Are we making German food?"

14

WELL, OLE MR. STANNUM'S cheeks flushed. Everybody else in the kitchen kept on about their business but leaned a keen ear in Frankie's direction. "German food," said Daddy. "What makes you ask that?"

"Leroy Price said—" started Frankie, but Daddy cut her off.

"That reminds me," he said. "The menus! Stay right here." Daddy strode into the main dining room and, a few minutes later, came back carrying a stack of rectangular menus printed on heavy paper stock. He handed one to Mother first, then to Elizabeth and Mr. Stannum, and then Frankie.

"Oh, in color, too, Hermann," said Mother, holding on to the menu tightly, as if she wanted to be sure it wasn't a dream and wouldn't suddenly dissolve into raindrops. She ran her finger over "Baum's Restaurant and Tavern" in black, regal-looking letters at the top. Below the name was an unusual scene: a line drawing of a white horse with a medieval soldier on his back, riding to war or to something else. He was holding a long trumpet to his mouth, a solid red flag hanging from its end. Behind him were a castle and two more soldiers—one with a smaller trumpet and the other carrying a cooked turkey on a serving platter. To the right, a young maiden holding a jug of wine, presumably, which was nearly half her size.

She was looking up, the young lady was, in the direction of the gal-loping horse, and right in that empty white space of the menu was this quotation printed in dark, scrolling letters: "An Eating Place of Wide Renown."

"It's beautiful, Daddy," said Elizabeth, predictably.

"What's it supposed to mean?" asked Frankie. "'An eating place of wide renown'? And what's the horse for? And why are there sol-diers?"

"Frances," whispered Mother.

"What?"

"They aren't soldiers," said Elizabeth. "For one thing, they would have guns if they were soldiers. They're musicians. You know, on horseback, traveling with the king."

"What king?" said Frankie. "We don't have any kings."

"Not a specific king," explained Elizabeth, trying hard to show her smarts. "A king, in general. Any king. Right, Daddy?"

"Well, where is he, then?" asked Frankie. "In the castle? And is this restaurant supposed to be a castle, because"—she looked around the room and then shook her head—"it is *not*."

Elizabeth rolled her eyes. "Honestly, Frankie."

Mother smiled at Daddy. "It does look like something out of a storybook."

Daddy turned his head slightly so that his one good eye had full view of the drawings. Then he held the menu at arm's length as if he were judging a work of art. "I think it shows the magic of the restaurant. When people sit at a table to eat, I want them to have an experience here like no other the world over."

Frankie opened the menu and looked over the food offerings. Under the heading **FRUITS AND JUICES**:

LARGE GLASS OF CHILLED TOMATO JUICE . . . 10 CENTS

EIGHT OUNCES OF PURE ORANGE JUICE . . . 15 CENTS

ONE-HALF SEEDLESS GRAPEFRUIT, CAREFULLY CUT . . . 10 CENTS

SELECTED PRUNES IN HEAVY HOME-COOKED SYRUP . . . 10 CENTS

"Blech, prunes," said Frankie. Hopefully they weren't Grandma Engel's stewed prunes, which she force-fed to Frankie whenever she was constipated. There was nothing that smelled or tasted worse. Grandma ate them by the tablespoonful until her teeth and tongue were coated with the thick brown sauce. It was, in a word, disgusting. And why anyone would pay money for them, let alone ten cents, was beyond Frankie.

"Oh," said Mother, smiling, "you've even put Mother's prunes on the menu. She'll be tickled."

Heavens.

Then this:

LARGE ITALIAN PURPLE PLUMS . . . 10 CENTS

FULL RIPE BANANAS, SLICED IN MILK, 10 CENTS . . .

IN CREAM, 15 CENTS

FANCY SPICED CRABAPPLES . . . 10 CENTS

Frankie read further and saw an assortment of cereals, hotcakes, club breakfasts, and eggs and omelettes.

Under **EGGS AND OMELETTES**, this note:

WILL YOU KINDLY GIVE YOUR WAITRESS EXPLICIT DIRECTIONS

AS TO HOW YOU LIKE YOUR EGGS

—WE KNOW YOU HAVE A PREFERENCE.

WE SERVE TWO EGGS—FRIED, BOILED, SCRAMBLED, POACHED,
OR SHIRRED—FOR 20 CENTS. CRISP BACON AND TWO EGGS
FOR 40 CENTS.
COUNTRY CURED HAM AND EGGS 65 CENTS OR, IF YOU LIKE,
SWIFT'S PREMIUM OR ARMOUR'S STAR HAM AND EGGS 50 CENTS.
ALL ORDERS SERVED WITH ROLLS OR
BREAD AND BUTTER. TOAST 5 CENTS.

Then a list of various omelettes made to order, all for 35 cents, except the plain for 25: ham, cheese, bacon, hamburger, tomato, Spanish, or onion. Then **TOASTS** and **SALADS** and **TAVERN SPECIALS**, which included hot blue plates, cold platter combinations, cold meats—full orders, and seafood in season, ranging from 25 cents for one dozen fresh shrimp to 65 cents for the genuine calf's liver (with onions or bacon), potatoes, and cabbage slaw. Frankie was happy to see "Toasted Cheese Sandwich" under **FAMOUS TAVERN SANDWICHES**, which was her very favorite, but most of all she was relieved to see that there wasn't any German food to be found, except for German fried potatoes under the heading **A LA CARTE**, whatever that meant. And considering that there were Italian plums, Spanish omelettes, and Gherkin dressing—whatever that was—Frankie didn't think one German thing on the menu made any difference. "So we're selling American food, then?" Frankie asked.

"Well of course, Frances," said Mother. "What else would we be serving?"

"I told you, German food," said Frankie. "That's what Leroy Price said, anyway." She knew better than to take Leroy's word for anything, but she also knew that Daddy's parents were German, and there was a lot of talk lately about the Germans—*those Germans* this and *those Germans* that!—and Daddy was always full of surprises.

Frankie thought she noticed Mother give a nervous glance in Daddy's direction, but if Mother did, Daddy didn't see it. He was still staring at the menus, paying attention to each word—from half fried milk-fed chicken to Philadelphia scrapple with syrup—as though he was adding up each printed letter on the pages, making sure all was accounted for. A missing letter, like a missing ingredient, you know, could really mess up a cake.

Then Daddy handed out menus to Julie, Mr. Washington, Amy, and Seaweed. He asked them, "What do you think?"

Julie answered right away that she had always wanted a horse. "A white one," she said, tapping the menu, "just like this one."

Amy, Mr. Washington, and Seaweed only nodded. But Daddy was full of encouragement. "Come on, now, don't be shy."

Seaweed was the only one to take Daddy up on this invitation. "Well, Mr. Baum," he said, clearing his throat, "I see what you trying to do here with those cats and their horns on the front. I mean, they ain't no Tommy Johnson or Blind Lemon Jefferson. But musicians are musicians, and the thing about musicians, you know, they be hungry a lot. Like for that turkey right there." He licked his lips. "That look good."

Frankie's stomach rumbled. It was getting close to suppertime. "With loads of gravy."

"And a side of potatoes," said Seaweed.

"And cooked carrots," Frankie added, nodding.

"Naw," said Seaweed. "Never could stomach carrots much."

"I don't think Mr. Baum is interested," said Mr. Stannum,

grabbing for the menu in Seaweed's hands. "And you all have jobs to do, as far as I know."

Daddy stepped in between Mr. Stannum and Seaweed. "I'm very interested. I wouldn't have asked otherwise."

Still, Seaweed, Mr. Washington, Julie, and Amy handed over their menus to Daddy and went back to work. Then Mr. Stannum leaned close to Daddy and said in a quiet voice, "Mr. Baum, can I have a word?" Daddy nodded and followed him a few steps until they were standing by the kitchen door.

Mr. Stannum towered over Hermann, but most people did, and Hermann wasn't the least bit uncomfortable. The same couldn't be said about Mr. Stannum, however. He had never been in such close proximity to Hermann before, and he couldn't help but stare at his glass eye.

The thing about that eye was that people felt as though Hermann were staring at them all the time. At least partially. And that's the sort of thing that made some people, well, anxious. They didn't know whether to stare back or look at their feet, and if they decided to stare back, which eye did they look at? It certainly was quite the predicament for some.

Hermann eventually got used to people feeling uneasy around him, and even learned to turn himself into somewhat of an attraction. Particularly for Frankie and Joan's friends, Hermann was happily obliged to entertain their curiosity about his glass eye by pretending to sneeze and then popping it into his hand. It was a perfectly gruesome trick. The first time he performed that trick in front of Ava and Martha, Martha turned the color of a pickled beet and then locked herself in the Baums' bathroom for five hours until the fire department arrived and had to break down the door with an axe. After that, Mother told him he could never do that trick again, to which he mostly agreed but reserved the right for special occasions.

This occasion might've qualified.

Daddy could see that Mr. Stannum was uneasy and gave serious thought to having a sneeze for his benefit, though he knew Mother's nerves were already worn thin and one good eye pop could do her in.

Mr. Stannum continued staring at Daddy's good eye, then shifted back and forth from one to the other, until he finally settled his gaze on his own shoes. That's when he noticed the spittle on the toe.

"Mr. Stannum?" said Daddy.

"Right," he said, keeping his head down while wondering if he had any shoe polish left in his cupboard at home, or if he needed to stop at Wexler's on the way. "The staff restroom," he said finally. "There's only one."

"That's right," said Daddy. "Isn't it working properly?"

"Oh yes, it is in fine working order," said Mr. Stannum.

"Then what seems to be the problem?"

"The problem," he said, "is that there seems to be only one." He stepped beside Daddy so Amy, Mr. Washington, and Seaweed were in plain view of Daddy's working eye. "Only one, for all of us."

Daddy sighed and then nodded. "I see."

"Now, the only toilets for whites you've got are in the dining room," said Mr. Stannum, "but me and Julie can't be traipsing through the dining room when you've got customers to use those toilets. It wouldn't be right."

"No," Daddy agreed, "that wouldn't be right. But neither would it be right for Amy, Leon, and Seaweed to do without facilities. I'm sure you're not suggesting they just go in the street, Mr. Stannum."

Mr. Stannum adjusted the collar of his shirt, which was feeling a bit like a lonesome boa constrictor. "Of course not."

"Then what *are* you suggesting?"

"Well," Mr. Stannum said after a few moments of thought, "the only thing to do as I see it is to make the kitchen toilet for whites only, in accordance with the laws of the city, and not to mention the laws of nature, and to put in a new lavatory for the colored staff. Not that I mind so much"—he cleared his throat—"but I'm thinking of *them*. It's just not what they're used to. There's a closet right beside the toilet back there, and we've got ample storage space already."

"That *is* one idea," said Daddy. He scratched the top of his head and then smoothed his hair, which was thick with pomade, so that it didn't stick up like a rooster's tail. "Putting in a new lavatory would take some doing, though, not to mention a good bit of money. I just don't think my pockets are that deep, considering all the construction going on in the dining room." He patted Mr. Stannum on the back. "So it seems to me, the better plan is to use the same one."

"The same one!" said Mr. Stannum.

"That's right," said Daddy. "I appreciate your concern for the others, as you say, but no one else has complained, and I shouldn't think the others will be bothered. And since you yourself said you didn't mind, I guess we don't have much of a problem after all, do we?"

"Well, er, but," grumbled Mr. Stannum. "No, I suppose we don't."

"Very good," said Daddy. "Then there you have it."

"Excuse me," said Mr. Stannum, heading back toward the

stoves, where Mr. Washington and Seaweed were up to their armpits in grease.

"Oh, wait," said Daddy. "One more thing." Then he stepped into the center of the room. "Everyone, give an ear for a moment, please." When he had everybody's attention, he said, "I'm inviting all the staff and their families here to the restaurant the night before we open. I thought it would be a chance to get to know everyone, and a good way to try out some of the things on the menu."

"But that's July the fourth," said Mr. Stannum.

"That's true," said Daddy. "I know some of you were planning on going down to the celebration on the square, but I thought we could all do some celebrating of our own right here. I know of a place in Baltimore that sells an assortment of fireworks, too. Just wait until you see the Whirling Dervisher and the Marble Flash Salutes. Spectacular."

Seaweed looked at Amy and grinned. "That sound all right by me."

"He don't mean us," whispered Amy. "Don't even think it."

"Sure he does," said Frankie, who couldn't help but overhear. "Don't you, Daddy?"

"That's right," said Daddy. "All are welcome."

June 21, 1939

Dear Frankie, who I remember very well,

You'll be relieved to know that all of my fingers are working just fine. Aunt Dottie won't let me near the tractor, which is all right by me. Incidentally, you shouldn't make a joke about such a thing. There are people who have lost fingers and other parts in tractor accidents, and I'm sure they wouldn't find that very funny.

Anyway, I'm sorry I haven't written, but I've been so busy settling into my new schedule here I barely have time for myself. Aunt Dottie, as it turns out, is quite strict. I have to get up at six o'clock to feed the chickens and turn the horses out to pasture. Then there are chores around the house, weeding the vegetable garden, cleaning the horses' stalls, and then and then and then and then . . .

My afternoons are free, so I really shouldn't complain, but lately I've been so tired from the morning activities that I fall asleep in a chair and don't wake up until suppertime. I think I now know how it feels to be Grandma Engel. (But please don't tell her I said that.)

Tell me how the restaurant is going. I bet it's really exciting. Will you get to work the cash register or seat the customers? Are you taking good care of Dixie? How's Bismarck?

Give my love to them and to Daddy and Mother, too. And Grandma Engel, of course. And everyone else. Even Elizabeth.

Oh, I miss you so.

With sisterly love,
Joan

P.S. Have you seen that no-good Leroy Price much?

15

"JOAN SAYS HELLO," Frankie told Elizabeth as she folded the letter in half lengthwise and slid it into the front pocket of her dress. She sat on the middle of the living room rug and slipped her shoes into her roller skates.

Elizabeth's head was buried in Mother's latest issue of *Ladies' Home Journal*. "That's nice."

"She also says that Aunt Dottie has her doing a lot of work around the farm." Frankie fastened the buckles and tightened the skates with her key. "She hasn't had any time to write before now, she's been so busy."

"Mmm-hmmm."

"She wants to know all about the restaurant, so I'm going to write her all about Amy and Julie and Mr. Washington and Seaweed. And that awful Mr. Stannum, too. And how Daddy is throwing a big Fourth of July party and has invited everybody."

Elizabeth laid the magazine open on her lap. The page, which featured a high-arched eyebrow with step-by-step how-to instructions, draped over her leg. "I don't know what Daddy was thinking."

"What do you mean?" asked Frankie. "Don't you think all the work on the restaurant will be done in time?"

"I'm not talking about all the work that needs done," said

Elizabeth. "I mean I don't know what Daddy was thinking inviting *everybody*."

"Why shouldn't he?" said Frankie. "We'll have plenty of food."

Elizabeth sighed and shook her head. "You don't understand. Just forget it." She returned to her page in the magazine.

"Forget what?" said Frankie. "What should I forget?"

Elizabeth put down the magazine once more in a huff. "All I'm saying is that inviting all the staff, you know," and then she brought her voice down to a whisper, "colored people along with the rest of us, people will talk. And I hope he doesn't get in trouble."

"Elizabeth Baum," said Frankie, getting to her knees, "you sound just like a snob talking like that."

"You take that back right now!" shouted Elizabeth. "I'm no snob. I'm only thinking of Daddy because of what other people might say. You're too young to understand. It matters what other people think."

While Frankie didn't give a fig about what others thought of her, Elizabeth strove for perfection in all that she did. When people took to calling you Princess since the moment you were born, anything less than perfection might disqualify you in their eyes and cause you to lose your crown. The expectation was set from day one, and Elizabeth worked hard to please everyone so that she could maintain her royal designation.

"And what do you think you're going to do on those skates?" asked Elizabeth, indignant.

"Um, roller-skate?" said Frankie, who wondered why it was that Princess, of the three of them, was considered to be the smart one. Such a question.

"No, you are not," said Elizabeth. "It's your turn to clean Dixie's shed."

"I'll do it later," said Frankie. "I've already got my skates on." She stuck her feet in the air and shook her wheels at her sister.

"Mother left me in charge while she and Daddy are taking care of some business at the restaurant," said Elizabeth. "And you need to clean the shed before you do anything else." She licked her finger and turned the page of Mother's magazine. The page made such a snap that it punctuated Elizabeth's command, and Frankie knew that was the end of the argument.

16

FRANKIE READ JOAN'S LETTER to Dixie twice. The pony stomped her hoof when Frankie got to the part about turning the horses out to pasture, and then once again when she said Dixie's name. "I *am* taking good care of you," she said, but Dixie shook her head back and forth in her stall. "I am too," insisted Frankie. "You're as bad as Elizabeth." And then she scooped a handful of oats from the metal bucket they kept in the food bin just outside the shed and held it out to the pony. Dixie immediately drove her nose into Frankie's palm and sucked up every last one of the oats quicker than Mother's Electrolux sweeper.

"Frankie!" yelled Elizabeth from inside the apartment. "Make sure you give her fresh water! And latch the door when you are finished!"

"I know!" Frankie shouted back.

"Last time you didn't and she got into the cider, remember?" yelled Elizabeth.

How could Frankie forget, when Elizabeth brought it up all the time? She made a face in Elizabeth's direction. "And it wasn't the last time," Frankie said under her breath, "it was last year." She stroked Dixie along her mane. "Joan will be back before you know it. And in the meantime, I'm as good as a Number Two as far as you're concerned."

But do you know, that pony shook her head again?

Frankie glared at her. *The Pony With the Human Brain, my word.* "What do you know?" She grabbed the saddle hanging on the wall and laid it across Dixie's back. Then she pulled down the leather driving harness from the shelf and spread it out on the grass. The pony snorted. Even she knew this was going to be a mistake. Frankie slipped the bridle around Dixie's head, grabbed the reins, and led her out of the shed. That part she had done a few times on her own, without Joan, but the driving harness and the cart, well, that was a different story.

For one thing, the driving harness had a lot of different parts and Frankie wasn't quite sure where they all went, how they fit together, and what they hooked onto. That was a lot of things to be unsure about. She tied Dixie to the hitching post by the cart and then stood over the pieces of harness. There was the browband, noseband, and throatlash, which she recognized right away, but had some trouble putting on. It didn't help that Dixie didn't really enjoy having those straps around her head and so kicked up a bit of a fuss. Still, after a brief struggle and some more handfuls of oats, Frankie managed to secure them. "There you go," she said, smiling. "I told you I could do it."

Dixie flicked her tail, which Frankie took to mean that she was impressed.

Frankie stared at the remaining pieces on the ground: wither strap with rein rings, breastplate, false martingale, false bellyband, girth, traces, breeching and breeching strap, hip strap, and crupper and dock. These, of course, were the proper names for the harness parts, but Frankie couldn't remember what they were called and didn't understand why they had to have such strange names in the first place. False martingale? Don't you think that sounds like a bird who tells lies?

Buoyed by her early success, Frankie moved on with confidence, hanging the other pieces of the harness all about the pony like garlands on a Christmas tree. Except that *this* Christmas tree wouldn't hold still and was getting tired of being tied to a post, snorting and whinnying and making enough of a racket that Frankie was sure Elizabeth would hear and come running. And speaking of running, Dixie wanted to very badly. She was itching to stretch those legs and hear the lovely clop-clop of her hooves on cobblestone. There was no sound that gave her as much pleasure, except for perhaps the clang of the metal feed bucket. "Quiet now," Frankie told her, and stuck the entire bucket of oats under her nose.

Frankie went back to work and was quite pleased with herself when she finished, until she saw two straps with buckles lying by her feet. "Oh," said Frankie, looking them over. "Where do these go?" By this time, Dixie had finished the oats—her thick tongue polishing the bottom of the bucket—and was back to rearing her head and raising a ruckus. Frankie told her to hush, but she didn't pay her any mind. A pony only has so much patience, and this one had run out of her very tiny supply many minutes before. If Frankie didn't untie her from the post that instant, there would be no telling what she'd do. The cobblestones were calling her name, and by golly, she was going to answer.

Leaving the two pieces of harness by Dixie's feet, Frankie yanked the cart from the corner of their yard and attached the harness traces to the tree of the cart. She tugged at the breeching and then untied the reins. "Now wait until I get into my seat," she told Dixie. "Just wait."

Dixie did wait. But only barely. Frankie got both feet on the footboard of the cart but had not yet turned around to face forward or to even sit down when Dixie, who could not possibly wait one second more, started into a trot. Frankie held tight to the reins and was knocked back into her seat as Dixie took off out of the yard and down the alley. Not wanting a repeat of the Hercules Beetle Scab Incident, Frankie pulled hard on the reins when they got to the front of the apartment building and slowed Dixie to a walk. The pony fought against the bit, wanting not to be held back, but to go, go, and keep on going. You can take a pony out of a rodeo but, as they say, you can't take the rodeo out of the pony. Yahoo!

By some miracle, Frankie managed to get by the apartment without Elizabeth noticing or coming to check on her. This was what Ava would call a clean getaway.

By the time the two turned onto Locust Street, there was the steady sound of clop-clop beneath them, enough to satisfy Dixie's itch. She settled down sufficiently that Frankie loosened her grip on the reins, but only a little. They continued through town as the afternoon wandered into evening, and before Frankie knew it, she was heading toward the restaurant. A good plan, she figured, because once Mother and Daddy caught a glimpse of her with Dixie, they'd see her differently. They'd see she was able to do a lot on her own, as much as Elizabeth, even, and perhaps they'd finally see that this Number Three didn't belong in the kitchen. No, sir.

As Frankie steered the pony closer to the restaurant, she could see Daddy's Studebaker pulling away from the curb, heading in the other direction. "No, wait!" she yelled. But alas, there was no point. The tires squealed as he rounded the corner, and a few seconds later he was out of sight.

She pulled Dixie to a stop and thought about whether to turn back home or keep on going. Rodeo pony or not, Dixie was nothing against the six-cylinder, ninety-horsepower motor of the Studebaker Dictator. Frankie would never make it home before Mother and Daddy. That was just a fact, plain and simple. And once she did get home and they discovered that she was gone, she would be in a hefty dose of trouble anyway. (Another fact.) Oh brother, there was no way around it. And so, she reasoned, that being the case, there was no point in hurrying back. She snapped the reins, and off they rode.

Frankie steered Dixie to the side of the restaurant and came to a stop. "This is the place," she said to Dixie. "Baum's Restaurant."

Dixie shook her head.

"I know," said Frankie. "You should see the inside. It's even worse."

Dixie shook her head again.

"Don't worry, we're not going in." She sat for a few minutes and stared at the place. Some of the lights were still on inside, which she figured meant that the men were still working on the dining room. They'd need to be if there was any hope of opening on schedule, what with the missing walls and such. Frankie didn't know a lot about restaurants, but people liked to have walls around them while they were eating, she was sure of that much.

Frankie watched the sun sink behind the Hoffman Meat Market building across the street. Then, when she figured Mother and Daddy would just about now be starting to worry, she yanked at the reins and clucked her tongue at Dixie to start moving. But that pony did not budge. Frankie snapped the reins against Dixie's hindquarters and yelled out, "Come on, girl. Giddyup!"

But giddyup that pony did not. There appeared to be no up in her giddy and certainly no giddy in her up.

Frankie had never seen Dixie do this before. She was always ready to get-along-little-dogie. "Dixie!" Frankie pleaded.

That pony had such a belly full of oats, she just preferred at that moment to have herself an old-fashioned rest. Frankie climbed down from the cart and checked Dixie over. She pulled at her bridle with both hands, but the beast might as well have been a statue cemented to the street. Frankie picked up each hoof and examined each leg for any sign of injury, or, well . . . cement. As far as she could tell, though, nothing but a stubborn head seemed to be the matter. "I swear," said Frankie, "you better get going!"

Then, the thought occurred to Frankie that maybe the animal was thirsty. All of those oats *would* make for a dry mouth, she thought. "Do you need a drink, girl? Is that what you're after?"

Dixie stomped at the ground.

"Well, why didn't you say so?" Frankie told Dixie she'd go inside the restaurant and fetch some drinking water. On her way to the door, she looked back and warned Dixie, "Now, don't you go anywhere."

But by the looks of Dixie, this was not going to be a problem.

Frankie jiggled the handle to the front door but found it inconveniently locked. She cupped her hands around her eyes and peered into the window, but saw only the bulbs in the chandeliers throwing shadows over the empty dining room. There were no men working tonight, at least not in the dining room, not even a trace of them. She went back to Dixie and checked on her once more, but Dixie flared her nostrils and whinnied, irritated that Frankie had come back empty-handed.

Then, Frankie remembered the door from the kitchen. She hurried around the back of the restaurant and squeezed through the narrow alley. She tried the door to the colored entrance. It swung open with hardly a pull, and Frankie made her way inside. Only one dim light in the kitchen was on, but it was bright enough for Frankie to get to the shelves of pots and pans without running into anything. She grabbed an aluminum saucepan and headed for the spigot at the sink, but as she did, she heard a voice coming from another room. Frankie dove into one of the cupboards closest to her and closed the door. Although once she was there, in the dark, with her knees pulled up to her chest, she wondered why she was hiding in the first place. This was her family's restaurant, for goodness' sakes. There was no reason for her to be inside a cupboard.

She started scooting out, nudging the door open with her knee, but then stopped when she heard another voice, one that she recognized.

"And this is the kitchen," said Mr. Stannum. He turned on the overhead lights.

Mr. Stannum. Great snakes! Frankie pulled the cupboard door closed. On second thought, hiding wasn't such a bad idea.

"This is some kind of operation," said a man, whose husky voice Frankie recognized as belonging to Mr. Price. There was also the musty scent of cigar smoke, which made her sure of it. "What is the total number under the employ of Mr. Baum?"

"Well, uh," said Mr. Stannum. "I'm not sure . . ."

"What I'm asking is," said Mr. Price, "just how many people are working for Mr. Baum here, at this restaurant? It's no secret, is it? I'd imagine a person in a position such as kitchen manager, like yourself, would be entrusted to know these kinds of things. And other things as well." His voice trailed off.

"Well, I'm not sure of the exact count, and there are more to be hired. Let's see, there's five of us in the kitchen, but we could use a few more good hands, and the bar staff, waitstaff. I'd say at least fifteen, maybe more."

"I see," said Mr. Price, writing that down in his notebook. "Like I said, this is no small operation you've got here. With the Depression on, a lot of folks have fallen on hard times. You'd have to wonder where a man gets money to start up such an enterprise." And then he laughed the way people do when they want you to think they are making a joke but are really as serious as a stiff wool suit.

Frankie didn't like his candor. How did he have the right to question where Daddy got his money to start the restaurant? Slowly and with ever so much caution, she nudged open the cupboard door just enough to have a look.

"Well, thank you for the tour, Mr. Stannum," said Mr. Price. "Mr. Baum told me to stop by the restaurant anytime so we could finish the interview, and yet once again I find that he's not here. I do hope he's not avoiding me. It would be a pity if that was the case."

"I'm sure he's not," said Mr. Stannum. "What I mean is, why would he be?"

"There's been some talk about town," said Mr. Price. "About Mr. Baum's loyalty."

"Loyalty?" said Mr. Stannum.

"That's right," said Mr. Price. "Some say he wasn't born here. His parents were German, you know."

"I didn't . . ."

"Well, ties to your country run deep," said Mr. Price. "The question is, in times such as these, which does he consider to be his country?"

Frankie covered her mouth with both hands so she wouldn't let out a yell.

"Now, I'm not saying he's done anything wrong," continued Mr. Price, "but I guess I'm not saying he hasn't, either. There are a few others in town of German ancestry, of course, but they've all been very cooperative and forthcoming, unlike Mr. Baum. Tell me, Mr. Stannum, have you by chance seen anything unusual around here?"

Mr. Stannum shook his head.

"Strange people coming and going? Witness any strange conversations between Mr. Baum and others?"

"Strange conversations?" asked Mr. Stannum.

"You know," said Mr. Price, "any talk in German, or any mention of Hitler. I've heard from some contacts, people inside the government, that Hitler is sending spies to America."

"Are you saying that Mr. Baum is a . . ."

"Like I said, Mr. Stannum, I'm not saying he is, and I'm not saying he isn't. I'm just asking that you keep your eyes and ears open. You know, now more than ever we've got to stay vigilant and protect this great country of ours. We won't be able to ignore what's happening in Europe for long, mark my words. We'll be in the thick of it soon enough, and when we are, we will need to know who we can trust and who we can't. And those we can't, well, we've got to bring the turncoats to their knees." He handed Mr. Price a calling card. "If you do notice anything suspicious, it is your duty to give me a call."

Mr. Stannum held the card gently in his palm.

"You've been very helpful, though, in filling in some of the blanks," said Mr. Price, smiling. "I better be on my way. Please tell Mr. Baum I stopped by and that I have a few more questions to pose to him."

Mr. Stannum nodded. "Will do, sir."

"Oh, I nearly forgot." Mr. Price unfolded an election poster from inside his jacket and retrieved a roll of tape from a pocket in his trousers. "I'll just fix this to the front window on my way out. And be sure to thank him for his support in the election."

Mr. Stannum said, "I'll be sure to tell him you came by."

"Incidentally, has my esteemed opponent paid a visit?"

"No," said Mr. Stannum. "Not that I've seen."

"You might've noticed there's not one single Robertson sign on the block," said Mr. Price. "George Robertson, let me tell you, is not equipped for the job. I say that not as his opponent, but as a man. He doesn't have the wherewithal to protect our town, our citizens, from outsiders. He's a do-nothing. A musician, a jazz lover no doubt, who, if elected, God forbid, will do nothing for us. Do you know that he is divorced?"

"Uh, no," said Mr. Stannum. "I didn't."

"Shameful," said Mr. Price. "Well, I better be on my way."

"Good evening, Mr. Price," said Mr. Stannum. "I'll see you out. I was just getting ready to lock up and head home."

Frankie slowly pushed open the cupboard door. But that Mr. Price would not stop talking.

"You a family man, Stannum?"

Frankie closed the door again.

Mr. Stannum hesitated. "I'm not married, no."

"Brothers or sisters in town?" asked Mr. Price.

"None to speak of," said Mr. Stannum.

"How strange."

"Well, I did have an older brother," said Mr. Stannum.

"Did?"

"He was killed in the Great War."

"Hmmm, that's too bad," said Mr. Price. "Then you know what it means to make sacrifices for your country."

"My brother, Tommy, he was the hero," said Mr. Stannum. "Not me."

"Yes, well, there are many ways to serve your country. An opportunity may arise in the future, and you may get your chance," said Mr. Price. "Good evening."

Frankie waited until the light in the crack of the cupboard door disappeared before she crawled out. Mr. Price had a lot of nerve saying those things about Daddy. And suggesting that he was a spy for Hitler! A spy! She was so fuming mad, she stormed out of the kitchen door into the alley. Before long she was beside Dixie, who was right where she'd left her, no surprise. What *was* a surprise, though, to both of them, was that Frankie had returned without any water.

"Oh, darn it all. I left the saucepan on the counter," Frankie explained.

Dixie shook her head.

"No, I'm not going back in there. It's almost dark and we need to go home. Mother will have her cake turner out, for certain. And this time she just might use it." Frankie climbed into the cart and snapped the reins. Alas, Dixie stood firm.

"Dixie!" Frankie yelled. "Move, you stubborn beast!"
Then, from somewhere nearby, they both heard music.
And wouldn't you know, that pony began to trot.

Don't tell me I'm scared, I done seen what you did
I said don't say I'm scared, I done seen what you did
You want me to look away, think I'm only a kid
You hopped a train, took yourself on a trip
I said you hopped a train, took yourself on a trip
Papa, you leave us alone, ain't coming back here
*   with that whip*
I'm a-countin' the days you been gone
I'm a-countin' the days you been gone
Someday, Papa, goin' to build me a railroad of my own

17

AS SHE AND DIXIE went on, the music surrounded them like a fog. The closer they got, the warm air became so thick with sound that Frankie nearly had to brush away the notes from her face. They followed the sounds for one block on and then Frankie tried to steer Dixie down Washington Street, but Dixie would not turn. They were about to go down Jonathan Street, about to go into the part of town where she was not allowed to be. Frankie pulled hard on the reins. Dixie reared her head, but she did not stop. "No, Dixie. No, no, no. Not this way."

Frankie pulled again. But as she did, one of the snaps on a line to Dixie's bit came apart and Frankie lost control. She held tight to the reins, but that did her no good. Frankie clung to her seat in the cart and yelled, "Whoa! Whoa!"

But music, even for a pony, has a way of taking you places.

They were heading into a forbidden part of town, and almost certain to wreck. Although Frankie wished she had something to throw at Dixie to get her attention—*Where's a stick of dynamite when you need it?*—and remind her who was in charge, the only thing in her dress pocket was her scab collection, and things weren't quite that dire yet. So, there was nothing to be done but hang on and hope that the lines to the cart held and that Dixie's legs would eventually grow weary.

Let me tell you, putting all your hopes into the Pony With a Human Brain may not have been the wisest decision, especially given Dixie's history, but what else was Frankie to do?

As Dixie trotted on, following the music, Frankie's own brain was thinking about the two pieces of harness she'd left lying on the ground in the backyard. She remembered there were buckles on them, not snaps. And what was it Joan told her about attaching lines with buckles? Something. She had told her something.

Dixie kept on until they found the source of the music on a sidewalk in front of a tattered apartment building. Three colored boys sitting on turned-over washbasins were carving out a stomping and grinding beat alongside a tune that was so full of gloom and agony, Frankie felt as though she were a stranger interrupting a funeral party. The Pony With the Human Brain apparently didn't feel the same way, because she stopped right in front of them and had herself a good listen. Although Frankie was relieved Dixie had finally come to a stop, she wished the pony had chosen a spot about a block or so away. For one thing, she wasn't sure these musicians wanted an audience. And for another, it wasn't polite to attend a funeral party without knowing the dead.

Frankie hopped off the cart and quickly grabbed the broken line. She kept an eye on the musicians as she tried to refasten the line at the bit, but the snap was busted and there was no way to put it back together. The musicians, well, they were deep into the place where music often takes people, and barely seemed to notice her. Moments later, though, the song ended abruptly, or so it sounded to Frankie, and then one of the boys, who had his head hung low over his cigar-box guitar, started singing something else.

Oh little girl, she got a boy's name
She workin' in the kitchen
Now ain't that a cryin' shame
She got the low-down workin' blues
And ole man Stannum he's to blame
Oh man, she got the low-down workin' blues

Frankie dropped the line and went over to the musicians to get a good look at the abercrombie who thought he knew so much.

"What you doing, Seaweed?" said the boy playing washtub bass. "We wasn't finished and that song is all wet."

The boy on the blues harp blasted out a sharp chord and said, "Shoot, hold it right there. I write the songs, dig?"

"I'm just messin', Shorty," said Seaweed. Then he grinned at Frankie. "What you doing out here by youself? Your daddy be knowin' you in this here part of town?"

"What was that song supposed to mean?" said Frankie.

"I asked you first," he said.

Frankie sighed. This boy was too much. "I'm just taking my pony out to stretch her legs. It's not good to keep her cooped up in her shed all day, you know." She tried to sound as though she did this all the time and that it was no big achievement, even though it certainly was. A Number Three trying to move up the ranks should never act like a Number Three, or that's all people will think of you.

"You best be going on home," he said, standing up.

Frankie planted her feet. "It's a free country."

Seaweed raised his eyebrows and nodded. Then he said under his breath, "You're right, it is. For some."

"For your information, I am aiming to go on home," said Frankie. "But a snap on one of the lines broke. And I can't go anywhere until I fix it."

"Hey, are we playin' or what?" said the boy with the blues harp. He started blowing, sounding like a train whistle bearing down the tracks.

Seaweed nodded at him. "In a minute." Then he stood and said to Frankie, "Let me have a look."

"I don't need any help," said Frankie. She made her way around Dixie and picked up the broken line. "Not from you or anybody else." She wanted to make that point very clear.

"All right," said Seaweed. "Then go on and fix the thing on you own and get on with youself." He sat back down on his washtub. "We tryin' to practice over here."

Frankie looked at the broken snap again. She tried to squeeze the metal ring closed, but it was no use. What she needed was some rope or wire. She checked the cart.

Emptier than a street beggar's tin cup.

Frankie shook her head. She could leave Dixie here and walk home. Or lead Dixie by the bit. Either way, with or without a pony, home was a long way to walk. A long, long way. And when she got there, oh, the trouble that would be waiting.

While she was trying to figure out what to do, Seaweed started picking at his guitar and the other boys were carving out another slow, gloomy tune. Frankie watched them sway their heads in time with the rhythm, the boy on the blues harp with his eyes closed, the boy with the bass making such a grimace, as if his appendix was having a spontaneous burst. Frankie's eyes were stuck on Seaweed's fingers. Or to be more exact, the strings on his cigar-box guitar.

"Excuse me," she said. "I'm sorry to interrupt."

"Aw, man," said the bass player. "What is this?"

"Lord Almighty!" yelled the one on the blues harp.

"Now you want help, do you?" said Seaweed, grinning. "Come to you senses?"

Frankie scowled at him. "No. I don't need any help. I just need to borrow one of your guitar strings."

"One of my guitar strings!" shouted Seaweed. "You crazy, girl."

"I'll give it back," she said. "Tomorrow, at the restaurant. I just need it to get home."

"Now I know you crazy," he said.

Frankie reached for his guitar. "You've got four others there. I'm only asking for one."

"Only askin' for one?" said Seaweed, his mouth hanging open.

"You don't know nothin' about no music if you think four strings ain't no different than five," said the boy on the blues harp. "Seaweed, are we practicing here or what?"

"Hold on a second, Shorty," said Seaweed. "I got me an idea." Then he looked at Frankie square in the eye. "Let's say I do give you a string to fix your horse. What you give me?"

"Your string back tomorrow, like I already told you," she said.

"Naw," he said. "I don't mean that. Let me think." He rubbed his chin. "All right. Here it is. I let you borrow a string if you promise— no, swear to it—here and now that you will get your daddy to let us play at his place."

"Play at his place?" asked Frankie.

"That right," said Seaweed. "His place. You know, the restaurant. And I mean when it's open for business, in front of a mess of people. Me and my band."

"*Your* band?" said the bass player.

Frankie looked from Seaweed to Dixie. The setting sun cast a light on Dixie's head in such a way that her eyes gave a sparkle. She flared her nostrils and nudged Frankie's arm with her nose. The pony liked it when the stakes were high.

"What you say?" asked Seaweed, sticking out his hand. "We got us a deal?"

Frankie shook his hand. "Fine."

"There you go, boys," he said, taking a bow, "I just got us a gig." Then he laid the cigar-box guitar across his lap and began to remove one of the strings. It only took a few seconds before the string was free and he was handing it over.

Frankie brought it to the broken snap. Seaweed followed. "Make sure you ain't gonna break it," he told her.

Frankie looped the string around the broken snap and tied it to the bit line. She tugged on it a few times to make sure it held, and as she did, a police car came to a stop beside them.

"Come on, let's go," said Shorty, as he and the bass player scrambled to pick up their washtubs and took off down the alley.

"Oh brother." Frankie shook her head, convinced that this was Mother's doing.

Officer McIntyre emerged from the police car and placed his hand on the billy club suspended from his leather belt. "What seems to be the problem here?"

"No problem here," said Seaweed, keeping his eyes down.

"I wasn't talking to you, boy," Officer McIntyre said. He eyeballed Frankie. "Miss, what are you doing there?"

"I'm sorry my mother troubled you, Officer," said Frankie. "I would've been home by now if this line hadn't broken. But I've fixed it now and that's where I'm headed."

"Your mother?" asked Officer McIntyre.

Frankie nodded. "Mildred Baum. Didn't she call you?"

"I received no such call, miss," he said. "Just on my routine patrol and spotted you here. This part of town is no place for a young girl like yourself." He looked at Seaweed. "Unsavory people around here." He stepped out of the way so that Frankie could climb into her seat on the cart.

Seaweed patted Dixie at her neck. "I better be gettin' on home, too. Ma be thinkin' I hopped a train to the Windy City by now."

Officer McIntyre grabbed the cigar-box guitar from under Seaweed's arm. "Aren't you the same Negro I caught last week on Church Street pestering a shop owner to let you play and disturbing the peace?"

"No, sir," said Seaweed. "Ain't me. Never been on Church Street."

Officer McIntyre swung the guitar like a baseball bat, waiting for one right down the middle. Seaweed's eyes were in a panic as he watched the policeman handle his most prized possession, but he held his tongue. "Best be quiet," his mother had always warned him. "The more you say, the deeper your grave. Anything more than *yes, sir* and *no, sir* be cause for trouble."

"You wouldn't be lying to me, would you, boy?" said the policeman, taking his billy club from his belt and a step toward Seaweed.

"No, sir."

"He helped me, Officer," said Frankie, interrupting the officer's questions. "He works at my daddy's restaurant, and wasn't doing anything but trying to help me get on my way. Honest."

Her heart was beating so loud in her ears she could barely hear Officer McIntyre ask, "Miss?"

"Baum," she said. "Frankie Baum."

"Baum?" said the officer. "Is your father Hermann Baum?"

Frankie nodded and then smiled, hoping that her father's name would lend credence to her words.

But the officer just narrowed his eyes. Finally, he tossed the guitar at Seaweed, who caught it by the neck and nestled it under his arm.

"I don't want to see you around here again," he said to Seaweed.

"No, sir," said Frankie and Seaweed at the same time.

As Officer McIntyre returned to his car, Seaweed picked up his washbasin and headed for the alley without looking back. Frankie flicked the reins and started Dixie in a trot. She tried to slow her racing heart and stole a glance at Seaweed as he disappeared between the buildings.

She wondered about many things on her journey home. Among them, what had almost happened? And, how on earth would she make good on her deal?

18

IT WAS A QUARTER past six o'clock when Frankie steered Dixie to the backyard of the apartment.

Ten minutes later she had Dixie securely tucked away in her shed, harness unfastened and returned to the shelf. She untied Seaweed's guitar string, wound it in a coil, and stuck it in her dress pocket. Dixie could not get to the water pail fast enough, and while Frankie was fumbling with the snaps, that pony was lapping up the water as if there were peppermints sitting on the bottom.

At half past six, Frankie was sitting on the stone steps that led to the alley alongside the apartment and thinking of what she would say to Mother and Daddy in defense of her whereabouts. Much of her thinking had to do with it all being Elizabeth's fault. After all, Elizabeth was in charge and hadn't been keeping an eye on Frankie as she should have. As everyone knew, that was one of the main responsibilities of a Number One.

A solid excuse, don't you think?

Frankie hadn't gotten very far along that line of thinking when Bismarck, who had been trying to keep cool under the shade of the side porch, caught her scent on the hot breeze—a mix of sweat and equine—and tracked her. He soon began announcing her arrival in the only way he knew how—howling and yipping, and licking at her face. Apparently, he wanted everyone in the neighborhood to know that he, and no one else, had found her, safe and sound.

Frankie tried to quiet him, but it was too late.

Mother was first out the kitchen door, followed by Elizabeth, and then Daddy. Frankie got to her feet and winced when she saw Mother with the cake turner in her hand. "I just took Dixie out for a bit," said Frankie, getting to her feet, careful to keep her rear out of Mother's reach. "She was in her shed all day. Elizabeth hasn't taken her out for a while . . ."

"Don't you dare pin this on me," said Elizabeth, with her hands on her hips.

Frankie ignored her. "And since Joan is gone, it was up to me to do. And look"—Frankie pointed to Dixie and then to herself—"we're fine. Except for a broken snap, which I fixed, nothing at all bad happened. We went out in the cart and everything."

"You hooked up Dixie all by yourself?" said Daddy. "To the cart?"

Frankie nodded, and she thought she saw a trace of a smile cross Daddy's face. "I can do a lot more than you think." She cleared her throat. "Even at the restaurant. I can seat customers or something like that. I know it."

"What does the restaurant have to do with anything, young lady?" said Mother. "We're talking about your leaving home without asking your sister, all by yourself, where nobody knew where you were. What if something happened?"

"Like what?" said Frankie. For the life of her, she didn't know what Mother was afraid would happen, only that there were fears of all sorts of things living inside her, fears that the worst could happen at any given moment, and then how do you go on when your worst fear comes true?

"Like *what?*" Mother said, her knees buckling slightly and throwing her off center, as if the ridiculousness of the question caught her by surprise. "That animal could throw you, leave you lying in an alley somewhere with your head cracked wide open. You could be run over by a car, kidnapped by Gypsies, roughed up by thugs . . ."

"Mildred," said Daddy, putting his arm around her shoulders. "Let's not get carried away."

"You just ask Mr. and Mrs. Lindbergh about getting carried away," she snapped. It had been seven years since the baby boy of Charles Lindbergh, the famous aviator, was kidnapped, held for ransom, and later found dead, but it still haunted Mother, along with much of the rest of the country.

Mother held up her hand, the one without the cake turner, and showed Frankie the very small distance between her thumb and index finger. "I was this close to calling the police. Don't ever do that to me again, you hear me?"

"I won't," said Frankie, keeping to herself the fact that the police had turned up anyway.

"Good." Mother took in a deep breath. "Now, you're on punishment for ten days."

"Ten days?" complained Frankie.

"Would you like to make it eleven?" said Mother.

Frankie shook her head.

"And I don't want to hear any talk about it," said Mother. "You're to be at the restaurant all day and then come right on home. No pony rides, no playing out back, no roller-skating, and no radio."

"No radio!" said Frankie.

Mother raised the hand with the cake turner ever so slightly, and Frankie relented.

"Supper's getting cold." Mother turned on her square heels and went back into the apartment without waiting for the rest of them.

Elizabeth followed close behind after shaking her head at Frankie, showing her disappointment—a classic Number One move. But it was Daddy whom Frankie was concerned about. "You gave your mother a real scare," he said, linking arms with Frankie as they walked the alley. Bismarck stayed by Daddy's other side.

Frankie nodded. "Daddy, I took Dixie to the restaurant to show you and Mother, but when you weren't there, I went inside to get her some water. I overheard Mr. Stannum talking to Mr. Price."

Daddy's steps slowed a bit. "Overheard?"

"I was in the cupboard."

"I see." Daddy nodded but didn't ask for any further explanation, as if being inside a cupboard was a very normal, run-of-the-mill kind of thing.

"Mr. Price was asking a lot of questions about the restaurant," she went on.

"Was he, now?"

"He wanted to know how many people worked there, for one thing," said Frankie. "And then he wanted to know how you had the money to start the business, you know, because of the Depression being on." She was about to step up onto the porch, but Daddy placed his hand on her arm.

"Yes, well, the Chamber of Commerce likes to know those kinds of things," said Daddy. "And Mr. Price thinks it's his job to know everything about everything. Not for you to worry."

But Frankie was worried. She knew she should tell Daddy about what else Mr. Price had said, about Hitler's spies and about whether or not Daddy was really born here in America, but she was afraid. It's not as though she believed those things were true. Of course she didn't. But if she said them out loud, if she repeated them, she worried that maybe—just maybe—they could be.

Daddy gently pinched Frankie's chin. "You run along now and eat your supper. You know how lima beans are when they get cold. Even Bismarck won't touch them."

Bismarck licked Daddy's knuckles at the mention of his name, and Frankie opened the screen door to the kitchen. But she turned back when she noticed Daddy wasn't behind her. "Aren't you coming?"

"I'll be along in a minute," he said, taking a seat on the porch step. "Just catching my breath."

"But the limas," said Frankie.

"I said, go ahead now," said Daddy. "Don't keep your mother waiting any longer."

Frankie did go ahead, and when she got to the dining room she found Grandma Engel, Mother, Uncle Hal, Aunt Edith, Ava, Martha, and Elizabeth all huddled around the table. "There she is," said Grandma Engel with a wink. "No need to send out the cavalry."

Frankie took her seat on one of the two empty chairs. The food was already on each of the plates: slippery potpie, boiled lima beans seasoned with ham, and buttered bread.

"Can we eat now?" moaned Martha, her face hovering just over the plate of food in front of her.

"Not yet," said Mother. "We're just waiting for Hermann."

"You shouldn't have gone off by yourself like that," Aunt Edith told Frankie. "Don't you care a thing about your mother's nerves?" Aunt Edith was short, like Mother, but more round and just as nervous. She liked experimenting with makeup, and never left her house without a fresh coat of red lips, and eyebrows painted pencil-thin and so high on her forehead that she always appeared surprised.

"Aw, come on now, Edie," said Uncle Hal. "It turned out all right."

"My girls always were worriers," said Grandma Engel. "You'd have thought they'd grow out of that."

Aunt Edith pursed her dark red lips and neither one said anything more.

"Where'd you go?" asked Ava, all wild-eyed and eager for information. "To the racetrack? Or to the cinema? Naw, don't say you went to the cinema. There's been no good show there since *Son of Frankenstein* played last winter."

Grandma Engel said, "So *you* say. That *Young Mr. Lincoln* picture is a good one, I'd bet. Henry Fonda is a fine actor, and nice looking, too." She fanned her face with her napkin.

As Grandma Engel was going on about the likes of Mr. Fonda, Martha had her tongue out and was letting it dangle across the pile of boiled dough on her plate. Then she let it linger over the pat of butter on her piece of white bread.

"He certainly is," said Aunt Edith. She reached across Ava and swatted at Martha's arm.

Martha retracted her tongue and then started to tear up. "But I'm so hungry," she sobbed.

Ava shook her head. "Henry Fonda ain't no Boris Karloff."

"Isn't," corrected Elizabeth.

"Remember the part when Baron Wolf von Frankenstein swings across his laboratory on a rope and knocks the monster into a fiery sulfur pit?" Ava sat back in her chair and smiled. "That was just about the best thing I ever seen."

"Saw," said Elizabeth.

"Where can you get one of those sulfur pits, anyway?" asked Ava.

"Just what would you do with a sulfur pit?" said Elizabeth.

"Let's change the subject," said Mother, who thought it best not to know too much about the inner workings of Ava's mind.

Ava shrugged. "All right. So where'd you go, then, Frankie?"

Frankie took a drink of milk. "To the restaurant."

"The restaurant?" said Ava, her mouth gaping. "The place where you were all day long?"

Frankie nodded.

"Man oh man," said Ava, folding her arms across her chest, "what a waste of freedom."

"And then down Jonathan Street," said Frankie.

"Jonathan Street?" said Mother.

"To where the coloreds live?" said Ava, her eyes widening. She was clearly impressed.

"Frances Marie," said Mother, "what have we told you about going to that part of town?"

Frankie started to answer, but Mother held up her hand. "Don't say a word until your father gets here. I want him to hear this straight from the horse's mouth." She gave Frankie a grim look and then turned her head toward the kitchen. "Hermann? You out there?"

"He said he'd be right in," said Frankie.

"I can go check on him, Mother," said Elizabeth, removing her napkin from her lap.

"No, I'll go," said Frankie. She pushed back her chair and jumped up before Elizabeth had a chance to beat her to it. On her way to the kitchen, Frankie heard a remark from Elizabeth about her animal-like behavior, which only made Frankie grin.

Daddy wasn't in the kitchen, though. Frankie checked the side porch and the alley. "Daddy? Are you out here? Everybody's waiting to eat. And Martha isn't going to make it much longer." The alley and porch were empty, except for Bismarck, who was preoccupied with licking the long fur between the pads on his front paw.

Frankie ran to the gravel lot behind the yard. Daddy's Studebaker wasn't parked there in its usual place. On the way back inside, Frankie wondered what would've made Daddy disappear like that. One minute talking about cold lima beans, and the next, vanished. Was it because of what she'd said about Mr. Price and Mr. Stannum?

"Well?" said Mother.

"Daddy's not here," said Frankie. "He's gone."

19

"DO YOU THINK DADDY is all right?" Frankie asked Elizabeth as she buttoned up her cotton nightgown and climbed into bed. She wouldn't normally start such a conversation with Elizabeth, but she needed to talk to someone, and Bismarck was asleep on the porch.

"What do you mean?" Elizabeth was already settled in her bed and propped up against the velvet headboard, a book in her lap. "Why wouldn't he be all right?" she said, opening the book and finding the last page where she'd left off.

"You know, disappearing like that." Frankie scooted herself to the center of her bed so she wouldn't have to see Joan's empty side.

Elizabeth didn't look up from her page. "You don't know the first thing about running a business, Frankie. He has a lot to do. Something you should think about the next time you go off gallivanting around town without telling anyone."

"But what business would he have to do all of a sudden? Just as we were about to have supper?"

Elizabeth snapped her book closed. "I don't know, but don't you go bothering him about it. He has enough on his mind these days."

"All right, fine," said Frankie. Was it possible for a Number One to refrain from bossing? No, it was not. "I won't go bothering him."

"Good." Elizabeth sighed and opened her book once again.

"Elizabeth?"

"What, Frankie?"

"Does anyone tease you, or give you trouble about Daddy?"

Elizabeth looked up. "About Daddy? No, why would they?"

"You know, about him being a German."

Elizabeth sat right up in bed. "What are you talking about, Frankie Baum? Daddy is no German."

Frankie got to her knees and gathered up a corner of the cotton sheet in her palm. "I don't mean one of *those* Germans, not those Nazi Germans, the ones making trouble and war. But I just mean being from Germany, or having his family there. Does anyone say anything to you about that?"

Elizabeth shook her head. Her eyes were opened wide, as if this were the first time she'd ever heard of such a thing. Frankie wondered how it could be that she and Elizabeth shared the same mother and father—the same bedroom, even—but lived on different planets in opposite universes. Just once, Frankie wanted to visit Elizabeth's planet, where life was easy and the biggest trouble was deciding whether to wear your hair in finger waves or pin curls. "Why, have people said something to you?"

"Not people, really," said Frankie. "One person."

"Who?"

"Leroy Price," said Frankie.

"What did he say?"

"He asked if we were going to make German food at the restaurant." Frankie winced at remembering and wished she'd gotten some swings in or a good kick up his backside. She would have, she knew, if that Seaweed hadn't interfered.

"Oh," said Elizabeth, looking relieved. "Is that all? Frankie, there are Italian restaurants in town, you know. Jewish delicatessens. I'm sure he was just curious about the food."

"I heard his father say some things, too," protested Frankie.

"Mr. Price from the Chamber of Commerce?" said Elizabeth. Frankie nodded.

"What did he say? Things about Daddy or the restaurant?"

"Both," said Frankie.

Elizabeth shook her head, dismissing Frankie's concerns. "Mr. Price, I'm sure, just wants to know about the restaurant because it's his job at the Chamber of Commerce to know about businesses in town. That's all."

"I don't know," said Frankie quietly.

"Look," said Elizabeth, "everybody loves Daddy. He's got friends everywhere—the Alsatias, the Owls Club, the Eagles. Do you think they'd let him into those clubs if they thought of him in . . . you know, that way?"

"You mean being a German?" said Frankie.

"Shh!" Elizabeth was very close to throwing her book at Frankie. "Would you stop saying that?"

Frankie wondered if Elizabeth had a point. "I guess you're right."

"Of course I'm right," said Elizabeth, leaning back against her pillow, as if there shouldn't be an ounce of doubt. "Now, go to sleep."

Frankie turned over so her back was to Elizabeth. But she did not sleep.

No, sir, she most certainly did not. For how can you sleep and listen for the door at the same time?

20

DADDY CAME HOME LATE that night.

Frankie heard the creak of the screen door in the kitchen and then Bismarck's toenails on the hardwood floor. She climbed out of bed and stood in the doorway of her room, peeking her head into the dark hall as she strained her ears to listen.

"Hermann," said Mother. "What happened? Where did you go?"

"Everything's fine, Mildred," said Daddy. "I had forgotten that I needed to see Fritz about some business matters, is all."

"Fritz? What business could you have at this hour? And to go without saying anything?" said Mother. "I don't understand. That wasn't like you, Hermann. First Frances disappears and then you? My nerves can't take much more."

"I should've telephoned, and I'm sorry," he said. "I didn't mean to worry you. It's not good to worry so much, you know. It does no good. No good!" Daddy's voice funneled down the hallway and woke Elizabeth.

"What's going on?" said Elizabeth, rubbing her eyes.

"Nothing," whispered Frankie. "Daddy came home."

"Oh, Frankie, go to sleep," she said.

Frankie ignored her.

"Shh," Mother said to Daddy. "You'll wake the girls."

"Whatever is going to happen is going to happen, worry or not worry," he said.

"Have you been drinking?" said Mother.

"Just one," he said, and then, "I might've had two, or three, but it was such a small glass it hardly counts."

"Please tell me," said Mother, "is something the matter?"

"What could possibly be the matter?" he said. "The place of wide renown is where dreams happen to regular people. The sky above us is as wide as it is high, Millie. We're in the dream business."

"I thought we were in the food business," said Mother.

"Everything's been taken care of, dear. Come on, it's been a long day."

Frankie heard their footsteps heading down the hall. She ducked back inside her room and slid under her covers. Bismarck joined her soon after, walking in circles over the empty spaces on the bed until finally deciding that Joan's pillow was an adequate resting spot. Frankie listened awhile longer but heard nothing more. Not that she could hear much over Bismarck's heavy breathing, but still . . .

Frankie rolled over and was just about to close her eyes when Elizabeth whispered, "Frankie, you still awake?"

"Yeah," said Frankie.

"Me too."

21

THERE WAS SOMEONE ELSE awake across town.

Mr. Sullen Waterford Price, Esquire, was working on his speech for the July Fourth festivities on the square. He stood in the center of his study and looked at his wife, Mrs. Price, who was perched quite delicately on the edge of their striped Victorian sofa, dabbing her nose with a pink-laced handkerchief and listening intently. Then he began to read.

"*Ladies and gentlemen, tonight as we celebrate our nation's independence, I would like to speak to you about peace in our time, of war being outlawed, and the laying down of arms across the world. That would be appropriate on this fourth day of July, the birthday of this great country: to celebrate peace. But friends, there is evil brewing in the world and there is talk that it may soon reach our shores. Well, I stand before you to tell you that it's already here . . .*"

Mr. Price, Esquire, looked up at Mrs. Price at that point. She nodded, blinked her eyes, and dabbed some more at her nose.

After he finished and Mrs. Price went on to bed, he removed a piece of paper from a drawer in his walnut desk and started to do some figuring. First, he tallied the number of campaign posters he had delivered to businesses around town, then he ticked the number of businesses that were displaying his posters in their windows, and lastly—and most severely—he ticked those that weren't.

George Robertson was gaining an edge with some in town, he feared. More of those blasted Robertson signs were cropping up in unexpected places. To shore up his win, his own campaign needed something more. Something that the citizens of Hagerstown couldn't afford to vote against. Something that struck fear in their hearts.

Then he took hold of his Wahl Oxford fountain pen and, emboldened by immense patriotism and sense of duty, wrote down this name: "Hermann Baum."

June 26, 1939

(Very early in the morning)

Dear Joanie,

I was so happy to have received your letter and am relieved you are not permitted to use Aunt Dottie's tractor. To think of you trying to drive such a thing when I know how much trouble you have with our radio set.

Farm work seems a lot more fun than working in a restaurant kitchen, believe me. I will gladly swap places with you anytime, just say the word.

Dixie and Bismarck say hello, and don't you worry, they are being well cared for by me. (Elizabeth hardly helps at all.)

Things are quite strange here with you gone, I must say. Daddy, for one, has not been himself. Do you know anything about Daddy being a German? I mean, not the bad kind, of course. Does Aunt Dottie talk about Germany at all? I know these are strange questions to ask, but that awful Leroy Price and his father have said some things, and with Daddy acting so strangely, I just don't know what to think. It's hard to think about these things without you here to think them with.

I miss you more-than-tongue-can-tell,

Frankie

Dear Frankie,

The postman has not yet delivered your reply to my last letter, but I am writing to you anyway. Writing to you makes me feel like we're in the same place, not miles and miles apart. Oh, how I wish the mail didn't take so many days to arrive.

Everything is so lush and green here, not at all like at home. Aunt Dottie's cornfield and bed of zinnias are so colorful, they nearly hurt my eyes. Honestly, I've been here almost a month now and I still am not used to it.

There are creatures here that I have never before seen or heard. Whistle-pigs, moles, and garter snakes. At night, I fall asleep to the sounds of coyotes and crickets, and in the morning I wake to a symphony of birds, not the pigeons and robins and crows at home, but goldfinches and bluebirds and purple martins.

Aunt Dottie and I went to the county fair a few nights ago. We watched the pig races and rode the carousel. My horse had a green saddle with a matching sash. You would have liked the one done up in robin's-egg blue right beside mine.

But you may be pleased to know that not everything here is enchanting. I made the mistake of telling Aunt Dottie how fond I am of Shirley Temple. She asked me if I'd mind if she fixed my hair in ringlets like Shirley's, and of course, I couldn't say no. I didn't mind so much at first, I confess, thinking it would only be one time. But now, Aunt Dottie wants to curl my hair every day, and to be truthful, I do not know how much more of it I can stand. She's even taken to calling me Shirley. She means no harm, I know, but the whole experience has caused me to sour on Miss Temple, and for that I know I will never be able to forgive Aunt Dottie.

I hope to receive a letter from you soon.

With sisterly affection,
Joanie

P.S. I am certain you are having great fun at the restaurant, and you will owe me ten cents. (I haven't forgotten our wager.)

22

"LOOK WHO'S HERE," SAID Seaweed, when Frankie pushed open the kitchen door. "Back to join us circus elephants." He was at the Frigidaires with Mr. Washington, loading in boxes of food. He juggled apples as he pulled them from the box, tossing them into the air two at a time and catching them. Or, *trying* to catch them. He did catch a few, to be sure, but it is a known fact that guitar pickers just don't play ball all that well.

Mr. Washington soon put a stop to the show. "Boy, I ain't gonna tell you again." He grabbed the apples from him and loaded them into the iceboxes. "More workin', less playin', if you aiming to keep this job."

"I am," said Seaweed. "I am."

Frankie retrieved the guitar string wound in a circle from her dress pocket and handed it to him.

"Held good?" he asked.

Frankie nodded and thanked him.

"You be holdin' good to our deal, too," he said. "Don't forget, now."

She hadn't forgotten. She had no plan about how to do it, but she hadn't forgotten.

Then Seaweed started humming the tune of some song that had

notes so low and mournful they sounded like they were climbing out of the dirt. Frankie wondered about that song, and how a boy who acted like such a clown could sing songs in the doldrums. But there was no time to ask. Because Mr. Stannum had a new job for her: cleaning the kitchen windows.

"Believe it or not," said Mr. Stannum, handing Frankie a metal bucket and a rag, "we should be able to see out those windows. They're covered in about an inch of grime, so you'll have to put some elbow grease into it."

"Yes, sir." Frankie stared into the empty bucket. *This is it.* She was convinced. This was what she'd be doing for the rest of the summer: it would take her at least that long to clean the layers of filth off the glass.

She filled the empty bucket with soap and hot water from the spigot and then climbed onto the countertops to reach the windows. She plunged the rag into the bucket and slapped it onto the window. Soapy water dripped down her arm and spilled onto the counter. She wiped her arm on her dress and pushed the rag around the windowpane until the square glass was doused. The dirt, though, stubborn as it was, stayed put.

"Like Stannum say," shouted Seaweed from the other side of the room, "you got to put your elbow into it."

Mr. Washington told Seaweed to go on and mind his own business, while Frankie gritted her teeth and pressed harder, until finally some of the grime started to loosen. She kept at it, but man oh day, after a while her arm started to ache. She dropped the rag into the bucket and caught the sweat on her face with her dress collar.

As she gave her arm a rest, she watched Amy scrubbing the floor and Seaweed and Mr. Washington cleaning the grease traps. She closed her eyes and imagined a cyclone blowing into town and lifting her away to the Land of Oz. She saw herself spinning and spinning way up, up, up into the sky, leaving these dirty windows and the kitchen and the restaurant to the wind.

Good-bye.

Be seeing you.

I'll write as soon as I get there.

"Would you look at that," said Seaweed, laughing. "She done gone to sleep standin' up. Like a horse." Instantly, Frankie fell from the sky, and when she opened her eyes, she was right back in Kansas like she'd never even left. Believe me, a drop like that could make a person a little dizzy in the head, and as she shifted her feet to steady herself, her sandal slipped on the wet countertop. Down she went. For real this time.

"Gracious, you all right, girl?" said Amy, kneeling next to her.

Frankie, who'd landed mostly on her backside, had wounded her pride more than her rear end. She got to her feet, wincing a little, and glanced at Seaweed. He was shaking his head at her and could barely hold back his grin. Frankie rubbed her hip. "I'm all right."

"Maybe you should have you momma tend to you to make sure ain't nothing got broke," said Amy.

Frankie shook her head. She knew Mother wouldn't settle for anything less than a whole lot of fussing and a trip to the doctor.

"You go on, now," said Amy. Then she lowered her voice to a whisper. "Don't you worry none; if Mr. Stannum asks, I'll tell him your daddy come calling for you." She winked at Frankie and nodded in the direction of the kitchen door.

Frankie didn't mind a break from the windows, and maybe now was as good a time as ever to talk to Daddy about what else she could do in the restaurant, seeing how dangerous things could be in the kitchen.

When Frankie pushed open the kitchen door, she saw the dining room crowded with workmen, tools, and an inch of sawdust. She found a path by the front door and headed up the stairs, taking them slowly on account of her aching behind.

At the top of the stairs, she glided her hand along the balcony railing until she reached Daddy's office and heard his voice. The door to his office was open partway, and she stood just outside, listening. "He knows nothing about us," said Daddy. "It's all for show. Simply politics."

"I think you underestimate him, Hermann," said Fritz. "Just tell him what he wants to hear and he will leave you alone. Put his sign up in your front window like I did, and you won't have any trouble. We have to be very careful these days."

"You don't think I'm being careful?"

"All I'm saying is that you shouldn't give Price any reason to be suspicious. What about the box? You don't have it somewhere he could find—I mean, if he or anyone saw where it came from—"

"No, no," interrupted Daddy. "I took your advice and put it someplace safe, out of town."

"Good," said Fritz. "Now come to your senses about Price, hear? I better get back. See you tonight."

Frankie bolted from the door and took the stairs four at a time. She didn't stop until she got to the kitchen, which was, incidentally, where Mr. Stannum was, asking about her. Amy was saying something to him, but what, exactly, Frankie didn't know, because all she could think about was what she had just heard. Why did Daddy have to be careful? And perhaps most important, what was in the box and why did he have to hide it?

23

DADDY CAME HOME LATE that night. And more than a few nights after that. Frankie had gotten good at staying awake way past the time she'd normally drift off, for it was easy to stay awake when you're trying to make sense of what's going on with Daddy and at the same time thinking of ways to prove to everyone that you don't belong in the kitchen, that you could do other, more important things if only you had the chance.

As good as Frankie got at keeping herself up until the wee hours of the night, she got even better at listening for the creak of the door to their apartment and Daddy's footsteps in the hall. She made Bismarck sleep by her bedroom door, instead of beside her in bed. For one thing, it was too hot to sleep next to a panting fur coat, and for another, Bismarck's ears were twice the size of Frankie's and could hear impossibly faraway things like the hiccup of a mouse.

Frankie suspected that Mother stayed awake long into the nights as well, but if she did, she and Daddy were careful to keep their talks at a whisper.

24

ON ONE ESPECIALLY HOT and humid morning, following an especially late evening, Frankie woke early. She found Daddy adjusting the knot in his tie at the dining room mirror. She watched him quietly from the hall for a while, watched him pull at his collar and straighten his vest, his good eye close to the mirror and stretched open extra wide.

She didn't know why exactly, but at this moment Frankie didn't feel quite at ease. Daddy looked the same to her, he did, and he seemed the same, straightening his tie and such as he always did each morning. But still, there she was in the hall, just standing there silent and watching, something she had never done before.

As she looked on, Daddy dropped his hands from his tie and for a long and quiet moment stared at his reflection. His mouth dipped down at the corners as he watched himself, his eyes becoming like slits, staring so long and hard that he became almost unrecognizable to himself. To Frankie, too.

Frankie grew uncomfortable there in the shadows of the hall, spying, and not understanding what Daddy was looking at, or looking for. She stepped into the light. Daddy jumped at the sight of her and his hand went to his chest. "Good Lord, Frankie, where did you come from?"

"Back there," she said, pointing toward the hall.

His mouth and eyes returned to their regular position as he undid his tie for the second time and shook it out to start again. "Well, you really shouldn't sneak up on a person like that. It's uncivilized, you know."

"Sorry, Daddy," she said.

He sighed and then got back to the mirror. "Very well." He looped the tie around his neck and fastened it at his throat after a number of twists and pulls. Then he turned toward Frankie. "What do you think?"

Frankie had been thinking, but not about ties. "Daddy," she said, "I'd like to try out another job at the restaurant." Then she added, just to be clear, "One that doesn't take place in the kitchen."

He frowned slightly. "Honey girl, we're a little short-staffed in the kitchen. That's where we could really use you most."

"But there's got to be another place where you could use my help," said Frankie. "I can do anything, you know." She took a few steps back so that he could see her, really see her.

Daddy smiled, but he couldn't see her, not really. It wasn't entirely his fault, Frankie knew. How could he see her for who she was with only one good eye?

"You do know that, right, Daddy?"

"Of course I do," he said. "You're a Baum, after all." Then he squeezed her shoulder. "Tell you what: stick it out in the kitchen just until we get more people hired, and then we'll see what else you can do."

"But when will that be?" said Frankie. "Today?"

Daddy sighed. "Not likely today, no."

"Tomorrow, then?"

Daddy shook his head. "Frankie."

But she was beginning to feel desperate. "When?"

"Patience, now," said Daddy. "Please."

But let it be known, it's hard to be patient when you are perpetually last and forever at the bottom.

"Now, I have to get going," said Daddy. "Tell your mother that I'll see you all down at the restaurant later this morning." He kissed her on the head as he passed by.

"All right," said Frankie. But things weren't right. And no one but Frankie seemed to notice.

AT THE RESTAURANT, DADDY and Inky were admiring the new neon sign out front that read "**BAUM'S RESTAURANT AND TAVERN**" when Mother, Elizabeth, and Frankie arrived. "There you are," said Daddy, pointing at the vertical sign as the neon lit blue. "Look there; now it's official."

"Would you take a look at that," said Mother, gazing up, in awe, as if her name were spelled out in stars.

Inky, who was just about Mother's size and always wore a grin on his face, said, "Guess who's going to be playing the organ during weekday dinners?"

"Who?" said Frankie. Despite everything she knew, there was a tiny place in the center of her heart that felt it might be her, that it could've been her, if things were just a little bit different. Certainly somebody would eventually recognize that she didn't belong in the kitchen, wouldn't they?

"My Margaret," said Inky.

Frankie's mouth fell open. "Mrs. Inkletter? I didn't know she knew how to play."

"Oh, sure," said Inky. "She's been playing since she was your age, Frankie. Though, she don't have much chance to practice these days since we sold our piano. We had to, you know, to make room for Margaret's mother when she came to stay two years back." Inky's grin was still there, but it dimmed a little.

"Well, does she know 'Chopsticks'?" inquired Frankie.

"I reckon she does," said Inky.

"What about 'When the Saints Go Marching In'?" said Frankie.

"Certainly does."

"Well, how about . . ."

"That's enough, Frances," said Mother, putting her hand on Frankie's shoulder and ending the quizzing.

"Why don't you all go on in," said Daddy. "They've just dropped off the new cash register, so Princess, you should give it a try."

Honestly, that is what he said.

"Really?" said Elizabeth, racing to the door.

"I don't believe it," said Frankie, following right behind. "She gets to work the cash register? How come *she* gets to work the cash register?"

Frankie never did get an answer, but she barely noticed anyway. Because once she got inside, lo and behold, there it was. The glorious cash register practically lit up the whole room. The nickel-plated brass sparkled under the chandeliers, and the five rows of buttons were so round and perfect they practically called Frankie by name.

Did I mention that it was glorious?

Mother stood in front of it and glided her hand along the word "National" etched in the brass on the marquee at the top. Then, ever so gently, she pressed the lever to open the cash drawer. The most delightful bell chimed as the well-oiled drawer slid open, but to tell you the truth, hearing it nearly made Frankie sick. It wasn't the sound of the bell, of course, but the realization that Elizabeth—not Frankie—was going to be pushing those buttons and counting change, and making that wonderful bell ring.

"Have you worked one of these before, Princess?" Mother asked.

"Sure," said Elizabeth. "Or something like it. One time Katrina Melvich let me play with the cash register at her dad's pharmacy. I'm sure this register works the same way."

Mother nodded, as if there was no doubt in her mind that Elizabeth could do anything. If Elizabeth said she could've piloted the *Hindenburg*, for goodness' sakes, no one would think otherwise.

Frankie watched as Elizabeth stood beside Mother and was about to push one of those perfect buttons. It was bad enough that Elizabeth was going to have the job of working the register, but that she was going to get to touch those buttons first, and press them down, well, that was simply too much for Frankie to bear.

Something inside her, you could say, snapped.

Frankie elbowed her way in front of Mother and Elizabeth and clung to the cash register like a starving dog holding on to a soup bone. "Let me" is what Frankie heard come out of her own mouth as she climbed up the cash stand and threw herself on top of the machine. It wasn't her best moment, certainly not her proudest, but she was overcome with the need to do something. And that, dear friend, is what she did.

"Frances Marie, come down off that register right now," shouted Mother. "What has gotten into you?"

"She's going to break it," said Elizabeth. "Daddy, do something."

But Frankie did not hear any of this. Because she was too busy pressing every single button on the cash register, sometimes two at a time, and then pulling down on the lever to hear that bell ring and ring and ring. The drawer opened each time, and when it did, Frankie slammed it closed again. She wasn't sure how many times she was able to open and close the drawer—thirteen, or perhaps fourteen—before she felt hands gripping her arms and pulling her off.

"She's gone mad," said Elizabeth.

"Frances Marie," said Mother, disappointment heavy in her voice.

The hands turned out to be Inky's and Daddy's, but Frankie managed to get in one more bell ring—*Fifteen!*—before relenting to their will. When she had both feet on the floor and they finally let go of her arms, she was feeling somewhat better.

"Frankie," said Daddy.

But Frankie didn't give him or Mother a chance to say more. "I know, I know," she said with a shrug. "To the kitchen."

26

IT WAS NO SOONER than Frankie opened the kitchen door that Mr. Washington told her to go right away to Hoffman Meat Market and help Amy bring back chickens. Dead ones, and a lot of them.

"Chickens?" said Frankie.

Mr. Washington nodded.

Seaweed said, "You know, the little birds that run around the barnyard, a-peckin' and a-scratchin' and tastin' real good breaded and fried with a heap of mashed potatoes?"

"I know what chickens are," said Frankie, indignant.

Mr. Washington said, "Amy done left for Hoffman's a half hour ago, and she might be needing some help getting those birds back here. We got stock to make and freeze. Seaweed and me got to work on that fan that quit runnin' again. And Julie's got a mess of bread she workin' on. Can you do that?"

Frankie nodded and told him that yes, she could. Just like Elizabeth, she could do anything. And maybe, just maybe, word would get back to Daddy.

She left the kitchen and headed across the street to Hoffman Meat Market. Stopping in front of the wide store window, she gazed up at the dead, skinless animals and their various parts hanging neatly on rows of deep hooks. Below them, a row of signs advertising the price of those parts per pound.

CHUCK ROAST, 15 CENTS PER LB!
BEST STEAK, ONLY 22 CENTS PER LB!
SPRING CHICKENS, 12 CENTS PER LB!

And then, between the signs for pork loin and pure lard, was one of Mr. Price's campaign posters. On the poster was a cartoon drawing of a man with torn trousers and an ill-fitting suit jacket, appearing down on his luck. Above him was a man in a hot air balloon—presumably Mr. Price—dressed quite sharply and clutching a sack full of money. YOU CAN'T AFFORD NOT TO VOTE FOR PRICE. THE COST IS TOO HIGH! VOTE SULLEN WATERFORD PRICE, ESQ., FOR MAYOR.

In truth, it wasn't clear to Frankie whether the man in the balloon was about to drop the money down to the poor soul, or if he had just robbed him of it and was floating away. That answer depended on whether you were planning to vote for Mr. Price or not, she guessed.

Which reminded her: she didn't see the poster that Mr. Price had taped to Daddy's front window. She'd had other things on her mind when she had gotten to the restaurant, namely the new sign, Mrs. Inkletter playing the organ, and, of course, the cash register. But she thought she would've noticed the poster, if it were still there. The one here in front of her at Hoffman's was hard to miss.

A man came to the window then, and right in front of her he hung a side of beef on an empty hook. Frankie winced. She knew, of course, where meat came from and had been by butcher shops many times before. But she had never stepped foot in one, and from outside looking in through the glass, she had the advantage of being separated from the death, from the blood, and from—oh my—the smell, and could let her mind imagine that those remnants were merely made of plaster, like mannequins on display from a ladies' department store.

It took a good bit of imagining on her part, for it takes a great deal of effort when you don't want to believe something you know in your heart to be true. But she'd had some help—you can't underestimate the power of three-quarter-inch plate glass.

On this day, however, she had to open the door and go inside. *Inside*, where there was nothing separating her from the recently deceased. She took a deep breath, held it in, and then turned the doorknob.

Quickly, she scanned the room for Amy, careful not to make eye contact with the pig head—that's right, there was a head of a pig— resting on a metal platter behind the counter.

Not real.

Made of plaster.

She told herself.

"May I help you?" said the man who was wiping his hands across the belly of his heavy white apron, leaving red and pink stains.

Tomato soup.

Catsup.

Nothing more.

She told herself.

While still holding her breath, Frankie managed to squeak out "Amy" and "picking up chickens."

"Ah, for Mr. Baum, right?" he asked. "Across the street?"

Frankie nodded. She was quickly running out of air and really didn't want to open her mouth and let in the same air that shared space with chopped-up animal chunks. She looked around again. For goodness' sakes, where was Amy?

"Are you one of his girls, then?" he asked.

Frankie nodded again.

"Thought so. I saw you over there yesterday. My son is in the same class as your older sister," he said. "Elizabeth?"

Another nod. Thank goodness for yes and no questions. They could really save the skin of a person who was trying hard not to breathe.

"You helping out?" he asked. "Looks like a lot of work to be done over there."

Frankie felt like her own head might pop off and join the pig's on the platter. She leaned against the glass display counter for support.

Now, unless you are like Harry Houdini, thirty seconds is about as long as you can hold your breath. Mr. Houdini famously held his breath for more than three minutes before escaping from an over-sized milk can filled with water. And what an escape it was!

But Frankie Baum, sadly, was no such magician.

She needed to take in some air soon or she would faint. And she couldn't think of a worse place to faint than a butcher shop. Suppose those butchers saw an opportunity to sell parts of her at 25 cents per pound?

Like the quick thinker that she was, she pinched her nose to at least avoid the smell and breathed through her mouth. "Yes, sir," she said, although she couldn't remember what the man had asked.

"Good," he said. "That's good. I saw your father on the street the other day and welcomed him to the neighborhood. About time somebody breathed some life into that place."

Breathed. Yes, breathing is good.

"You mind the smell?" he asked.

She shrugged, but continued to pinch her nose. "A little."

"Funny," he said, "you get used to it after a while."

"The chickens?" said Frankie. She didn't want to be rude, but she needed to get going.

"Right," he said. "We're rounding them up for you. It's not often we get such large orders. A colored girl came in a while ago. She's waiting out back for them."

"Amy?"

The man shrugged. "I'll see what I can do to speed things up."

Frankie headed for the back door of the shop. "You can wait in here, young lady," he said. "It's awful hot out there today."

Frankie shook her head and smiled. "That's all right; I'll wait with Amy outside."

Amy was leaning against the brick building, wiping her forehead with her dress sleeve. "What you doing here?" she asked.

"Mr. Washington thought you might need some help," said Frankie.

"I been waiting out here so long, I coulda hatched my own chickens and raised 'em up," Amy said.

"The man inside said they'd be ready soon."

"That be Mr. Hoffman." Amy shook her head. "Mr. Stannum be real mad as long as I been here."

"It's no fault of yours," said Frankie.

"Don't make no difference to Mr. Stannum."

Minutes later, Mr. Hoffman returned to the door with a crate full of chickens wrapped in parchment. "Here you are," he said. "A dozen whole chickens."

"These fresh?" asked Amy.

Mr. Hoffman looked at Frankie when he answered, "They don't get any fresher. That's a Hoffman guarantee."

Amy unwrapped a corner of the parchment to have a look. Her mouth fell open.

"What's wrong?" asked Frankie.

"These birds ain't been cleaned," said Amy. "They got the feathers on and everything. Mr. Stannum wanted them cleaned."

"I don't believe that's so," Mr. Hoffman said, rocking back on his heels.

"I don't mean no disrespect," said Amy, "but I placed the order myself the day before yesterday."

"Well," said Mr. Hoffman, "we seem to have a difference of opinion." He adjusted his rolled-up shirtsleeves, exposing his thick forearms. Then he spoke directly to Frankie. "Look here, you want a dozen chickens, here they are. But if you want them cleaned, we can do that for you, for an additional cost. But it's going to take another day."

"Another day?" said Amy. She looked at Frankie, too.

Frankie didn't know what to do. She'd only been working in the kitchen just over a week, which wasn't long at all. And considering that fact, what difference would one day make to wait for clean chickens?

"What's it going to be?" said Mr. Hoffman.

On the other hand, if Mr. Stannum wanted chickens today, he

would not be pleased if they returned empty-handed. Amy would be in trouble, and Frankie didn't want that. What difference did it make if they were cleaned or not?

"I don't know," said Amy.

Then Frankie thought of Elizabeth and that cash register and how sometimes you have to act like you know things even when you don't. "We'll take them," she said.

"We will?" said Amy.

Frankie nodded and grabbed one side of the crate while Amy took the other.

"I don't know about this," whispered Amy as they lugged the heavy box across the street.

"Don't you worry," said Frankie, feeling more confident with each step. "It will be all right."

27

AS PERHAPS YOU GUESSED, it wasn't all right.

Frankie and Amy dragged the box of birds into the kitchen. They heaved the crate onto the butcher-block counter, and just in time, too. Although the chickens were young and each weighed just under two pounds, two pounds multiplied by a dozen chickens equaled aching, tired arms that found it difficult to hold anything one second longer.

"Thought you run off," Seaweed said to Amy, "been gone so long." He was on a ladder, looking at the fan mounted in the wall, which had stopped running.

Amy wiped the sweat from her face with her apron and scowled at him.

"Better get four of those birds chopped up and into the pots for stock," said Mr. Washington, filling a stockpot with water from the tap. "Two into the oven for roasting. And the rest in the freezer to keep. Mr. Stannum be wanting us to make some things on the menu for him to taste. To make sure we doin' right. Then I got a list as long as my arm of other things he want done today." He turned to Julie, who was twisting dough into loaves of bread and laying them on the counter near Frankie and Amy. "How you coming on the bread?"

Julie, whose nose and cheeks were dusted with white flour, said, "I've got four loaves ready to go into the oven and enough dough for about a dozen dinner rolls rising over here." She nodded in the direction of the tall metal shelves alongside the butcher-block counter. "Plus half a dozen fruit pies for the freezer."

"That good." Mr. Washington nodded. "That real good."

Amy twisted the string of her apron around her fingers, causing her nail beds to lose some of their color. "Sorry to say I can't do none of that yet, Mr. Washington."

He shut off the spigot. "What you mean?"

Amy pulled off the top layer of parchment and held up a chicken by its limp neck. Its head was gone, but everything else seemed to be in place, including the feathers and feet.

"Oh no, no, no. That ain't no good, girl. That won't do, I say." Mr. Washington left the stockpot in the bottom of the sink and gripped the edge of counter.

"The order got all messed up. Mr. Hoffman said we have to wait one more day if we want 'em clean," Amy explained. She looked at Frankie and then took the rest of the chickens out of the crate and laid them on the counter. "Look. They all like that. All of 'em."

"Can't you just clean them here?" offered Frankie.

"Clean 'em *here*?" said Seaweed, climbing down the ladder to have a closer look at the birds. "Do you know what kind of stink and mess cleanin' chickens is? Especially when we got the rest of the menu to get ready for in this place? You ever cleaned a chicken?"

Frankie gave it a moment's thought. "Sure have," she said, trying to sound as confident as Elizabeth. "All the time."

This was, of course, a pure lie.

Seaweed picked up a chicken and swung it gently toward Frankie. The bird looked like a headless marionette suspended onstage, ready to do a tap-dancing number.

Now, wouldn't that be something to see?

"You took off the feathers before?" he said.

Frankie swallowed. "Yep. That's right."

"Then you know that ain't no easy job," said Seaweed. "And you pulled off the skin and took out the windpipe?"

Frankie winced. No matter how much you pretended to know about these kinds of things, hearing a person say "pulled off the skin and took out the windpipe" did something to you.

"Then," continued Seaweed, "you sliced the thing open and pulled out the gizzards and everything else inside?"

Frankie nodded. At least, she thought she nodded. Her mind was still stuck on *gizzards*. What a word.

"That enough, Seaweed," said Mr. Washington. "Since you know so much about it, you can help Amy get going on 'em." He grabbed some pinning knives and handed one to Amy and one to Seaweed. "I'll mess with the fan awhile."

"Aw, man," said Seaweed, shaking his head. He laid the knife on the table. "Shoot."

Julie moved her bowls of rising dough down the countertop away from the chickens. "There isn't enough room in this kitchen to be cleaning birds, Leon. Not when I got all this baking to do." She wiped her forehead with the back of her floured arm. "Just be sure to keep those birds away from my dough, you hear?"

Mr. Washington looked at the list. "Frankie, how about you peel potatoes?"

Amy and Seaweed started pulling out the feathers while Frankie sat on a stool by a bag of potatoes as big as a laundry bin.

Mr. Washington flicked the switch for the fan back and forth, listening for the motor to start turning, but the fan blades gave a halfhearted rotation every now and again and then stopped.

"We gonna be needing that fan right soon," said Seaweed, turning his head away from the chickens.

The smell had just reached the other side of the kitchen, where Frankie was peeling. She didn't know how Mr. Hoffman could get used to it.

Have you ever smelled the insides of a dead chicken? How about twelve? Not for the faint of heart.

Julie untied her apron and laid it on top of a stool by her work area. "I need to get some air," she said. "Nobody touch these sheets of dough. They're scored and ready to go into the oven just as soon as the other batch comes out." She fanned her face with a dish towel as she pushed open the kitchen door.

Mr. Washington peered into the fan. "It got a short in the wiring." He flipped the switch again, and the blades turned slowly, but only for a few seconds before coming to a stop. "I be needing some other tools for this job." Then he left.

Seaweed, Amy, and Frankie kept working, but no one got very far, and certainly not far enough, by the time Mr. Stannum appeared. "What in the blazes is going on in here?" Only, he didn't say *blazes*.

Frankie dropped the potato she was peeling onto the floor. She didn't want to make a move to retrieve it and call attention to herself, as Mr. Stannum's gaze was fixed on the pile of feathers and carcasses covering most of the butcher-block counter. So she stayed as still as—well, you could say, one of those chickens.

Amy tried to explain. She only got as far as the part about there being a mistake with the order before Mr. Stannum cut her off. His fingers started tap-tapping, trying to find the beat of that drum once again. "Where's Leon?"

"He went for his tools to fix that fan," said Seaweed. "It quit workin' again."

Mr. Stannum brought his lower jaw forward and scraped at his mustache with his bottom teeth.

"We done got through three birds already," said Amy. "Me and Seaweed. We only have . . ." She counted the chickens in the pile. "Nine left to do."

"Nine left," Mr. Stannum said. "Only nine left." His fingers were really going now. "Well, that's nine more things we have to add to a very long list. And let me tell you how lists work, Amy. Because you must not know." He pulled a piece of folded paper from his trouser pocket and waved it in her face. "Once you make the list, you want to cross things off the list, not put more on. That's the only way things get done!"

Amy cleared her throat. "But Mr. Hoffman woulda took one more day to have 'em done," she said.

"And you decided all by yourself, with that pea brain of yours, to just bring them here and clean them yourself. Didn't you?" he said.

Amy kept her head down, picking at a feather with the point of her knife.

"Didn't you?" said Mr. Stannum again.

"Not exactly," whispered Amy.

"Then who did?" shouted Mr. Stannum.

Amy stole a glance at Frankie across the room just as Frankie hopped off the stool and said, "I did, Mr. Stannum." And before she could say anything more, wouldn't you know that shorted-out fan wire caught a spark.

What a spark it must've been, because the blades of that fan started turning at high speed, blowing such a breeze as a hurricane toward the center of the kitchen, right at the pile of feathers. It only took a second for the wind to reach them and they lifted into the air, swirling and floating until the room was so thick with feathers, Frankie could hardly see anything else. Like a million dizzying hummingbirds in flight.

Seaweed covered his eyes and then Amy did the same, neither one having been inside a feather pillow before and not knowing what else to do. Also, there was screaming, to be sure, but the muffled kind, because no one wanted to open their mouth for fear of letting in chicken feathers. Mr. Stannum just stood as if his body were rusted stiff, watching in disbelief. Then Frankie spotted Julie's bread dough, all six beautiful loaves lying on baking sheets out in the open. She ran at them, grabbing a dish towel on the way and waving it in the air to knock away feathers, but when she got to the counter, she saw that those loaves were already tucked under a cozy down blanket.

In all the commotion, no one could think to turn off the switch. At least not until Mr. Washington returned with his tools, alongside Daddy. They both yelled when they saw what was happening, then Mr. Washington ran toward the fan. He flipped off the switch and slowly, gracefully, the wind died and the feathers started to fall.

Everyone stood quiet and still until the last of the feathers settled, afraid to move and stir up a breeze that would cause another feather storm. Frankie spit out two feathers that had gotten in her mouth and looked from Daddy to Mr. Stannum, who both had enough feathers in their hair to look like they were wearing ladies' hats. She waited for someone to say something, and she didn't have to wait too long. Mr. Stannum brushed the feathers off his head, then his shoulders, pulled out one feather that was stuck in his mustache, and finally clasped his hands together at his waist. Then he yelled with a good bit of satisfaction, "You are all fired!"

28

HOW LONG DOES IT take to clean up a million chicken feathers? Just about as long, in fact, as it took Daddy and Mr. Stannum to come to some sort of understanding in one of the restaurant's back offices. Daddy, alone, finally emerged as the last dustpan of feathers was swept up and thrown away. "Mr. Stannum and I have talked," he said, with a few feathers still stuck in the lapel of his suit jacket, "and there was a misunderstanding of sorts. None of you will be let go of your jobs. I'd like you to stay." He glanced behind him. "*We'd* like you to stay."

Amy, who had been crying the whole time, threw her arms around Daddy. "Thank you, Mr. Baum. Bless you now, oh, bless you. And I was thinking that even though there's a big ole mess here, these birds are fresh as a crocus. I bet delicious, too. And I know that Mr. Hoffman don't want to be losin' your business, so if you the one that doin' some talkin' with him I bet he knock down the price a good bit."

Daddy patted her on the back and nodded.

"All that bread," said Julie, leaning over the counter with her head in her hands, "and those pies." She wrung her hands. "They're as good as garbage now."

Mr. Washington kept his head down but shook Daddy's hand. Seaweed did not move, but instead folded his arms across his chest.

"No reason we shoulda been let go in the first place," he said under his breath. He looked at Frankie. "Wasn't our fault about them birds being brought here like that. We done nothin' we shouldn't't've."

Frankie's cheeks burned. Seaweed was right; that she knew. Daddy seemed to know it, too, because he looked at her then and his face was heavy with disappointment. "I'm sorry," she told him. "I'm the one who said we'd take the chickens that way."

Daddy pinched her chin and sighed. "What's done is done. Like I said, a misunderstanding. Now, let's get back to work. We've got a restaurant to open in a few days."

Seaweed and Amy got back to the chickens without speaking a word, while Mr. Washington set down his tools by the broken fan. Frankie looked at the bushel of potatoes, which were still waiting to be peeled, when Daddy said, "Your mother and Elizabeth are out looking at material for curtains, and I have a meeting with Yancy Biggs across town. He's agreed to have his orchestra play here for our July Fourth party and on weekends and we need to go over a few details. Do you want to come along?"

"Really?" said Frankie. "Me, come along with you? To a meeting?"

"If you'd like," he said. "Let's see, now, the car's parked around back." He patted the pockets of his trousers. "Oh dear, I must've left my keys upstairs. Give me a minute."

"I'll get them for you, Daddy," she said. "You wait right here." Frankie took the stairs two at a time and slid her hand over the dark wooden railing that ran along the second-floor balcony, overlooking the dining room. She leaned over the railing and waved down to Daddy, who was standing by the cash stand and talking to a pair of men putting the finishing touches on the plaster walls.

Frankie followed the railing past the banquet room to Daddy's office. She opened the door and went inside. Daddy's desk took up most of the room, and piles of papers took up most of his desk. Frankie looked around for the keys to the Studebaker, but she didn't see them. She opened his desk drawers and lifted up the piles, accidentally knocking a few folders to the floor. As she bent down to pick them up, she noticed Mr. Price's election poster, the one he had hung in the front window, sticking out of the waste can.

So *that's what happened to it*, she thought.

Frankie finally found the keys on the seat of Daddy's chair. Just as she grabbed for them, she heard a voice. She turned around, startled, but there was no one.

A ghost, that was her first thought. It had to be. A building that old and standing empty for so long was bound to be haunted with lost, restless spirits, she figured. But just as she was starting to get excited about the possibility, she heard the voice again and determined that it was coming from the heat register in the floor. She got closer and put her ear up to the metal grate.

Frankie could hear Mr. Stannum's voice clear as a spring day from the office downstairs. "I don't mean to bother you, sir," said Mr. Stannum. "But remember the other night when you came by . . . Yes, well, you said to let you know if I noticed anything . . ."

There was a short period of silence, and Frankie strained her ear to hear.

"Yes, well, I found something."

Frankie pressed her ear closer to the grate.

"I don't know exactly," said Mr. Stannum, his voice lowering. "It's in German."

Frankie held her breath.

"No, he's leaving now for a meeting. But . . . I don't know, sir. I don't know who he's meeting with. He is my employer, and I . . . yes, but I do need this job. Right. Yes, all right," said Mr. Stannum. "I understand my duty, sir. I will, then. I will. You can count on me. Uh, good day."

"Did you find them?" called Daddy from downstairs.

Frankie got to her feet. "Coming!" She ran across the balcony and down the stairs. "Here you go," she said, dropping the keys into Daddy's open hand.

"Thank you," he said. "Ready to go?"

Frankie looked behind her toward the kitchen, toward the closed door of Mr. Stannum's office, toward whatever he was up to. She would need to stay close if she was going to find out. "I changed my mind," she told Daddy. "I think I'll stay here. I've got potatoes to peel."

"Are you certain?" he said.

Frankie nodded. "There's a good bit I need to do."

29

AS UNPLEASANT AS IT was, Frankie had no choice but to stay close to Mr. Stannum for the rest of the day. It wasn't easy, either, because he spent a good deal of time in his office with the door closed. But that didn't deter Frankie. You see, at the moment when she told Daddy that she wasn't going to go with him to the meeting, when she made the decision instead to stay at the restaurant, she decided that she would learn exactly what Mr. Stannum had found. She would find out, no matter what. And when she did, she would . . . well, to be honest, she didn't know what she would do.

But she would do something, because Number Threes, in absence of Number Twos, had no choice.

30

MR. STANNUM LEFT THE restaurant at four o'clock. While Seaweed and Amy were tossing the last of the cleaned chickens into pots for stock, while Leon was testing out a new switch for the fan, and while Julie was pounding more dough to replace the loaves she'd lost to feathers, Mr. Stannum grabbed his leather satchel and hat and slipped out the front door without telling anyone where he was going or when he'd return.

Frankie followed him.

He walked down Washington Street and onto Locust Street for a few blocks more. Then, he crossed over to East Avenue and ducked inside Barnard's Pharmacy. Frankie waited a few minutes just outside the door. She didn't want to run into him, or let on that she was tailing him. So she waited until the next customer came along, a woman who happened to be of considerable width carrying a substantial pocketbook, such that Frankie could easily hide behind her silhouette all the way into the store. The woman headed toward the soda counter with Frankie close—*very close*—behind. But the woman had her mind on an ice cream soda and was none the wiser.

Frankie peeked around the woman's midsection as they approached the counter, long enough to see Mr. Stannum perched on a stool and sipping a fountain soda. "Tilly," said Mr. Barnard, behind the counter. "What'll it be? The usual?"

"I see no reason to make a change," said the woman. "And go ahead and put a dollop of cream on top, would you?"

"Cherry?" he asked.

"Make it two," she said.

Frankie held her breath and imagined herself no bigger than a toothpick so as not to be discovered. She also said a quick prayer that Tilly would not all of a sudden bend down to adjust her slip or have the urge to tighten the buckle on her shoe, leaving Frankie out in the wide open to be picked off like a whistle-pig in a vegetable garden. Whether the toothpick imaginings or the prayer did the trick, no one could say. But neither Mr. Barnard nor Mr. Stannum seemed to notice Frankie.

Instead, Mr. Barnard nodded and smiled at Tilly and went over to the cooler to scoop the vanilla ice cream. Mr. Stannum returned his attention to his drink. Frankie took that opportunity to slip away from the woman and slide into one of the booths along the wall a few feet away. She pulled out the menu that was tucked behind the salt and pepper shakers, and propped it up on the table in front of her.

From behind the menu, she watched Mr. Stannum as he took a few sips of his drink, and then glanced over his shoulder. After a few times alternating between glancing at the door and nursing his soda, it was obvious to Frankie that he was waiting for someone. Mr. Price, most likely.

Frankie watched for him, too. She was doing such a fine job at it that she didn't see Mr. Barnard come up to her table. "What can I get for you?" he asked, pad and pen in hand.

Frankie was so startled, she dropped the menu. She scrambled to pick it back up again before Mr. Stannum looked her way. Then she held it open in front of her and ordered the first thing she saw. "Root beer float."

Mr. Barnard said, "Coming right up."

Before he could make it back to the counter, in walked Mr. Price. "Afternoon," said Mr. Barnard. "Have a seat anywhere you like."

Mr. Price chose the stool next to Mr. Stannum. The two men didn't say anything to each other for the longest time. No *Hello*. No *Good afternoon*. No *What have you got on Mr. Baum?* They were silent so long that Frankie thought they might be passing notes on napkins or talking in Morse code.

Mr. Barnard delivered Frankie's root beer float. "Thank you," whispered Frankie, from behind the menu.

"Is there something else you want to order?" he asked.

"No, that's all," said Frankie.

"You sure?" said Mr. Barnard. "You're studying that menu awful close."

"I'm sure," said Frankie, keeping her head and her voice low.

"Suit yourself," said Mr. Barnard. Then he stood near Mr. Price and asked, "So, what will it be? Whatever you'd like, it's on the house, of course."

Frankie rolled her eyes. How these people went out of their way to please this man was really something.

"Just a cup of coffee," said Mr. Price. "And maybe a doughnut."

"You bet," said Mr. Barnard.

Then Mr. Price leaned toward Mr. Stannum. "You brought it?" he said in a low voice.

Mr. Stannum nodded.

"Let me have it," said Mr. Price.

Frankie only heard mumblings from the men's conversation.

She scooted to the edge of the booth so she could better hear them, but they were doing a masterful job of keeping their voices from drifting beyond the counter.

What a pity. But do not worry, my dear friend, you shall know all that was said. Read on.

Mr. Stannum hesitated and drained the last of his soda. "You know, I've been thinking. It's probably nothing. I shouldn't have bothered you."

Mr. Barnard set down the glazed cake doughnut at Mr. Price's place, along with an empty porcelain cup. Then he poured coffee from a steaming pitcher into the cup, sloshing a little into the saucer. "There you are, sir. Anything else?"

"Not at the moment," said Mr. Price.

"How about for you?" he said to Mr. Stannum. "Another soda?"

Mr. Stannum shook his head. "We're fine," said Mr. Price. "We'll let you know if we need something else."

Mr. Barnard gave a nervous smile and nodded. He backed away to return the coffeepot to the burner. Then he pulled the white towel from his apron pocket and, with no other customers to serve, he polished a spot on the counter by the soda fountain.

"I'll be the judge of what is nothing and what isn't," said Mr. Price. "Now, let me have a look at what it is you found."

Mr. Stannum stared into his empty drinking glass. From this exchange, you might wonder if he were having a change of heart, which would only be possible if he had any heart at all. Finally, after a few long moments, Mr. Stannum reached into his leather satchel and pulled from it a piece of paper. He didn't even have a chance to unfold it before Mr. Price snatched it from him.

Frankie strained her eyes to see. Although she couldn't make out anything more than dark squiggly print from her vantage point, at the top of the paper were these strange words: *"Deutsher Unterstükengs Bund von Hagerstown."* Mr. Price's eyes lit afire. Below, there were more words in German, but the only word on the entire page that the two gentlemen recognized was *Hagerstown*. It didn't matter that they couldn't understand the rest of the words. Mr. Price knew just what they were: evil. What's more, he believed this document, no matter what it said, certainly confirmed his suspicions about Mr. Baum. And he was delighting in it.

"Do you know what it means?" asked Mr. Stannum, looking worried.

Mr. Price held up the paper and gave it a little wave. "Yes, Mr. Stannum, I do know what this means." He took a last sip of coffee. Then he grabbed his doughnut in one hand and the German words in the other. He stood.

"What are you going to do?" asked Mr. Stannum.

"What any person who wants to protect his country from Nazi sympathizers would do," said Mr. Price. "Don't you worry, Mr. Stannum. You've done your part to make this great nation proud." Then he reached into his trouser pocket and pulled out a handful of tin buttons. On the front, bright red letters on a navy blue background spelled three words: PRICE FOR MAYOR. He tossed one at Mr. Stannum and watched it land on his cocktail napkin. Then, without giving much care to aim, Mr. Price flung two more down the counter toward Mr. Barnard and Tilly like he was sowing seeds in a plot of land. It didn't much matter where they fell or who caught them, because it was just like his politicking grandpappy, the late Maurice Waterford Price, always said: "If you throw enough seeds at the dirt, some will eventually take root."

Before leaving, Mr. Price strode past Frankie's booth and tossed a button at her table. It sailed under her menu, which she still held in front of her face, and kept on going until it came to a stop in her lap.

Frankie wanted to holler. A real, loud, honest-to-goodness scream that might shake the world back to its senses and make Mr. Stannum undo what he had just done, whatever that was. The thing was, Frankie didn't know. Daddy had something written in German. Something. What was it and what did that mean about Daddy? And what was Mr. Price going to do now that he had it?

Mr. Stannum paid his bill and picked up his satchel. He left a small tip and the tin button behind.

Frankie waited until he was gone before she got up and headed for the door. She had to get back to the restaurant before Mr. Stannum did and before Mother and Daddy noticed she was gone. She needed to talk to someone about what to do next. But with Joan gone, who was that somebody? Frankie was trying to sort it all out when Mr. Barnard interrupted her.

"Young lady," he said. "I think you forgot to pay your tab."

Frankie looked from him to the root beer float sitting untouched at her table. "Oh," she said, her face getting hot. "My tab." She patted her dress pockets, but the only thing she had on her was her blue silk bag that contained her scab collection. She held it out to him so he could see she wasn't fooling. "I seem to have forgotten to bring my money purse."

Mr. Barnard, who tolerated children almost as much as he tolerated customers who skipped out on the check, looked at the silk bag she was holding. "No money, you say. Then what do you have in there?"

"Nothing," she said. In her experience, her particular collection was not something that those over the age of thirteen appreciated.

Stamps? *With certainty.*

Coins? *Absolutely acceptable.*

Dolls? *Simply endearing.*

Scabs? *Did you say scabs? Well, that's just positively disgusting.*

"Let me see," said Mr. Barnard.

Frankie shook her head.

"Thief!" he yelled, pointing at her.

Tilly raised her hands in the air like Frankie was holding up the place.

"But, look!" said Frankie, pointing to the root beer float at the table. "I didn't even have a sip of it. I swear it's the truth."

Mr. Barnard took a step closer to Frankie and she was afraid he was going to grab her by the ear, drag her to a chalkboard, and make her write *I will remember to bring money for floats* one hundred times in her best cursive. That's just what her teacher at school would have done, anyway.

But Mr. Barnard did not grab her ear. He grabbed the blue silk bag. Then he pulled at the drawstring and shook out the contents onto the counter.

It took him about a minute to realize what he was looking at. "What the . . . ?"

It took Tilly a second or two longer. She gagged first, then screamed, "Holy mackerel!" and nearly slid off her seat.

"I told you," said Frankie. She swept her prized scabs back into the bag and returned them to the secure quarters of her dress pocket before Mr. Barnard did something barbaric like knock them to the ground or throw them in the garbage.

Then Mr. Barnard demanded she give him her father's name and phone number, and if she didn't or tried any tricks, he swore to God Almighty that he was going to call the police and have her hauled off to jail.

Jail is no suitable place for children, she knew, especially for those who picked at their scabs. And so, reluctantly, she gave up the number.

What number, you ask?

Frankie did intend to give Mr. Barnard the number to the restaurant. But at the last minute, she thought better of it and gave him another.

31

OVER AT UNCLE HAL and Aunt Edith's apartment, the telephone was ringing. Uncle Hal had already gone out in his taxi for his shift, and Aunt Edith was in her bedroom painting on her eyebrows. She was experimenting with a more severe arch, a technique that she had seen in a recent issue of *Ladies' Home Journal*, and she was finding it to be quite tricky. Meanwhile, Ava and Martha were in the living room playing with paper dolls; Martha was dressing them up and Ava was holding them for ransom.

Martha had named the prettiest one Mary Beth, and Ava had just nabbed her before answering the telephone. "Leave the money in a briefcase under the bridge or the girl gets it," Ava said in a deep voice.

"Pardon me?" said Mr. Barnard.

"Only the governor can pardon you," said Ava, "and I hate to be the one to tell you, but he's in on the job."

"I'm calling from Barnard's Pharmacy," he said, clearing his throat. "This is Mr. Eugene Barnard speaking. Is there a Mr. Hermann Baum at home? I have his daughter here and she does not seem to have enough money to pay for what she ordered."

"Is that right?" said Ava. "What did she order?"

"What? Oh, well, a root beer float."

"Good choice," said Ava. "What kind of ice cream?"

"Excuse me," said Mr. Barnard, "but may I speak to Mr. Baum about this matter?"

"I don't think that's such a good idea," said Ava. "He's a very busy man, and I'm afraid he doesn't take kindly to being disturbed, if you know what I mean."

Mr. Barnard turned to Frankie. "Hold on one moment; is your father the same Hermann Baum who's opening the new restaurant in town?"

"That's right," answered Frankie.

The color in Mr. Barnard's face began to pale. "Oh, I see."

"Do you know him?" asked Frankie.

Mr. Barnard shook his head slowly, the handset still pressed against his ear. "Not directly. But I've heard about him."

On the other end of the phone, Martha and Ava were deep in a row. "Where did you put Mary Beth?" shouted Martha. "Give her back!"

Ava put her hand over the phone and whispered to Martha, "Like I already told you, you'll see Mary Beth again after I get the money. That's how a ransom works. And if you don't deliver, the boss told me to turn Mary Beth into spitballs."

"What boss?"

"*The* boss," said Ava. "The head of my crime family, who do you think?"

"Oh," said Martha. "Is he nice?"

"Nice? I just told you he wants me to turn Mary Beth into spitballs, and you're asking if he's nice?"

"You wouldn't do such an awful thing," said Martha.

"Oh, wouldn't I?" Ava cradled the phone under her chin as she produced paper Mary Beth from under her dress and promptly ripped off her head.

Martha screamed bloody murder.

"Look," said Ava, returning the phone to her ear, "you don't want to make him angry. He's got connections, see? He'll turn you and everyone you know into mincemeat. Minced!"

Martha picked up Mary Beth's head and ran down the hall, screaming for their mother.

Mr. Barnard swallowed. Then he slowly returned the handset to the base while Ava went on about her mobster connections. "You know," he said to Frankie, "why don't we just forget this ever happened."

"Really?" said Frankie. "I'll bring you what I owe. Honest."

Mr. Barnard shook his head. "Don't think a thing about it, really. Like you said, you didn't even touch it. It wouldn't be right to charge you for something you didn't drink." He escorted Frankie to the door. "And tell your father that I didn't know. I mean, I didn't realize who he was."

"What do you mean, who he was?" asked Frankie. "Who is he?"

It seemed like a strange question to ask, but Frankie was beginning to think that maybe she didn't really know.

32

IT WAS A FRIGHTENING thing for Frankie, realizing that her father might not be who she thought he was. That he could be . . . well, something—or someone—else. That he could be, of all things, spying for Adolf Hitler. What it did was make her wonder if everything she knew to be true wasn't true at all. Indeed, that was something to wonder.

Tell the truth, is there anything in this world to be more frightened of?

33

FRANKIE HIGHTAILED IT TO the restaurant, taking alley-
ways to try to get back before Mr. Stannum did and before Mother
notified the police. She needn't have bothered, though, because
everyone was so engrossed in preparations for the Fourth of July
party and grand opening that they didn't seem to notice she had
been gone. And if they had noticed, they didn't seem to mind. That
being the case, she made her way to the banquet room, where there
was a nice buffet table along the wall, which just so happened to be
covered by a long tablecloth that reached the floor.

She crawled underneath.

What she needed was to think. What she needed was Joan.
What she needed was a pencil and some paper.

What she didn't need was Seaweed.

He lifted up the edge of the tablecloth and stuck his head under.
"What you doin' there?"

"Nothing," said Frankie, climbing out.

"Nothing?" Seaweed folded his arms across his chest and
grinned. "Now, I seen people do nothin' before, lots of times. I like
to do a lot of nothin' myself sometime after I'm done workin'. But
you there, under that table? Well, that ain't nothin'. Look to me like
you were hidin' from somebody."

Frankie just stared at him, trying not to give anything away.

"You hidin' from Mr. Stannum? Don't you worry none, he shut up in his office since he got back. So he won't be askin' you to go get more chickens."

"Mr. Stannum?" said Frankie. "Is he back already?"

"That right. What you mean *already*?" said Seaweed. "He been gone more than an hour. Just like you."

Frankie shook her head. "How did he get here so quick?" she said under her breath.

"What you been doing," said Seaweed, "tailin' him?"

"Who, me?" asked Frankie.

"Nah, George Washington," he said. "Do you see anybody else in here?"

Frankie put her hands on her hips. "What are you doing in here anyway?"

"Your momma came round the kitchen lookin' for you," said Seaweed. "And I seen you come in here while I was takin' a break. What she nervous about all the time for, your momma?"

Frankie shrugged. That was an ancient mystery. "I've got to go." She bolted for the door, but Seaweed grabbed her arm.

"Take it easy now," he said. "Take it easy. Good thing I covered for you and told her where you was."

"Where I was?" Frankie shook him off and raised her eyebrows. "Where *was* I?"

"Around the corner picking up eggs for the tater salad," said Seaweed. "We was a dozen short." Then he added, grinning like a goat, "Did you done forget?"

"Thanks." Frankie smiled. "You saved my skin."

"Again," he said. "That makes two by my count."

Frankie started past him, but Seaweed held up his hand. "So, you talk to your daddy yet and work it out?"

"Not yet," said Frankie. "I've been a little busy."

"Busy?" he asked. "Deal was, you get us a gig. Look, I make it real easy. Seeing how there's a big party here on the Fourth and everybody's welcome, just like your daddy say, I was thinkin' that would be the night me and my boys could play." He rocked back on his heels while letting the idea float in the air between them awhile.

"Daddy told Mrs. Inkletter she could play the organ and he's already got an orchestra," said Frankie.

"We had us a deal, remember?" Seaweed said, his eyes serious and his grin gone.

"I know," said Frankie. "I know. I'm just saying that it might not be so easy, is all. You have just as much chance of getting him to say yes to you. Better chance, probably. I'm still in the kitchen, after all." She rubbed the toe of her sandal over a dark spot in the wood floor. "Besides . . ."

"Besides what?" said Seaweed. "No way I can ask him. You know your daddy better than me."

Frankie shook her head. If only that were true.

Dear Frankie,

Oh, that Leroy Price makes me fume. What did he and his father say to you?

On the morning I left for Aunt Dottie's, while Daddy was picking up a package at Fritz's, he came around, that Leroy Price, I mean, and ogled Daddy's car. And then, and I remember this part very well, he said Daddy was a German. A German! That was the first time I have heard anybody call Daddy that word, and I was so surprised, I couldn't think of a comeback fast enough. I kicked myself the whole way to Aunt Dottie's, thinking of things I ought to have said to him.

I did ask Aunt Dottie after I received your letter, but to tell you the truth, she's kind of funny. As much as she sits with her ear at the radio, listening to any reports about what's going on in Europe, she doesn't want to talk about her and Daddy's parents or Germany or anything like that. She told me I shouldn't concern myself with such things and that Germany is as far away from her mind as it is from Pennsylvania. That's just what she said.

But the thing is, Frankie, the package that I told you about, the one that Daddy picked up. He left it here with Aunt Dottie. I stole a look at it while Aunt Dottie was getting dressed for bed. She had stuck it — or hid it, more like it — in the pie safe. She didn't know I saw her put it there, but I did. Anyway, it's still in brown paper wrapping, unopened. It's got Daddy's name on it, but Fritz's address. And here's the thing that's so strange, Frankie. It's marked "airmail," and the return address reads Germany.

Why do you think he left it here with Aunt Dottie? And what do you think is inside? And before you even get the thought in your head, no, I'm not going to open it. If Aunt Dottie found out, she'd grind me up and feed me to her animals, who, incidentally, need to be fed, so I must go.

Love and miss you more each day,

Joan

P.S. Even though we aren't really acquainted with Uncle Reinhart, perhaps you should write to him in California. He might be more eager than Aunt Dottie to give you some information.

July

34

ON THE THIRD DAY of July, this was how things stood. First, Frankie was still in the kitchen. She had not yet found a way to convince Daddy that she was just as good as Elizabeth and could be doing other things. Second, she had not yet told Daddy about Mr. Stannum. She didn't know what she was waiting for, only that telling Daddy about Mr. Stannum meant having to tell Daddy that he was suspected of being a spy for Hitler and that thanks to Mr. Stannum there was some sort of proof of it, which was now in Mr. Price's hands. And when delivering all this bad news to Daddy, it would almost certainly come out that Frankie could have stopped this all from happening if only she'd been anything other than a Number Three and didn't just sit by and watch.

And why had she been such a do-nothing, anyway? Was it because she wondered, even just a little, if Mr. Price was right?

Oh, and lastly—as if there weren't enough troubles—she hadn't yet worked out how she was going to make good on her deal with Seaweed.

This was what you could call a tight spot.

To make matters worse, all day long she had watched Mr. Stannum play the part of a loyal and trustworthy employee, being so agreeable to everyone that Amy was convinced he had come down with the fever. It really burned her up. Perhaps that is why Frankie decided it was time to talk to Daddy. In truth, it was past time, but better late than always a do-nothing Number Three, she figured. So, after she finished work in the kitchen and hung up her apron, and after checking to make sure Mr. Stannum was nowhere in sight, she climbed the stairs in search of Daddy.

Elizabeth and Mother were in the dining room taking inventory of what was needed for tomorrow's party, and so didn't notice Frankie in the least as she went past. She climbed the stairs and found the door to Daddy's office open enough that she could see his shirtsleeves at his desk, as well as his fingers paging through a folder. "Daddy?" she said as she stepped inside. "Can I . . . ?"

But those weren't Daddy's shirtsleeves at all.

"Mr. Stannum," said Frankie, "what are you doing up here? Where's Daddy?"

"Oh, well, uh," he said, dropping the folder. "I was just looking for an order your father wanted me to place. For fresh fish and seafood, you know; he found a shop in Baltimore he wanted me to inquire about." He cleared his throat and then raked his dirty fingernails through his silver hair. He came toward Frankie and the door. "Uh, no luck, though. I'll just have to wait until he returns and ask him directly."

Frankie stood firm in the doorway, inspecting him. Those eyes of his were having quite a blink.

Mr. Stannum gave a brief smile and tried to get by. "I think he ran out to the bank. Your father, I mean." He squeezed by her as she glared at him. What she really wanted to do was check his pockets for anything belonging to Daddy. The rotten thief.

She watched him all the way down the staircase, and once he

was gone, she looked around for anything out of place on Daddy's desk. But the thing was, every last thing was out of place. Heaps and piles, piles and heaps.

Frankie trailed after Mr. Stannum and waited outside his office. He left soon after to talk to Mr. Washington about ground hamburger, and when he did, she snuck in and real quick checked his brown leather satchel.

Empty, except for a small, framed picture of a young man in a military uniform.

She checked the pockets of his jacket, which was hanging on the back of his desk chair.

Empty times two.

"What you doing in here?" said Amy, sticking her head inside.

Frankie jumped. "Nothing."

"Snoopin' is more like it," said Amy.

"Where's Mr. Stannum?"

"Kitchen," said Amy. "Lookin' for what we ain't done. I reckon he be back right soon."

"I'm going," said Frankie. She tore off a piece of paper from a tablet on his desk and wrote in block letters a question that had been on her mind since her first day in the kitchen.

Frankie folded the paper in half, then in half again.

And she slipped it into his jacket pocket.

What was this question? Of course you'd like to know, as it's only natural to be curious of such things. All will be revealed in due time, my friend. In due time.

35

LATER THAT SAME EVENING, Mr. Price convened an emergency meeting of the council of the Chamber of Commerce. Council members met in the back room of the chamber, where a mahogany desk, long enough to seat the seven council members as well as the president, had been a fixture of the chamber since its founding in 1873. Carved into the top were the initials of each of the presidents who had served. "SWP" was at the bottom, number sixteen.

At precisely seven o'clock, Mr. Price raised the gavel and struck it hard against the mahogany. "I, Sullen Waterford Price, Esquire, sixteenth president of the chamber, hereby call this emergency meeting to order." He puffed on his fat cigar. "Gentlemen, we have ourselves a grave problem."

The council members nodded and whispered to each other, acknowledging that yes, there certainly must be a problem to discuss. However, none knew just what that problem happened to be. No matter, though; the Council members had unwavering confidence in their leader, and if Mr. Price said there was a problem, then a problem there most definitely was. That was the way of it, as always had been.

Mr. Price struck the gavel down once more. "Gentlemen, gentlemen, please."

The men quieted down immediately. If only Dixie were so obedient.

"Gentlemen, it has come to my attention that there is a business-man in town, one who calls himself an American but has ties to Nazi Germany, and perhaps to Hitler himself," said Mr. Price.

Puff.

Puff.

The men gasped and looked at each other, returning to whispers and grumbles about the audacity of such a traitor.

"Who?" said Mr. Merr, scratching his graying sideburns. "Who is this man?"

"Name him," said Mr. Marks. "Tell us, please."

"Yes, name him," shouted the others.

Mr. Price sucked on his cigar like a pacifier, relishing the moment as well as his fine tobacco, and then let the name *Hermann Baum* pass from his lips.

"Baum?" said Mr. Merr. "The new restaurateur?"

Mr. Price nodded. "One and the same."

"I don't believe it," said Mr. Travers, who was the oldest of the council members.

"I know," said Mr. Price. "This was as much of a shock to me."

Puff.

Puff.

Puff.

The men were raising their voices and talking on top of one another as they tried to make sense of what Mr. Price was saying. The council members knew of Hermann Baum, and had some of the same friends, but none of them knew him personally. None of them, that is, save Mr. Travers.

"Now, wait a moment," said Mr. Travers. "I have known Hermann for years. He's been an Elk as long as he's lived in Hagerstown, and I just don't think that it could be possible that he's . . . that he's . . . well, that he's what you say he is. With all due respect, of course, Mr. Price."

Mr. Price tapped the ashes from his cigar into his marble ashtray and held it firmly between his fingers. "Of course, Mr. Travers, I do respect your opinion on most matters. But you may want to refrain from making any further statements until you see what I'm offering as proof." He reached into a drawer to the right of his chair and pulled out the paper that Mr. Stannum had given him. Then he stood, lifting the paper with both hands as if the words written on the page were weighted with lead. Starting at the far end of the long desk, he stopped briefly at each council member's seat so that every man could observe the evidence.

"What does it say?" asked Mr. Merr.

"I don't know," said Mr. Pearson, shaking his head. "Does anyone here read German?"

"I'm sure I do not," said Mr. Gaines. He pounded his fist against the mahogany desk, insulted that such a question could be posed in present company.

Mr. Travers put on his round eyeglasses and studied the paper. He cleared his throat. "Then if no one knows what this document says, what does it prove, exactly?"

Mr. Price remained calm. "Gentlemen, pardon me for saying so, but you are all being as naïve as schoolchildren. You are missing the point entirely." He laid the paper carefully at his seat and then leaned on the desk in front of Mr. Travers. "It makes no difference what this says. The facts are these: This document, in German, was found in the possession of Mr. Hermann Baum, a man who, upon repeated attempts to contact him, refuses to answer any of my questions about his birth country or how he has come upon his considerable assets, such as a new restaurant requiring substantial construction and that employs nearly twenty people, including coloreds. Just what are we supposed to make of that, Mr. Travers?"

Even if Mr. Travers had a reply—which he did not—he wouldn't have had an opportunity to respond, because Mr. Price had a great deal more to say. "Has anyone seen today's newspaper?" Mr. Price picked up his copy of the *Daily Mail*, which he had brought with him from home, unfolded the front page, and read aloud this headline: "'Nazis Arming in Danzig, House of Commons Told.'" He threw the paper at Mr. Travers. "Read for yourself. Hitler is sending in weapons to the Free City, and let me assure you, friends, if he takes Danzig, he will take Poland next. There will be no stopping him."

"But you are talking about Europe," said Mr. Merr. "What stake does America have in this?"

Mr. Price picked up his cigar once again. "Mr. Merr, what do you think will stop Hitler and the Axis powers from attempting to conquer us, once they have conquered Europe? It's no secret that Hitler is recruiting spies in cities all over the world, even in America."

Puff.

Puff.

"A spy?" said Mr. Travers. "Is that what you are saying Hermann is? Is that what you are accusing him of? Surely you don't think . . ."

"Baum *is* without a doubt a German name," offered Mr. Gaines.

"It is indeed," said Mr. Price.

"As are Mueller and Hoffman, and a dozen other surnames in town," said Mr. Travers. "Are you accusing all of them of the same thing?"

"Right you are, Mr. Travers," said Mr. Price, "but both Mr. Mueller and Mr. Hoffman have been interviewed and are deemed acceptable, honorable businessmen, and—not to mention—supporters of mine." He cleared his throat. "And when you consider all of the other facts I've laid out before you, I don't see how you could doubt the danger that Mr. Baum poses to this town, to all of our businesses, and to our families."

Mr. Gaines held up the paper with the German words. "Why, this could be instructions from Hitler himself to do us all in!"

"What are we going to do?" asked Mr. Merr. "Should we go to the authorities? Alert J. Edgar Hoover?"

"Hoover would take care of him, all right," said Mr. Gaines.

"Perhaps in time," said Mr. Price. "But I am quite confident that this matter can be handled locally. If I may make a suggestion." He reached into the drawer beside his chair once again and removed a stack of flyers. "It really is quite simple. If we make it clear to Mr. Baum that his business is not welcome here, that he is not wanted, then he will have no choice but to leave." He divided the stack of flyers by seven and handed a pile to each council member. "The surest way to rid yourselves of the rat in your basement is to make the basement, shall we say, undesirable to the rat."

Puff.

Puff.

36

OF COURSE, NOT ONE of the Baums knew about the emergency meeting of the council. Only Frankie knew that Mr. Price had whatever it was of Daddy's and would do something bad with it, but when, what, and exactly how remained a mystery to even her most imaginative mind.

Something else that was occupying her imagination? Exactly what was inside the package Daddy had left at Aunt Dottie's. Joan's letter had arrived the day before, and Frankie could think of nothing else. Frankie had never before seen a parcel that was carried all the way to Maryland by airplane across the Atlantic. How important it must be, but what was it, and who sent it? The woman in the photograph? Was this the box that Daddy told Fritz he had taken out of town to be safe?

And what was wrong with Joan, anyway? For goodness' sakes, how could she resist opening that package when there were enough mysteries already to drive Frankie mad?

July 3, 1939

Joan,

I'm sorry all that country air you're breathing in is clouding your judgment, but if you do not open that package this minute and tell me what is inside I will be forced to hand over your Patsy doll to Ava for her torture experiments.

With regret,

Frankie

37

FRANKIE SAT ON THE edge of Mother and Daddy's bed and watched Mother slide a long beaded necklace over her dark hair. "Please can I go with Aunt Edith and Ava and Martha?" asked Frankie.

Mother, who was sitting at her dressing table, shook her head. "The answer is still no. You are on punishment, remember?"

How could she forget? Honestly. For the last ten days she'd been at the restaurant and at home—*with the exception of Barnard's Pharmacy, which doesn't count*—with no fun before, after, or in between. Today was the last day of it, but that did her no good. "But they are going to see *Tarzan Finds a Son!*"

"You should've thought about that before your disappearing act," said Mother. She slid a sapphire ring on her finger and pinched Frankie's cheek. "You only have a few more hours. Things will be back to normal tomorrow."

"But the picture is playing tonight," said Frankie, "and tomorrow is July the Fourth; the cinema is closed." She played with the powder puff on Mother's dressing table.

"There will be other picture shows," said Mother.

Frankie sighed. That was not at all the point.

Mother brought her hand to her ear. "Oh dear."

"What is it?"

"Ear itch," said Mother. "Somebody's talking about me. I hope it's not those women at the Ladies Auxillary." She shook her head and then stood. "Mind your grandmother this evening, hear?"

"Where's Elizabeth?" said Frankie.

"Spending the night with Katrina Melvich," said Mother. "Now, I mean it, don't make me have to worry about you running off or getting into trouble."

Frankie shook her head. "I won't."

Then Mother took one last look in her mirror and closed her eyes. "Lord, give me the strength to deal with the women in the Ladies Auxiliary tonight and help me hold my tongue so that I won't tell them where I think they ought to spend eternity." Then she opened her eyes and winked at Frankie.

"Amen," she and Frankie said together.

Grandma Engel was waiting for Frankie at the dining room table. "How about a game of poker?"

"No, thanks," said Frankie.

"Setback?"

Frankie wrinkled her nose.

"Suit yourself," said Grandma Engel. And she started laying out the cards for solitaire.

"Can we turn on the radio?" asked Frankie. "*The Shadow* is coming on."

Grandma Engel flipped over a set of three cards. "Your mother told me no radio." She eyed the eight of hearts on top. She needed a nine and she clucked her tongue. "Your punishment and such."

Frankie watched Grandma Engel's hands, all puffed up and

crooked with arthritis, fumbling the cards as she moved them. Like a crab trying to pick up a piece of dental floss. After a few more turns Grandma Engel said, without looking up from the cards, "But your mother isn't here, and what she don't know means more fun times for us."

Frankie smiled and leaped up from her chair to turn on the Philco. The set hummed, and while Frankie waited for it to warm up, she said, "I wonder what villain the Shadow will uncover today."

"Who knows?" said Grandma Engel.

"The Shadow," said Frankie. "The Shadow knows." Then she laughed—"*Wah-ha-ha-ha!*"—just as the radio announcer's voice came through the speaker. "*Who knows what evil lurks in the hearts of men?*"

If only she could know.

She closed her eyes. Inside her heart, in the tiny pocket that was tucked away underneath the layers of ribs and muscles and skin, the place so deep within that it knew nothing of the talk and accusations that lurked on the outside, *that* was the part of her, perhaps the only part, that knew what was right, that knew what was the pure truth. Daddy was in there, in her heart, and when she thought of him in that place, she saw the man who sometimes hid behind the sofa to surprise her when she came home from school. The man who'd rescued Bismarck from that ditch. The man who'd stayed up all night singing to her that time she got the mumps.

And when she opened her eyes, this is what she knew: Daddy was no German spy.

She knew something else, as well. She knew that she needed to find something that would prove his innocence. So, after Grandma

Engel retired to the upholstered easy chair, Frankie turned down the volume on the radio and switched off the table lamp. Then, although it was hotter than blazes outside, Frankie pulled the crocheted afghan from the back of the couch and draped it over Grandma Engel's knees.

"My goodness," said Grandma Engel, "aren't you a dear to look after me like this." And then, "What are you up to?"

"Are you comfortable, Grandma?" asked Frankie in a soft, soothing voice that was almost a sweet whisper.

"I am," she replied, "but why are you talking that way?"

"I'm sure I don't know what you mean," said Frankie softly.

Grandma Engel covered a yawn with the back of her wrist. "Stop doing that. You'll have me out in no time."

And she certainly was. Out, that is. Barely a minute or two more and her eyelids drooped. When she began making the *puh-puh-puh* sounds with her mouth like she always did when she was in deep sleep, Frankie tiptoed down the hall and into Daddy and Mother's bedroom.

She went straight to Daddy's desk. Unlike his desk at the restaurant, the one at home was tidy and spare, with only an oil lamp, a desktop calendar, a framed photograph of him and Mother on their wedding day, and a fountain pen. She opened the top drawer and sifted through a pile of papers, mostly receipts for things like the weekly milk delivery, repairs to the coal-fired boiler, and Mother's wringer washer, which Daddy had bought as an anniversary gift. She opened the other two drawers and found mostly the same kinds of things.

As she sat in Daddy's chair, it occurred to her that she had no idea what she was looking for. It seemed that it was much easier to find evidence proving you were indeed a spy than to find evidence proving you weren't. She doubted that she'd find a certificate signed by Adolf Hitler or President Roosevelt verifying that Hermann Baum was not now nor ever employed as a spy for the Nazis. That would be too darned simple.

So what *was* she looking for, then? A tooth in a giant bin of corn kernels comes to mind. One single grain of sand on the ocean's floor. One chicken feather in a million plucked birds.

After all the desk drawers had been checked and she had run out of places to look, Frankie gave up and decided she'd better check on Grandma Engel. On the way down the hall, as she was thinking of what to do next, her foot ran smack into the side of that old walnut dresser. Frankie winced and hopped on one foot while rubbing her sore toes, which she was sure were broken. "Stupid thing," she said, cursing it.

Then she noticed that the cupboard door at the bottom of the dresser was hanging open. She sat before the dresser cross-legged, pulled open the door, and began to root. Old issues of *Time* magazine were stacked in the corner behind table linens and boxes of candlesticks. A tin box filled with sewing notions. Also, old drinking glasses wrapped in newspaper.

Just as she finished looking at all of these things and was returning the sewing box to the spot where she'd found it, her hand clipped the edge of something else in the far right corner of the cupboard. She reached in—*way, way in*—and pulled out a small framed photograph covered with dust. Frankie blew at the dust, but most of it stayed right where it was.

Dust that has some age to it, don't you know, becomes quite comfortable where it settles, and it takes more than a bit of breathy wind to uproot it.

So, Frankie balled up the hem of her skirt and wiped at the glass and its tin frame. Black-and-white images of two people, a man and a woman in wedding attire, began to appear under the dirty glass. The woman was wearing a lacy dress and clutching a bouquet. She was pretty, with light-colored curls that framed her face, and young, but Frankie did not know her.

Frankie spit on her skirt hem and rubbed harder at the stubborn dust. She could almost see the face of the man, who was dressed in a dark suit and cradling the woman's waist with his arm. Frankie rubbed harder still, and as the man's face finally started to peek through, she stopped rubbing. She knew that face.

It belonged to Daddy.

38

"WHAT YOU DOING, SUGAR?" asked Grandma Engel. Her tall, stocky frame took up most of the narrow space at the end of the hall, and with the dim lamplight from the living room shining behind her, Grandma Engel's silhouette had the makings of Frankenstein.

Frankie jumped. "For the love of Pete!"

Grandma Engel clapped her hands and slapped the wall. "Scared you, did I?"

Frankie was tempted to throw the photograph back into the cupboard, forget what she'd seen, and challenge Grandma Engel to a game of setback. That certainly would have been the easiest thing to do. But by her count she had more questions than answers, and the questions were still coming. For example, in the last few seconds, this one: Did Daddy have another wife someplace else? And this one: Did he have a different family? A different life?

Alas, the real question was, what would happen if the answer turned out to be *yes*?

39

MEANWHILE, JUST A FEW blocks away, Elizabeth and Katrina Melvich were sharing a glass of iced lemon water on the front stoop of the Melvichs' apartment building. Katrina was going on about tomorrow's Fourth of July celebration on the square and how her little brother had been practicing his tap-dancing routine for hours upon end the last eight nights—make that nine!—and had driven their mother and father to cotton-stuffed ears and Katrina to take refuge out of doors.

"You're so lucky to have younger sisters," Katrina told Elizabeth. "Who don't tap."

"You wouldn't say that if you had to share a room with them," said Elizabeth. "You should have seen Frankie with the new cash register at the restaurant. Honestly, her behavior was so embarrassing."

And speaking of embarrassing, it was about that time Robbie McIntyre and his friend Albert Linden walked by. Robbie leaped on the top step of the stoop and hung on to the cast iron railing while screeching like a howler monkey. Katrina and Elizabeth screamed and then giggled. Katrina dipped her fingers into the drinking glass and flicked some lemon water at Robbie's face. Elizabeth followed suit.

Robbie opened his mouth wide and bit at the spray, grunting.

You'd have to wonder why Elizabeth, a smart and sensible princess, would be entertained by such a thing. By such a boy. Albert Linden was wondering the same as he simply stood by with his hands in his pockets and watched.

"Thanks for the bath," said Robbie. He hoisted himself up on the railing and straddled it. "Nice of you two to wait out here for us." And then he grabbed the glass of lemon water right out of Elizabeth's hands and drained it dry.

"Animal!" said Katrina, laughing. "Maybe they'll have an opening for the likes of you at the square tomorrow."

"Yeah," said Elizabeth, "too bad you don't tap-dance; you could join Katrina's brother and put on a good show."

"You both going to be there?" said Robbie.

Katrina looked up toward her apartment window, where her brother was all but certain to still be slamming his shoes into the floor. "Yeah."

Elizabeth kept her head down.

"What about you?" asked Robbie.

She shook her head. "My daddy is throwing a party at the restaurant."

"Oh yeah," said Robbie, adjusting his flat cap. "So I heard."

"You heard?" said Elizabeth.

"Everybody has," said Robbie. "People have been talking a lot about your father lately. Isn't that right, Al?"

Albert Linden nodded and then shrugged. "Seems so."

Elizabeth felt something get caught in her throat. "What do you mean?" she managed to squeak out.

"You know, about him being a German," said Robbie. He said it so matter-of-factly, as if he were talking about shoelaces. "Some people say he might even be working for—"

"My daddy is no German!" shouted Elizabeth. "I wish people would stop saying that horrible thing. I don't know who started that ugly lie, but people shouldn't be allowed to say such things. And what's worse is that people believe them!" Whatever was in her throat was starting to come dislodged.

Katrina, Robbie, and Albert stared at her cautiously. Never before had they heard Elizabeth Baum raise her voice and turn such a shade of red.

"I didn't mean any harm, Elizabeth," said Robbie. "I'm just telling you about the talk going around. It's got nothing to do with you, anyway."

"I don't care," said Elizabeth. "I'm telling you it's all a lie. Daddy is not a German. He's got nothing to do with Germany, so if you want to spread something around, why don't you spread that? The idea that Daddy is any different than anyone else in this town, any different than your fathers, is just plain wrong!"

"You're saying he was born here?" said Albert, leaning against the railing. "In America?"

"Of course he was," said Elizabeth, narrowing her eyes on him and trying to discern his meaning.

"But he lived there," said Albert. "In Germany, for a couple of years. That's what I heard."

"He did not," said Elizabeth, descending the steps and facing Albert square on. "That's an outright lie. Who told you that?"

Robbie stepped between them. "We didn't mean to upset you. Like I said, it's got nothing to do with you."

Elizabeth wondered how he could say such a thing. It had everything to do with everything, and nothing less.

Katrina scowled at both boys and then put her arm around Elizabeth's shoulder. "Don't worry. It's just talk. That's all. Come on, let's go inside." She led Elizabeth to the door.

"Aw, come on," said Robbie, "don't be mad."

Elizabeth stopped. "If people were saying these things about your father, what would you be?"

Robbie shook his head, confused. "But, Elizabeth, my father isn't a German."

40

THINGS WERE JUST AS confusing back at the Baums' apartment. Maybe even more so.

"What you got there?" said Grandma Engel.

Frankie placed the tin-framed photograph in Grandma Engel's swollen hands.

"You got all the lights turned down so low in here, I can't even see my own elbows," said Grandma Engel. "Come over to the lamp so I can see what's what." She carried the photograph over to the dining room table and took a seat while Frankie flipped the switch on the chandelier.

Grandma Engel tilted the frame to catch the light and then brought it close to her face. Her green eyes widened, Frankie noticed, as she looked it over, but there was something in her eyes and the way she gently set the picture down on the table that told Frankie she had seen this before, or at least recognized the light-haired woman.

"You know who that is," said Frankie. It wasn't a question.

Grandma Engel nodded. "I do."

"Then who is it?" said Frankie, sitting next to her at the table. "Tell me."

"I can't." Grandma Engel patted Frankie's hand. "It's not my story to tell."

"But . . ."

"Put that back where you found it, hear?" said Grandma Engel. "Your daddy will tell you when the time is right."

"Tell me what?" Frankie pulled her hand away from Grandma Engel's.

"I already told you, sugar, it's not my story to tell."

Frankie's whole body started to tremble. "He has another family, doesn't he?" she blurted out. "In Germany. A wife and probably other daughters or maybe a son. That's why he travels a lot, isn't it? He goes to visit them. And that's why he's been on the telephone in the middle of the night." It was all making sense to her now, finally. The package he left at Aunt Dottie's was from his other family.

He wasn't a spy for Hitler.

He was a stranger.

The door to the Baums' apartment flew open then, and in rushed Ava and Martha, out of breath. "Frankie, you'll never guess what we saw hanging on the wall at the cinema!" said Ava.

Martha collapsed in the middle of the woven rug. "Make her guess," she said, panting.

Frankie was tired of making guesses about things. For once, she wanted someone to tell her outright.

"Girls," said Grandma Engel. "Now may not be the best time for games."

"Aw, come on," said Ava. "You gotta guess."

"She'll never guess it," said Martha, rolling from side to side. "Never in a bazillion years."

Frankie said nothing.

"All right, fine," said Ava. "I'll just tell you."

"A poster of Judy Garland!" shouted Martha, before Ava had a chance.

"Martha, you scamp!" said Ava. "I was going to tell her. And it's not just a poster of Judy Garland, dummy, it's a poster of *The Wizard of Oz* picture show."

"Well, Judy Garland is on the poster," said Martha. "I saw her myself. Along with the scarecrow, the tin woodman, and the lion. Just like in the book." Martha sat up. "Even the great Oz himself."

Ava rolled her eyes. "Yeah, but no witch. You'd think they would have put the witch on the poster. I can't wait to see what she looks like." She drew back her mouth into a frightful grimace and squinted her eyes until she could barely see out of them. "Anyway, you should go have a look at the poster. The picture's coming to play next month and Momma said she'd take us to go see it the first day it opens. You want to see it with us?"

"Maybe," said Frankie. "But I'll probably have to work at the restaurant."

"Your mother and father will let you have a day off at the restaurant to see that picture show, Frankie," said Grandma Engel. "I'm sure of it."

Frankie wasn't sure of anything. And not even the promise of Judy Garland as Dorothy could change that.

41

FRANKIE TOOK OUT THE letter she had written to Joan earlier in the evening and added a postscript.

Then she stuffed it back into the envelope and sealed it shut.

July 3, 1939

Joan,

I'm sorry all that country air you're breathing in is clouding your judgment, but if you do not open that package this minute and tell me what's inside I will be forced to hand over your Patsy doll to Ava for her torture experiments.

With regret, Frankie

P.S. There is more, Joan. I just found something and I don't know what it means, but Daddy has a secret, maybe more than one. Before now, I could not believe what people are saying about him. I couldn't. And I don't mean that I didn't want to believe what they are saying to be true, I mean that I knew it couldn't be true because Daddy would never do anything against this country. But, Joan, what if Daddy is not the person we think we know? What then? What do we really know at all to be true?

42

PREPARATIONS FOR THE FOURTH of July celebration on the square were going as planned. Mr. Price was instructing the photographer about where to stand to capture the best moments during his speech. He even made a copy of his speech for the photographer and underlined each sentence that was expected to generate an enthusiastic response from the audience. "I'm expecting a big crowd," he said, "and I want some pictures of the audience with smiles on their faces and looking patriotic. Have you got any of those wide lenses?"

"Yes, sir," said the photographer.

"Good. Because I'd like a shot of me, right up there at the stage, along with all of my supporters. Like I said, I am expecting a big crowd. All the businessmen in the chamber and their families, and probably a lot more."

"Yes, sir."

"Can you do patriotic?" said Mr. Price.

"Will there be flags?" asked the photographer.

"Of course," answered Mr. Price.

"Then I can do patriotic."

"That's what I want to hear." Mr. Price looked around the square. "Now, where did I put those flags?"

Mrs. Price, meanwhile, was by his side listening and nodding at the appropriate times and occasionally looking over her shoulder to see how Leroy and Marty were getting along with the banner that was to go across the stage. IN HONOR OF OUR NATION'S BIRTHDAY! VOTE PRICE FOR MAYOR!

Leroy and Marty were getting along about as well as a honey badger and springhare stuffed in a paper sack. The banner was lying at their feet while they acted out the Fight of the Century between Mickey Mouse's Mechanical Man robot and the rabid gorilla called The Kongo Killer. Not surprisingly, Leroy was Kongo Killer, and he was giving Marty a serious beating.

"Look at them," Mr. Price said to his wife. "Would you do something? Don't they know how important tonight is for me? And tell them I have a job for them once that banner is hung."

"Yes, dear," said Mrs. Price, dabbing her nose with her pink handkerchief. "I'll just . . ." Then Mrs. Price hurried over to her sons. "Boys," she said in her quiet voice. "Now, boys. Your father asked you to hang up his banner, remember?"

At that moment, Leroy clobbered mechanical Marty with a gorilla punch to the gut. Then he raised his arms above his head and feigned being held back by a referee. Seeing his chance, Marty wound up his arms in wide circles and yelled, "Beep bop beep!" But after extending his arms into punches that didn't connect, he had a mechanical failure that rendered him defenseless and he collapsed in an imaginary pile of wires and circuits.

"Boys," said Mrs. Price when the match was over and Leroy stopped grunting and pounding his chest, "your father would like the banner to hang right in front of the podium where he'll be speaking. He'd also like me to remind you how important this evening is for him and for our family."

"But the Mechanical Man demands a rematch," said Leroy, kicking Marty with his foot. "Don't you, Mechanical Man?"

Marty nodded helplessly and gave a single, defeated "Boop."

"I see. Well, how about hanging up the banner and *then* having the rematch?" suggested their mother. "And report back to your father when you are finished. He has another job for you, understand?" She didn't wait for an answer and simply hoped the boys would comply. Then she hurried back to Mr. Price, who was poring over the list of things he needed to do before the night's festivities. He crossed off "Photographer" and underscored the next item on the list: "Flyers."

And underneath that, he circled what was written in capital letters: "BAUM'S RESTAURANT."

43

OVER AT BAUM'S RESTAURANT, Frankie stood on a wooden milk crate and leaned over the deep sink, scrubbing the caked-on bacon grease from an iron skillet. Mr. Washington, Amy, Seaweed, and Julie had been at the restaurant since dawn, cooking for the night's festivities and dirtying more dishes than Frankie had ever seen in her life. They were waiting for her, incidentally, those dishes. All of them, just for her.

Daddy and Mother had been at the restaurant early, too, she guessed. Frankie had waited for Daddy to come home the night before so she could ask him about who it was in that photograph standing next to him. But he either came home very late and left very early, or hadn't come home at all. Mother, too, was gone when Frankie awoke that morning. She had made arrangements for Uncle Hal to take Frankie in his taxicab to the restaurant.

And so it was: as Frankie was just getting out of bed, the day had started without her. The sun was barely up and she had already been left behind.

She was behind on the dishes, too. The pots and pans kept piling up and she couldn't scrub them clean fast enough.

"So," said Seaweed, adding a dirty stockpot to the pile. "We all good?"

"What do you mean?" asked Frankie, wondering how on earth anyone could think she was good when there was a mountain of grime all around her.

"About me and my boys playin' tonight," he said, grinning.

Frankie dropped the dishrag into the sink. "Oh, that." She fished around the bottom of the basin until she found it. "I, uh, well . . ."

"You didn't talk to your daddy," said Seaweed, the smile fading from his face so fast, there was no trace of it left.

"I'm sorry," said Frankie, and she was. "I meant to, but . . ." If he had any idea what other things she needed to talk to Daddy about, serious things of a spying nature, he wouldn't be bothering her about something as small as playing his music.

Seaweed shook his head. "You said yourself you owed me. I heard you."

"I know it," she said.

"We had a deal."

Frankie nodded.

"I see." Seaweed scrunched up his face. "Guess a deal don't mean the same when it's with a Negro. Ain't that right?"

"No," said Frankie, shaking her head. "That's not fair."

"It ain't fair," he said quietly. "You be sure of that." He held out his hands and looked them over, his dark skin stretched thin over his knuckles. "Forgot for a second what I look like to you. What you see out of those green eyes of yours ain't nothing like what I see. And what you see ain't nothing like it is."

"Seaweed Turner, why you flappin' your gums and you ain't boilin' those string beans like I told you?" Mr. Washington said.

"There ain't no clean pot left in the place," said Seaweed, looking right at Frankie. "What you want me to do, boil them in my shoe?"

"Watch yourself, Seaweed," said Mr. Washington. Then he softened his voice a little and said, "Frankie, I knows you doin' your best, but if you could just work a little faster. We got a mess of things to get done today."

Frankie nodded and plunged another pan into the gray dishwater. She was up to her elbows, quite literally, in grease, and her fingertips were as waterlogged and withered as raisins.

Seaweed turned away and untied his apron. He pulled it over his head and laid it on the counter.

"Where you think you going?" said Mr. Washington.

Seaweed didn't answer. He just ducked out the back door and into the alleyway.

Frankie wondered what he meant when he said that what she sees is nothing like it is. What was it like, then? Frankie didn't know what to say to Seaweed to make things better. She knew, of course, what she needed to *do* to make things better, but there was a lot she needed to do or figure out before things got better. And sitting between her and any figuring was this sink full of pots and pans.

Mr. Stannum came into the kitchen when she reached the halfway mark in her pile. He cast his eyes about the place, asking if This was done and if That was finished and where were These and why were Those. He did not speak to her, which was a relief—because if he had, Frankie wasn't sure she could hold her tongue. Even so, Frankie noticed that Mr. Stannum didn't have the usual sharp edge to his voice.

Perhaps because he had a victory over Daddy with his betrayal and was feeling satisfied and smug, as people often do when they accomplish something. When they set the wheels in motion. They can just sit back in their easy chair with their feet propped up and watch the cars go off the track. Or, maybe he had found the note she'd slipped in his pocket and was worried that someone was onto him. *Let him worry,* thought Frankie. *If he likes spying on Daddy so much, let him see how it feels.* And then she thought of something else to write on another note for him: "TRAITOR."

Frankie found that thinking of Mr. Stannum and what he had done—let alone seeing him and his awful mustache when he came into the kitchen to check on Things—helped her scrub with such ferocity that she got through the second half of the pile much quicker than the first. When she finally finished, just as she drained the water and hung the dish towel across the faucet to dry, Daddy stepped into the kitchen.

Frankie watched as he spoke to Mr. Stannum and Mr. Washington, looked over some receipts and put his signature to them. Mr. Stannum, she noticed, stiffened when Daddy asked him questions, and kept his eyes on the floor. Daddy noticed it, too. "Is everything all right with you, Mr. Stannum?" he asked.

Mr. Stannum cleared his throat. "Yes, sir. There's just a lot to do before the big opening."

"Indeed there is." Daddy slapped him on the back and smiled. "Don't worry. We're all working together and looking out for each other, isn't that right?"

"Yes, sir." Mr. Stannum coughed like he was choking on the words.

"That's what families do," said Daddy, raising his voice as if he were making an announcement. No, a declaration! "And we are all family here."

Frankie couldn't help but notice how Mr. Stannum's eyes were blinking like there was no tomorrow. G-U-I-L-T-Y.

Daddy kept on. "They will be talking about us in the papers, wondering where we've been all these years and just how they could have lived without our fine dining experience. People will be lined up all the way down Jonathan Street to Potomac, mark my words." Then he slapped Mr. Stannum on the back once again.

Mr. Stannum winced. "Yes, sir," he said again. Blink, blink, blink. And then he excused himself to his office.

Frankie saw her chance to try for some answers. "Daddy, wait. I need to talk to you."

Daddy looked on Frankie, and as he did, his shoulders sagged as if the burden of whatever secrets he carried with him suddenly took on more weight. "I know," he said. But he made no move toward her.

"You do?" Maybe Grandma Engel had gotten to Daddy and told him about what Frankie had found in the dresser. She swallowed and felt her heart drumming in her ears. Talking to him about this would be much easier if Frankie didn't have to actually say the words, if she didn't have to speak at all.

It would be easier to do if *he* brought up the photograph. And then she could talk about the other things. And ask him questions. As long as he didn't say that the woman in the photograph was indeed his wife and that he had another family someplace else—in Germany, maybe, with two daughters, not three, and they would both be working the cash register . . .

As long as he didn't say that, she would be all right.

Daddy took in a long breath and nodded. But just as Frankie came out from behind the sink, Mother stuck her head into the kitchen. "Hermann," she said, "Dolores and BettyAnn have got the summer complaint. They just telephoned. They won't be coming in."

"But we're already short on waitresses," said Daddy, mopping his forehead with his handkerchief. He sighed and shook his head. "Well, I suppose Princess can fill in."

Mother nodded, and before slipping back into the dining room, she said, "Are you feeling all right, Hermann? You look a little peaked."

"Fine," he said, leaning against the counter. "Just minding the heat."

"I can help," Frankie told Daddy. She drew herself up as much as she could and was sure she stood at least three inches taller. "With the waitressing."

Daddy said, "I'm afraid not. Now, you wanted to talk to me, is that right?" He pulled his shirt collar away from his neck.

"That's right," said Frankie.

"You want to do something other than work in the kitchen, Frankie. I understand. I really do. But I need things to stay as they are right now."

"But . . ."

Elizabeth came into the kitchen then. "Daddy, Yancy Biggs is on the telephone for you."

"Biggs?" said Daddy, looking at his pocket watch. "On the telephone? Why, he should be here and setting up by now."

Elizabeth shook her head. "He's not coming."

"Not coming!" shouted Daddy. "Not coming! And why the hell not?"

The entire kitchen went silent, as if the anger in Daddy's voice, which was rarely heard, snuffed out everything else. Even the Frigidaires, which usually chugged and grumbled, seemed to know better than to make a sound. Elizabeth's face turned red. "I don't know," she said quietly. "He wants to talk to you."

Daddy started toward her. "Fine," he snapped. "I'll see to this."

Seaweed returned from the alley then and put his apron back on. He glanced at Frankie and Daddy and then grabbed the bowl of string beans from the counter and headed for the stove. There was something in the way his shoulders slumped, carrying those beans across the room, something that Frankie recognized in herself. Seaweed was right, after all. She wasn't seeing things like they really were. In truth, she wasn't really seeing *him*, just like everybody else wasn't seeing her.

"Daddy," said Frankie.

He turned. "Frankie, please, can't this wait?"

"No," she said, swallowing. "I can help. Even if Mr. Biggs isn't coming, it'll be all right."

"What are you talking about?"

Elizabeth shook her head at Frankie to try to get her to stop. But Frankie couldn't stop, not when she knew how to help and come through for Daddy and Seaweed like no one else could. "There's plenty of other bands out there who would jump at the chance to play here. I happen to know of one"—out of the corner of her eye she could see Seaweed watching her—"and I can make all the arrangements. Just leave it to me."

Daddy rubbed his head. "Frankie, I have a lot on my mind right now, so would you please just stop . . ."

"But if you just listen, I know I can—"

"For the love of . . . please, stop being such a bother!" he yelled.

Elizabeth got out of the way as he stormed past her, leaving

Frankie standing there in the middle of the kitchen. Daddy had never raised his voice like that at her before. Mother, sure, lots of times, but never Daddy. In fact, Frankie had never heard him raise his voice like that at anybody.

In the middle of the kitchen, she was the size of a teacup.

After a moment, Frankie turned around and saw Mr. Washington and Amy and Julie taking way too much time plating the food. Without looking up from stirring a bowl of slaw, Amy said, "Don't you worry none, Frankie, he didn't mean that, no how."

"It's the heat," said Julie. "It makes you act crazy."

Seaweed stepped out from behind the stove. "Yeah, it ain't no thing we can't play here. I'll just explain it to the boys."

"This ain't about you, Seaweed," said Amy, giving him a look. Then she squeezed Frankie's arm. "Your daddy got a lot in his head. Takes a lot to do what he done, startin' up a new place like he is. He is up at the tippy top, and if one thing below goes out from under him . . ."

"Like the orchestra," said Frankie.

Amy nodded. "In the blink of an eye the whole place turns into a pile of rubble."

"In the blink of an eye," Frankie said to herself.

"What I can't figure is why the orchestra would cancel a paying gig at the last minute," said Julie. "That Biggs sounds like a fool to me."

But Frankie had an idea why. And she thought she had an idea *who*, as well.

44

FRANKIE HEADED STRAIGHT FOR the city square.

There she dodged a mess of Fourth of July planners who were busy wrapping streetlamps with red-white-and-blue ribbons and draping American flags at each corner. A wooden stage had been constructed in the square's center, and a VOTE FOR PRICE banner was hanging crooked—oh, those Price boys!—below the makeshift podium. Alongside the stage, there was a cart holding a block of ice nearly the size of Bismarck for selling penny sundaes.

Frankie usually loved the Fourth of July. But these days, there was no more *usually*.

She weaved in between the rows of hay bales that were meant for audience chairs and rested her legs on one right up front. She didn't see Mr. Price anywhere, but she knew he would turn up if she waited long enough. He had everything to do with the orchestra canceling, she was sure of it.

While she waited, a quartet of singers, two men and two women, all wearing matching stars-and-stripes outfits, rehearsed a few patriotic songs to the tune of a banjo, and Frankie couldn't help but think of Joan and how different things would be if she hadn't gone away. Why, oh why, oh why couldn't she be there, too?

Frankie lay down on the hay bale and looked up at the clouds that seemed to be playing keep-away with the sun. She watched those clouds for a long time, watched them while a brass band took the place of the quartet, watched them while Little Bobby Melvich rehearsed his tap-dancing number, and watched them while Joyce Sempleton practiced reciting Walt Whitman's poem "I Hear America Singing."

Joyce Sempleton, incidentally, needed the practice—because America, so it seemed, couldn't get the words right.

Frankie wished she could reach up and touch those clouds. She wished she could grab hold, pull herself through them, and come out on the other side—where there was more than just a piece of sky; where it was wide enough for her to soar. Where there were no dishes to wash, potatoes to peel, or secrets to be kept from her. Where she was not just a Number Three, but a person who wasn't a bother, who wasn't in the way. Where she could make things the way they should be.

She reached up and closed her eyes, hoping that what she dreamed for herself could really come true. And then, as if the clouds had heard her request and wasted no time in providing an answer, something fell out of the sky and hit her squarely—*smack!*—in the forehead.

Her eyes flew open and she sat up. On the ground next to her bale of hay was a piece of paper crinkled into a ball.

"Direct hit!" yelled Leroy Price from the stage.

Frankie got to her feet. "What do you think you're doing?"

"I think I should ask you the same," said Leroy, hopping down from the stage. Marty followed him, holding a penny sundae in one hand. But he had some trouble with the jump and fell into Frankie's hay bale on the landing. "Saved it," Marty said, admiring his snowball, which was still upright, before taking a bite. He brushed the hay from his hair and sat beside her. "Are you coming tonight to watch the fireworks, Frankie?"

That's when Frankie saw two waitresses from the restaurant, Dolores Hemphill and BettyAnn Chase, each holding penny sundaes, walk by not even twenty feet away and disappear behind the stage. What were they doing here? Didn't Mother say they'd called out sick with the summer complaint?

"So, are you, Frankie?" asked Marty again.

"What?"

"Are you coming to watch the fireworks?" he said.

"No, Marty."

"Why not?" said Marty. "The whole town is going to be here watching. We've got fireworks and food and music. Daddy's got the Metropolitans playing here. So why won't you come?"

"Because she's not invited," said Leroy. "That's why. Only Americans celebrate the Fourth of July."

For a second, just one, she was taken aback. "I am an American," she said.

"You ain't," Leroy said.

"I am too," shouted Frankie. "You take that back right now, Leroy Price."

Leroy grinned. "Why should I take it back? It's the truth."

And then she said, "Wait a second. Who did you say was playing here?"

"The Metropolitans," said Marty.

"Yancy Biggs's orchestra?" she asked. "Daddy hired them to play at the restaurant!"

"I guess they don't want to play for no Germans, either," said Leroy. "Can't say that I blame them."

Frankie threw the crumpled-up paper, which bounced off his shoulder and fell to the ground. She was aiming for his mouth. "I said, take it back!"

"Come on, Leroy," said Marty, taking another bite of his snowball. "Leave her alone."

"Shut your mouth, Marty," said Leroy. "You heard what our daddy said. There's no way we're gonna let no-good Germans take over our town. They're worse than the coloreds." Then Leroy Price cleared his throat, gathering up as much phlegm as he could, and spat at Frankie. A gob of mucus the size of a fifty-cent piece landed just below her eye and began to ooze down her cheek.

A fire lit inside her. Without taking the time to think or wipe her face, Frankie lunged at Leroy, pushing him backward until he fell onto another hay bale at the far end of the stage. "Get off!" he screamed at Frankie, but she kept pushing down on him like a steam-powered roller.

"Take it back!" she yelled again. If she yelled loud enough and pushed him hard enough, maybe she could undo everything and start all over. Maybe she couldn't change things all on her own and be anything more than a Number Three, but she could do something to make Leroy Price see her, like she wanted Daddy to see her and know that she was as good as anybody else. *Look at me! Look!*

With his back still on the hay bale, Leroy kicked at Frankie. She grabbed fistfuls of hay and threw them at him. He tried to bat them away, but she did not stop until he was completely covered, until she could no longer see his face. Then, when she could do no more, when all of her steam had been used up and she had nothing left but tears, she grabbed Marty's snowball and dumped it on top of Leroy's head.

Marty stood next to her. "Aw, man, what a waste of egg custard."

"Sorry, Marty," said Frankie, wiping the hair out of her face.

"No, I'm sorry," he said in a low voice.

"It's not your fault you have a monster for a brother." Then she yelled "Monster!" at Leroy to finish him off.

"No," said Marty. "I don't mean that. I mean this. I'm sorry for this." He picked up the balled-up paper and unfolded it, smoothing out the wrinkles on his stomach. Then he handed it to Frankie.

BOYCOTT GERMAN BUSINESSES!

BOYCOTT BAUM'S RESTAURANT!
Our fair city is under threat from evil forces. But do not
be mistaken, these forces are not just overseas, they are
right next door.
To keep Hagerstown citizens, businesses, and families
safe, we must NOT patronize German-owned
businesses, whose loyalty is to Germany and ultimately
to Adolf Hitler himself, rather than this
great nation of ours.
We must keep our wallets closed to those who seek to
contaminate our town!
Thank you for your cooperation.

Hagerstown Chamber of Commerce Council

45

MR. STANNUM SAT IN his office at the restaurant with the door closed. Ever since he met with Mr. Price at the pharmacy, he'd been having strange feelings. He had thought he was doing the right thing, for his country, for his brother. He had, hadn't he? Done the right thing? After all, it was his duty, just as Mr. Price said. His duty!

But now, well . . . he *tap-tap-tapped* his fingers to some odd beat.

What if he were wrong?

He pulled his handkerchief from his jacket pocket to dry his face, and as he did, a slip of paper fell to the floor. He picked it up and unfolded it.

He swallowed, then wiped the sweat from his neck as he read the handwritten words: *WHERE IS YOUR HEART?*

46

YOU NEVER HAVE SEEN so much red, white, and blue as was in the dining room of Baum's Restaurant that night. The sheer number of adornments would have rivaled those in the nation's capital. Streamers, garlands, and paper chains *galore* were strung from the chandeliers to each wall and back again. Under that canopy, three long tables had been fashioned together, side by side, each seating twenty-four. At every place setting there were vases of red, white, and blue flowers with tiny American flags tucked in them, and ribbons in the same color scheme were tied around the backs of each chair.

There was no way Mr. Price would doubt Hermann Baum's loyalty if he saw all this. But perhaps that was the point.

Fritz and Inky had already taken their seats at the end of the first table and were debating President Roosevelt's domestic policies. "Welcome, welcome," said Hermann, shaking their hands. Then he nodded toward the bar and said, "Mr. Dench will make you whatever drink you'd like."

"I highly recommend a rickey," announced Grandma Engel, who was sitting on a stool at the bar. "Mr. Dench here makes the best in town." Then she gave him a wink.

"You all right, Hermann?" asked Fritz.

"Why does everyone keep asking me that?" he answered. "I'm fine, I'm fine."

Mother, who was perched at the door, ready to greet the guests as they arrived, gave Grandma Engel a disapproving look. To which Grandma Engel replied by sticking out her tongue.

Elizabeth grabbed the water pitcher and starting filling Fritz's and Inky's glasses at the first table, while Aunt Edith and Uncle Hal, along with Ava and Martha, arrived and took their seats beside them. "Oh, thank heavens," said Aunt Edith to Uncle Hal, looking at the eighteen empty chairs at their table. "I thought for sure we'd be late."

Martha grabbed a dinner roll from a basket on the table in front of her. Ava tied her napkin around her head to cover her nose and mouth. She stuck her finger into Martha's side and said, "Give me that roll or else."

"I will not," declared Martha, starting to take a bite.

"I'm warning you," said Ava. "I said *or else.*"

"I don't care," said Martha, chewing with her mouth open. "Go ahead and shoot. I'm not playing; I'm hungry."

Ava yanked off her napkin in a pout. "You're no fun."

At the far end of the second table sat Mr. and Mrs. Bulgar, Julie's father and mother. As Elizabeth filled their water glasses, they sipped on mixed drinks and sampled a basket of breads and muffins that Julie had brought out special for them. "Delectable," they said. "Just scrumptious."

The only other person at that table was Mr. Dench's sister, Fern, who had just been to the dentist the day before, where she'd had all of her teeth extracted due to a severe gum problem. She wouldn't be fitted for dentures until the following week, so until then she was unable to eat any foods other than, say, applesauce and rice pudding, and was too embarrassed to converse with anyone lest they see her pink, swollen gums and missing bicuspids. No one else knew this, of course, except for Mr. Dench. As Fern just sat quietly, staring at her water glass and waiting patiently for the ice to melt, the Bulgars whispered about her unsociable character and ill-begotten manners. But toothless Fern Dench wasn't the only thing they were whispering about.

"What should we do?" Mr. Bulgar asked his wife. "I didn't know there would be coloreds here. Not in the same room. Never in my life have I dined right next to Negroes." He looked over his shoulder at the table behind them, where Mr. Washington's wife, Henrietta, and their two young boys were seated, alongside Amy's mother, father, grandmother, aunt and uncle, and her eight cousins. Katie Resden, the Baums' housekeeper, was there, too, chatting up Seaweed's mother and sister Peaches about the oppressive heat.

"It's a shock to me, too, dear," replied Mrs. Bulgar quietly. "Julie never mentioned this would be a mixed affair. Let's just eat quickly and then leave. We don't want to disappoint our Julie."

And speaking of disappointment, there was a good bit of that going around. By Daddy's count, there were forty-three empty chairs. The Wexlers, the Hoffmans, and plenty of others had said they were coming, and yet they were almost an hour late, if they were coming at all. Daddy had tried telephoning many of them, but he could not get a single answer.

Forty-three no-shows, with enough food to feed seventy-five. Daddy rested his hand over his chest to calm his racing heart.

Since there hadn't been any more guests to greet in a while, Mother left her position at the door and took his side. "Where do you think everyone is?" she whispered.

"I don't know," he said. "Something is not right."

"Should we go ahead and serve the food?" asked Mother.

"Let's give them a little while longer," said Daddy. "They'll be here."

"All right," said Mother, giving his arm a squeeze. "I'll get back to the door."

Aunt Edith took a sip of her iced tea and said, "Hermann, I'm so excited to hear the Metropolitans play tonight. What a treat!"

Daddy winced. "About that," he said. "There's been a change of plans." He raised his voice so that everyone could hear. "We had an arrangement with Yancy Biggs and his Metropolitans to play for you tonight, but as you can see, they aren't here. And the reason they aren't here is that they aren't coming. Mr. Biggs called me earlier today to inform me that he has another, more fruitful opportunity, as he put it, and he apologized for not being able to make it."

Aunt Edith's high-arched eyebrows said it all.

This was a blow to Daddy, a kick in the gut. And as the guests looked at the empty corner of the room where the orchestra was supposed to be playing, and then at all of the empty chairs, they started to wonder, as Daddy did, just what was going on. Some of them, the Bulgars, for instance, had heard talk around town about Mr. Baum having ties to Germany. But there was quite a bit of talk about a lot of things these days, and the Bulgars were so pleased that Mr. Baum had employed their only daughter that they were willing to overlook what they viewed as just rumors.

The rumors hadn't spread so far as to reach those on Jonathan Street, though, so Henrietta Washington and others at the third table attributed the poor showing to Daddy not knowing much about running a restaurant.

Regardless of what anyone believed about Daddy, they all could agree on this: the party was not much of one.

"Biggs is a second-rate bum," said Fritz, pounding a fist on the table and breaking the silence, which had gone on too long.

"I never did hear them play none," offered Katie, "but I know they ain't no Duke Ellington. They ain't nobody like the Duke."

"Except Cab Calloway," said Amy's father, clearing his throat. "That there's a bandleader."

"Now, Benny Goodman," said Mrs. Bulgar, "there's a man who knows how to lead an orchestra."

"Amen," said Mr. Bulgar.

"The King of Swing," said Grandma Engel. She slid down from her bar stool and wiggled her hips.

"That's it, call up Benny," said Uncle Hal, laughing. "That'll show old Yancy Biggs he's nothing but a bum."

Seaweed's mother stood up. "Now, hold it one second." Her mouth was pulled tight in a straight line. Finally, after a long couple of seconds, when she was sure she had everyone's attention, she said, "Let's get one thing straight in here. The king ain't got nothin' on Lady Ella. Fitzgerald, I mean," and her face broke into a wide grin.

Everyone laughed, and the room—at least for a few minutes—had the flavor of a celebration.

Now, it was around this time that Inky whispered to Hermann and pointed up toward the balcony. There, perched at the Hammond electric organ, was Mrs. Inkletter, cracking her fingers and waiting for her cue. "Right," said Hermann, hoping that Mrs. Inkletter's playing would help spur on the guests' good humor. And so he made another announcement, introducing Mrs. Inkletter and her fine musical talents.

Mrs. Inkletter sat tall in the center of the bench and let her fingertips rest gently on the keys. In all fairness, she started out strong with "God Bless America," an appropriate, if not lively, selection.

"There's my girl," shouted Inky. "Listen to those notes."

Alas, while no one, *and I mean no one*, could follow the greats—Ella, Duke, Cab, and Benny—in a performance, Mrs. Inkletter proved that it's disadvantageous to follow a *conversation* about them as well. When you've conjured up musical legends in people's minds, your playing better be legendary, too, or you might as well pack up and go home.

But packing up and going home wasn't in Mrs. Inkletter's blood. Like I said, she started out strong, but about halfway through, she hit a wrong note. It was a whopper of a wrong note, too. A dilly. A beaut. A corker. A real humdinger. One that could be heard from the mountains to the prairies to the oceans white with foam, just like was written in the song. Then she stopped playing altogether, God bless her.

"Mercy!" said Grandma Engel.

"She just needs to get warmed up, is all," explained Inky. "You should keep going, dear," he called up to her.

"Don't encourage her," whispered Grandma Engel.

Mrs. Inkletter shook her head and waved him away. And then she started, oh yes she did, right back from the beginning. If it's not perfect, you do it over again until it is. This was her life's philosophy.

While everyone's necks were craned up toward the balcony, Daddy said, "Uh, let's see how the food is coming along. I think it's time to eat. Excuse me for a moment while I check." He pushed open the kitchen doors. "Mr. Stannum," he called. "Go ahead and have everyone bring out the food. Let's all eat." He stuck his head in farther. "Mr. Stannum?"

Mr. Washington, who had just filled platters of baked ham sandwiches, cold platter combinations, hot sliced chicken breasts, and frankfurts with sauerkraut, said, "Stannum ain't here. He left a while ago. I don't know where or why."

"Left?" said Daddy.

"Out that way," said Julie, pointing to the door leading to the alley.

"He look real bad, too," said Seaweed. "Worse than he usually do."

Amy nodded and then added, "Like he just lost something."

Hermann was suddenly overtaken by a feeling that he had lost something as well. He glanced around the room. "Where's Frankie?"

No sooner had he uttered the words than Mr. Travers appeared in the doorway with a piece of paper in his hands. "Hermann," he said, "I need a moment of your time."

47

OFFICER MCINTYRE ARRIVED ON the scene. First, he eyed the cart with the block of ice near the stage. *A penny sundae would taste divine in this heat,* he thought. *Dee-vine.* Then he pulled at the waist of his pants, which were giving his middle an uncomfortable squeeze—a reminder that his pants were one and a half sizes too small.

Egg custard, vanilla sugar. He would have one of each. *Dee-vine.*

Officer McIntyre always made a point of dismissing any notion that his waist was one and a half sizes too big.

Which it was. Anyone could see that.

He hitched up his trousers and was heading for the cart when he saw a young boy covered in hay. Not too far away from that boy was young Frances Marie Baum, the girl he'd been charged to locate. The same one, in fact, that he'd found weeks before while on patrol in the colored part of town. Trouble, this girl was turning out to be. As soon as he spotted her, he knew the penny sundae, delicious as it may be, would have to wait.

Duty before snowballs.

Officer McIntyre had the young Baum girl in his sights and he would bring her safely home, just as he'd promised her mother. All in a day's work. Dear Mrs. Baum had been a nervous wreck when she noticed her daughter had disappeared and she telephoned the police. Terrible thing, a young girl disappearing like that without her folks knowing where she'd run off to. What a worry children could be to their parents.

He knew that firsthand. Good thing his son, Robbie, was not the kind of boy to get in trouble. No, sir. A more perfect angel there was not.

"Frances Baum," said Officer McIntyre as he approached Frankie and Marty.

"Oh, Mother," said Frankie under her breath.

"I didn't do anything, Officer," said Marty. "It was all Leroy. He started the whole thing. Tell him, Frankie."

By that time, Leroy Price had finally gotten to his feet and brushed the hay from his clothes. He gave Marty and Frankie such a look that Marty hid behind Officer McIntyre and clutched his leg.

"Is that so?" asked Officer McIntyre.

"We were just leaving," said Leroy. "Our father needs our help with some important business." Then he smirked at Frankie as a reminder of just what business he was talking about. "Come on, Marty."

Marty reluctantly let go of the officer's leg and followed Leroy, who knuckle-punched him in the arm before they both left the square.

Then Officer McIntyre turned to Frankie. "Your mother is worried sick about you," he said. "You've given her quite a fright."

"Sorry," said Frankie. "I didn't mean to."

"Mean to or not, it's what you did. And I'm not the one you need to say sorry to." He put his hand on her shoulder. "Well, come along. I'll see that you get home."

"No, wait," said Frankie. "I can't go home."

"Nonsense," said Officer McIntyre. "I've my orders to find you and return you to your quarters safe and sound."

Frankie fished the BOYCOTT GERMAN BUSINESSES! flyer from her dress pocket. "Not home," she said. "I need to go to our restaurant right away."

48

MOTHER AND ELIZABETH WERE on the sidewalk in front of the restaurant when Officer McIntyre delivered Frankie in his police car. "She was at the square," Officer McIntyre told them. "She claims she wasn't running away from home, just lost track of the time is all."

Frankie felt the burn of Mother's glare but kept her eyes on her sandals. "Thank you for your trouble, Officer," said Mother, trying to put a lid on her anger for the officer's benefit. "My husband just left in the car to look for her."

"Ah, well, leave it to the police to get the job done," he said, puffing out his chest. "All in a day's work."

Frankie took a step toward the restaurant, but Mother caught her by the wrist. My goodness, Mother had such a grip. Frankie looked up at the sky and cursed the clouds she had wished on.

"When you are off duty, why don't you come by this evening?" Mother said to Officer McIntyre. "We're having a party here, with good food and entertainment."

"And fireworks," added Elizabeth.

"That's right, fireworks imported directly from Baltimore," said Mother. "You haven't seen anything until you've seen the Whirling Dervisher." She smiled. "You are more than welcome."

Officer McIntyre tipped the bill of his hat with his finger. "I thank you for the offer, ma'am. But I promised Robbie and the missus that we'd go to the square for the festivities. I don't want to disappoint."

Elizabeth looked away at the mention of Robbie's name.

"Well, then, I hope to see you tomorrow for our grand opening," said Mother. "Dessert is on us. It's the least we can do." She nodded in Frankie's direction.

Officer McIntyre cleared his throat. "I'm afraid I have to work tomorrow evening."

Mother nodded. "Well, some other time, perhaps."

"Perhaps," said Officer McIntyre. Then he looked directly at Frankie. "Now, don't make a habit of running off, young lady."

"I won't," said Frankie. She felt her cheeks get hot.

Officer McIntyre tipped his hat once more and then got back into his police car and pulled away from the curb.

Before Mother had a chance to get out even one word, Frankie pulled the wrinkled flyer from her pocket and held it out to her. "They're all over town," she said. "I saw them hanging on doors and windows of shops on the way back here with Officer McIntyre."

Mother's face lost its color. "Good Lord," she said, covering her mouth with the back of her hand.

"What does it say?" asked Elizabeth, snatching the paper from Mother's hands. "What's going on?"

"It says that people shouldn't come to the restaurant because Daddy is a supporter of Hitler," said Frankie. She couldn't help but smile a little when she got to the end. Not because of Hitler, of course, but because for once in her life, Frankie knew something before Elizabeth.

Mother said, "Frances Marie." Then she looked around to make sure no one heard.

"There's more," said Frankie.

"Heavens," said Mother. "What more?" Elizabeth made a grab for Mother just in case she went down. "I'm all right," said Mother, widening her stance and resting her hands on her knees as if she were getting ready to catch a curveball. "Let's hear it."

49

HERMANN CIRCLED THE SQUARE a few times in the Studebaker before setting out on foot. He had no idea where Frankie would be, but he would find her. At least he hoped he would. That girl could hide like none other. For all he knew, she could be tucked away in a cupboard somewhere.

He made his way through the crowd that was starting to fill up around the stage. It was quite a turnout, and no hay bale sat empty. Bobby Melvich was tap-tapping all over the place and giving a good show when Hermann walked up to the stage, pushed the VOTE FOR PRICE banner aside, and pulled back the red-white-and-blue drapes that hung down in front. He checked under the stage, but nothing.

He hadn't meant to raise his voice at her like that. He just wasn't himself today, and it certainly wasn't her fault things were falling apart at the restaurant. She had only been trying to help, after all. But there was so much riding on the restaurant's success. So much at stake.

Hermann turned back into the crowd. He spotted Mr. and Mrs. Wexler watching the young dancer and eating frankfurts. "Happy Fourth," he said. "Have you seen Frankie anywhere?"

"Oh, Hermann," said Mr. Wexler, nearly choking on his sandwich. "I did not expect to see you here."

"Yes, well, I didn't expect to be here. I'm looking for my daughter."

"We were, uh, planning to come by the restaurant like you asked," said Mr. Wexler, wiping his mouth with a handkerchief.

"We certainly appreciated the invitation," offered Mrs. Wexler, whose face was becoming flushed. "But Mr. Price came by and . . ."

"What?" said Hermann. He wasn't following.

"What she means," said Mr. Wexler, "is that we were going to stop over, but Mr. Price and some of the council members paid a visit to the store this morning, and, well, we've always come here to the square for the Fourth, and in the end, we felt it was best. You understand, don't you?"

Hermann certainly did understand. The flyer, which Mr. Travers had brought to the restaurant, was tucked in Hermann's shirt pocket. Mr. Price's influence had a far greater reach than Hermann had imagined. But the one thing Hermann hadn't counted on was that people, the people he thought he knew—friends, for Pete's sake— would believe these things about him. It occurred to him then that perhaps you can't really know people at all. And that realization was perhaps worse than anything Mr. Price could do to him. He took a deep breath, for the air around him seemed to be as thick as burlap.

"Are you all right, Hermann?" asked Mr. Wexler.

Hermann wiped his forehead with his jacket sleeve. "Fine, yes," he said. There were more urgent matters at hand. "Frankie. Have you seen her today?"

Mr. Wexler shook his head. "No, not here. Sorry."

Hermann pushed past, and a few steps beyond them he saw Mr. and Mrs. Hoffman. They saw him, too, but do you know, they pretended they didn't. You didn't need two good eyes to see that. Like the Wexlers, the Hoffmans had been invited to Baum's for the Fourth of July party and said they would come. And yet, here they were.

Hermann shook his head, hoping they would see that, too, and kept on searching.

The crowd applauded for the young tapper when he finished his routine, and then, lo and behold, Mr. Price took the podium. "Wasn't that just wonderful!" said Mr. Price, clapping his hands.

Hermann, who was scanning the crowd for Frankie, turned to look at him.

"I wonder if I could give that a try." Mr. Price laughed, along with most of the audience. Then he shuffled his feet about the stage, knocking ashes from his cigar as he went. The harder the crowd laughed, the more disgusted Hermann became. Finally, Mr. Price patted the boy on the head and said, "I think I'd better stick with public service."

"Public service," grumbled Hermann under his breath. "Is that what he calls it?"

"And speaking of public service," said Mr. Price. "You may have heard that I'm running for mayor." The audience roared and waved their flags, and Mr. Price scanned the crowd for the photographer to make sure he was getting the best shots. And that's when he locked eyes with Hermann Baum. Mr. Price cleared his throat after a moment or two and began his well-rehearsed speech. "My dear ladies and gentlemen, today as we celebrate our nation's independence . . ."

Hermann turned his back and began walking away. He stumbled a few steps, the heat making it increasingly difficult for him to get his breath. Through the crowd, he saw Mr. Stannum heading toward him. *A friend*, he thought, *finally*. *A friend*. He lumbered toward him, but just as Mr. Price got to the part in his speech about "the evil that has already reached our shores," Hermann heard nothing else and fell to the ground.

50

THERE WAS NOTHING ANY of them could do but wait.

51

OVER AT THE BAUMS' apartment, Grandma Engel held tight to Elizabeth's hand. Aunt Edith was in the kitchen putting the kettle on for tea while Uncle Hal held a sleeping Martha on his lap at the dining room table. Next to them, Katie was teaching Ava how to cut a deck of cards with one hand, while Amy and Mr. Washington sat on the sofa in silence.

They could hear the fireworks from the city square and winced at each boom, which rattled the apartment windows. They were already on edge, as they waited for the telephone to ring or for Mother to come home from the hospital with news, and the sound of their sky exploding only made things worse.

Bismarck paced from one end of the apartment to the other and could not get settled. "I never did care much for fireworks," said Grandma Engel. "Would somebody stop that dog? All his back and forth is making me a nervous wreck."

"Dogs don't like fireworks much, either," said Uncle Hal.

But Frankie knew different. "He knows something is wrong with Daddy," she said from under the dining room table. She barely had enough room for herself under there, what with Uncle Hal's, Ava's, and Katie's legs there, too, but still, she called Bismarck to her and, when he came, she coaxed him to crawl under Ava's chair and lie down beside her. Frankie stroked his velvety ears as he panted, and she whispered to him over and over that everything would be all right.

Whether he could tell she was lying, she wasn't sure. But perhaps he couldn't, because afterward, he lay there next to her and rested his head on her knee, quite content.

Every now and then, Grandma Engel would check on Frankie from her easy chair. "You doing all right over there, honey girl?" she'd call out from the living room.

Each time, Frankie told her that she was.

Until finally, when Frankie's worries got so bad they made her start to tremble, so much that Bismarck began to whine, she instead answered, "No, Grandma. I need to know about Daddy."

"We all do, sugar," said Grandma Engel. "We just have to wait."

"That's not what I mean," said Frankie. "I need to know about that photograph. Who is that woman? And why was it at the bottom of the dresser?" She was glad for the cover of the table and legs around her and found it easier to ask questions from under there than if she were out in the open. She hoped that being under the table would also make it easier to hear the answers.

"Oh, Frankie," said Grandma Engel in a weary voice.

Ava stuck her head under the table. "What woman?"

"I know you said it isn't your story to tell," said Frankie, ignoring Ava, "but I can't take not knowing." Frankie's voice started to crack.

"What woman?" asked Ava again.

"What are you talking about?" asked Elizabeth.

After a few quiet moments, Grandma Engel said, "Fine. But come out from under that table. This isn't the kind of story that should be told from across the room or heard while under furniture."

Frankie climbed over Bismarck and scrambled into the living room. She sat on the floor by Grandma Engel's feet. Ava soon joined her, and Elizabeth moved to the upholstered chair closest to her. Aunt Edith brought two cups of tea for Amy and Mr. Washington. "What's going on?" she asked.

"I'm telling them about Hermann and Victoria," said Grandma Engel.

"You aren't," said Aunt Edith, nearly spilling the tea.

"You just hush," said Grandma Engel. "There's no reason they shouldn't know. And their father would tell them if he were here and able." She looked at Frankie. "This one here already knows something of it and has nothing but her imagination to fill in the blanks."

Mr. Washington stood up. "Maybe me and Amy shouldn't be around to hear." He nudged Amy to put down her tea and get up.

"Nonsense," said Grandma Engel. "You're here, you're family. Now sit back down."

They did.

"Now," began Grandma Engel. "Frankie, go get that photograph."

Frankie ran down the hall to the walnut dresser and opened the bottom cupboard. She pulled out the table linens and box of sewing notions and reached back into the far corner where she had left the picture. She grasped it and, leaving everything else where it was, raced back to the living room.

"Let me have it," said Grandma Engel.

Frankie handed it over.

Grandma Engel turned the frame over in her swollen hands and then rested the picture on her lap so that it faced Frankie, Ava, and Elizabeth. "But that's Daddy," said Elizabeth, looking confused.

"It is," said Grandma Engel.

Ava put her face real close to the picture. "Aunt Mildred don't even look like herself."

"That's because it isn't her," said Frankie, looking at Grandma Engel.

"This was your daddy's first wife," said Grandma Engel. "Her name was Victoria."

"First wife?" said Ava. "How many does he have?"

"Ava," said Grandma Engel, "would you please?"

"Would I please what?"

Grandma Engel shook her head. "Victoria and Hermann were married before he and Mildred were married."

"I didn't know Daddy was married before," said Elizabeth.

"What happened to her?" asked Frankie. "Where is she now? Does she live in Germany?"

"Germany?" said Grandma Engel. "Why in the world would you think that? For goodness' sakes, she lived right here in Maryland. She was a lovely girl."

"You knew her?" asked Frankie.

"I did," said Grandma Engel. "Not too well, but this was a smaller town back then and most people knew of each other at least. Not like today. Anyway, she and your father were married a few years and they were expecting a baby."

This was all too much for Frankie to hear. "A baby!"

"Does Mother know?" asked Elizabeth.

"Well, of course she does. What do you think?" Grandma Engel said.

Frankie didn't know what to think, and apparently neither did Elizabeth.

Grandma Engel lovingly patted the photograph. She sighed. "And, as sometimes happens, sadly, Victoria died while giving birth. They lost the baby, too."

The words, all of them, hung in the air like smoke.

Frankie found it hard to swallow. "Was it a girl?" she whispered. "The baby, I mean?" She didn't know exactly why she wanted to know this, or why it mattered, just that it did.

"Frankie!" scolded Elizabeth, as if such a thing were nobody's business, especially hers.

Grandma Engel cocked her head to the side as if she were trying to understand the reason behind Frankie's question. "No," she said finally. "It was a boy."

A boy.

There weren't any boys in the Baum family, only girls. Which made Frankie wonder if it was an even bigger disappointment to Daddy that he never got to have *that* boy, or any other. Three girls, that's what he ended up with, but was he hoping for a boy each time?

"Huh," said Ava, and then she went back to the table to practice her card trick.

"Is that it?" asked Frankie.

"That's all she wrote." Grandma Engel handed the photograph back to Frankie. "Now the story has all been told. You can go ahead and put that back."

Frankie was about to return it to the cupboard. But then she wondered aloud, "Why did Daddy put it at the bottom of that dresser? It was all covered with dust."

Grandma shrugged. "You'd have to ask him about that. But sometimes you don't want to be reminded of painful things. Sometimes you just want to put them away somewhere and forget they ever happened."

Frankie wasn't sure she understood, and she felt bad for Victoria that she was left in the dresser that Daddy hated, in the thing that left him with bruises. So she went to the kitchen and, with a damp dish towel, wiped off the rest of the dust. Then she laid it carefully on the pile of table linens in the dresser and closed the cupboard doors.

52

THE RAIN CAME THAT night and continued into the next morning. Frankie lay in her bed facing the window and watched the rain shadows dance down the curtains in crooked lines. Her body ached with sorrow, as if from a bad dream that she couldn't remember. Her eyes still heavy with sleep, she blinked away the fog and tried to call up the events of the day before in her mind.

When they came, oh my, they came. Like horses breaking free of their pen, the memories ran through her. She sat up in bed, wondering how long she'd been sleeping and if Mother had come home from the hospital with any news of Daddy. Across the dark room, Elizabeth's bed was empty and made up. Frankie pushed against the lump beside her as she pulled her legs from under the covers. "Come on, Bismarck," she said. "Move."

"I'm not Bismarck," said Joan, sitting up and rubbing her eyes.

"Joanie!" yelled Frankie. "You're here!" She threw her arms around Joan's neck and knocked her back on her pillow. "What are you doing here?"

Joan squeezed Frankie tight. "Fritz came up to Aunt Dottie's to get me, you know, after. We got home late and you were already asleep. I tried to wake you up, but you just kept calling me Bismarck." Frankie let go and they sat across from each other on the bed, knees to knees. Joan turned on the bedside table lamp. "I'm really glad to be . . ." And then she looked at her pillow and her side of the bed, which were covered in dog hair. "Didn't I tell you not to let Bismarck get too used to my side?"

"Didn't I tell you to stop bossing me so?" Then Frankie stared at Joan's curls. "Oh no, your hair!"

"Don't you dare laugh, Frankie. It's awful, I know." She pulled at her curls to try to straighten them, but as soon as she let go, they snapped back into perfect ringlets.

"You do sort of look like Shirley Temple."

"Frankie!" said Joan.

"All right," said Frankie. "I won't say anything else about it."

"Thank you." Joan stretched out her legs, which nearly reached to the foot of the bed. "I don't know how it happened," she said, "but this bed got smaller."

They both laughed, but then immediately felt bad for doing so, and were quiet. "Did you see Mother?" asked Frankie.

Joan shook her head. "She wasn't here when I got home."

"She must be home by now," said Frankie.

Their feet hit the wood floor at the same time, and when they reached the hall, Frankie was two steps ahead.

Elizabeth and Grandma Engel were on the living room sofa, sitting on either side of Mother. She was pale, except for her eyes, which were puffy and pink. She clutched her eyeglasses in her hand, and without them on, there was a trace of young Mildred Engel, scared and alone among the garbage cans, hiding from the truant officer.

"Girls," said Grandma Engel, when Frankie and Joan came into the room. "Have a seat."

"Joan," said Mother. She opened her arms and brought her in. "Welcome home, dear. It's wonderful to see you." Joan kissed her damp cheek.

"What about Daddy?" asked Frankie. Her breath caught when she said his name.

"That's what I want to talk to you about, girls," said Mother.

Then Joan went back to Frankie and grabbed her hand. They squeezed into the easy chair together. And they waited.

53

DADDY'S HEART HAS A *disease*. That's how Mother explained it to the girls, and that's how the doctors at the hospital had explained it to Mother. Daddy was a very sick man, and there was nothing anyone could do for him to make him better, other than keep him comfortable and in bed. Until.

After Mother got all that out, she laid her head on the back of the sofa and wept.

That was the gist of it.

But it made sense to no one.

"He's so young," said Elizabeth, wiping away her own tears. "I don't understand."

"He's going to die?" asked Frankie, squeezing Joan's fingers. That couldn't be right. There must be some kind of medicine that could help. And then she wondered if the doctors at the hospital had seen those flyers and had heard the rumors about Daddy. They wouldn't decide *not* to help him if they could, would they?

Mother moaned into her hands, and Elizabeth stroked her arm to soothe her. "Frankie, please," said Elizabeth, giving her a look.

"Everybody's going to die sometime," said Grandma Engel. "Hermann's alive right now, and I don't care what those doctors say, they don't know a plum thing more than any of us do about it. When it's your time, it's your time."

"Can we see him?" asked Joan.

Mother blew her nose into a handkerchief. "In a few days," she said. "You all can see him in a few days."

"That will be the best medicine for him," said Grandma Engel, nodding.

"What about the restaurant?" said Frankie. "The grand opening is supposed to be tonight."

Mother got to her feet. "As far as I'm concerned, the restaurant is closed." Then, without saying another word about it, she made her way across the room, pausing once. "It's just as well. If last night was telling, there wouldn't be anybody to show up tonight anyway." She went on down the hall to her room to lie down.

"This is all Mr. Price's fault," said Frankie. "And Mr. Stannum's."

"Mr. Price from the Chamber of Commerce?" said Grandma Engel. "And Mr. Stannum from the restaurant? What do they have to do with anything?"

Then Frankie explained about how she followed Mr. Stannum to the pharmacy and saw what she saw. And about the BOYCOTT GERMAN BUSINESSES flyers that the Price boys were handing out.

Elizabeth wiped her cheeks with the back of her hand. "If you're talking about whose fault this is," she went on, "you might want to look in the mirror."

"What do you mean?" said Frankie, dropping Joan's hand and getting to her feet.

"I mean, Daddy was out looking for you when this happened," accused Elizabeth.

"Elizabeth!" said Joan. "That's not fair."

Grandma Engel stomped her foot on the floor. "Stop it now! Just stop! What happened to your father was nobody's fault. Didn't you hear what your mother said? He is sick. Now, I don't want to hear any more of this kind of talk, do you understand?"

Elizabeth, Joan, and Frankie nodded.

"Let me hear you," said Grandma Engel.

"We understand," the girls said at the same time.

"Good," said Grandma Engel, standing up. "Now, let's get some breakfast going. We'll all feel a little brighter with full stomachs. Elizabeth, why don't you help me?"

When Elizabeth and Grandma Engel were gone, Frankie whispered to Joan, "What Elizabeth said. Do you think she's right?"

"Of course not," said Joan.

"But Daddy wouldn't have been out there at the square looking for me, if I hadn't . . ." The thought sickened her.

"I'm certain that had nothing to do with it," said Joan.

Frankie nodded, succumbing to tears. "He must have been so worried and upset." But there was more to Frankie's grief. She also felt terribly guilty for having wondered if Daddy was really a spy for the Germans. That he could have been. She no longer believed that to be true, of course, though she still couldn't explain the piece of paper that Mr. Stannum had found. But thinking that she'd doubted Daddy, even for a short time, well . . . how was she any different from Mr. Stannum or anybody else who was swayed by those rumors?

Joan shook her head. "Aunt Dottie told me that their father was sick a lot while they were growing up. So maybe Daddy has the same kind of heart problem. Frankie, nobody is to blame."

"Maybe not for his heart," said Frankie. But there was plenty of blame to go around for everything else.

54

THE HOSPITAL WAS FOUR blocks away. Visiting hours began at nine o'clock sharp, and Mother made sure she and the girls were out the door, in formation, and moving at a brisk pace by ten minutes till. She had also made them dress alike this morning, in flower-printed cotton dresses that Daddy had brought back from a business trip to Philadelphia several months earlier.

The girls would normally have protested such a thing, but they were well aware that Mother's nerves were in a fragile way, and so they held their tongues. There was, in fact, only one thing they hated more than Mother making them wear matching dresses, and that was walking down the street with her.

The three girls had to walk side by side—Elizabeth on the left, Joan in the middle, Frankie on the right—and never behind one another. Behind was where Mother walked, for that position had the vantage point of seeing and correcting any mischief-making, as well as setting the pace with the rhythmic *trip trap* of her heels on the sidewalk. Mother's legs may have been petite, but they could move like nobody's business. To Mother, walking was not a leisurely sport or done for pleasure; it was a means of getting from place to place in as quick a manner as possible.

Walking behind also helped her improve the girls' posture.

"Keep your head up, Frankie," said Mother before they had even gone one block. "Shoulders back, Joan. You're not on the farm."

Joan and Frankie exchanged a look, but in truth, Frankie was relieved to have something else to concentrate on other than Daddy and what he would look like in that hospital bed.

When they got to the front door of the hospital, Mother took the lead. They climbed three flights of stairs and wandered down a long hall with white walls, passing nurses in all-white dresses and matching socks and lace-up shoes. Frankie had only been to the hospital one other time, when Joan had her tonsils out a few years back. The smell of ammonia and urine, the one thing that stuck out in Frankie's memory of the place, was the same and as strong as ever. Frankie pinched her nostrils closed until Mother saw and told her to act like a lady.

"I can't hold my nose?" asked Frankie.

"It's not polite," said Mother.

"Are you telling me that no lady holds her nose, ever?"

"That's right," said Mother.

"Not even if she's around the most awful smell you could imagine?" said Frankie. "Like if she was down in the sewer pipes?"

"Don't be smart," said Mother. "When was the last time you saw a *lady* down in the sewer pipes? And you shouldn't be talking about sewer pipes in the hospital. It's unsanitary." Then she took a deep breath and stopped in front of a wide door, number 303. A nurse came out of the room and smiled at Mother and then at the girls. "Good morning, Mrs. Baum," she said in a quiet voice. "He's ready to see you all."

Mother thanked the nurse and gently pushed open the door.

She went inside first, followed by Elizabeth and then Joan. Frankie lingered in the doorway. Daddy may have been ready to see them, but Frankie was not sure she was ready for whatever was in that room. At home, at least, she could imagine him as he'd been the last time she saw him, or every other time before that. But if she went through that door, whatever he was in there, lying on that bed, that's what she was afraid she would never be able to rid from her mind.

She knelt down and adjusted the buckle on her sandal, for something to do. Then she did the other one. Perhaps there was a bathroom nearby that she could use. But then, Daddy called her name.

She straightened her legs and went inside.

The curtains were drawn closed, except for a narrow gap that let in a thin ray of sunlight. It took a few moments for Frankie's eyes to adjust to the dark after the bright lights in the hallway. There were two beds on either side of the room, and Daddy was in the one closest to the window. In the other bed, there was an older gentleman with thin white hair combed over his otherwise bald head. His eyes were open, gazing up at the ceiling, and his hands were folded neatly above the covers, as if he were patiently waiting for something to happen.

Frankie rushed by him, for if something was going to happen, she didn't want to be nearby to witness it. Mother, Joan, and Elizabeth were crowded around Daddy, and there was no place for Frankie, so she stayed back by the foot of the bed.

"There you are, Frankie," whispered Daddy. He smiled and moved his shoulders as if he wanted to sit up, but then winced and lay back down again.

"Does it hurt?" asked Mother.

"It's nothing," he said, keeping his eyes on Frankie.

It was a relief to see that he looked more like himself than the frightening thing Frankie had imagined he might, though he was pale and his eyes were cradled by dark moons. He seemed so small, stretched out in that bed, and Frankie wondered if it was merely the size of the mattress that made him look that way, or if life had already begun to leave him.

He touched Joan's face and then squeezed Elizabeth's hand. Mother sat down in a chair beside the bed. Daddy asked Joan about Aunt Dottie's and about how she liked the farm, and then he quipped about all the pretty nurses who brought his meals right to him without him even having to get out of bed.

"How is the food?" asked Mother. "Are you eating?"

"Well, it isn't Baum's Restaurant," he said. "But they say it's food, so I'm inclined to believe them."

Mother's mouth turned down at the mention of the restaurant, and she pulled the curtain closed so that the thin piece of sunlight was no more.

"Joan," said Daddy, "just wait until you see it. A place of wide renown is what it is." He looked at Mother. "Mildred, maybe you can all go by the restaurant to show her, and check on things."

Mother gave a brief smile. "Did you sleep well?" She fussed over his blankets, smoothing out the folds. "Didn't get too chilled?"

"I don't know how anyone can sleep in here," he answered. "Someone was in to check on me every ten minutes or so, waking me."

"As they should," said Mother. "I'm glad to hear you're getting good care."

Daddy looked from Elizabeth to Joan to Frankie. "So, girls, tell me what you've been up to."

None of them knew what to say. Frankie knew better than to say what she'd been up to with Mother in the room. Anyway, Mother didn't give any of them the chance.

"Reinhart is making arrangements to come," Mother said.

Daddy grimaced. "You shouldn't have written him."

"I didn't," said Mother. "Dottie did."

"He'll just put his nose where it doesn't belong," said Daddy, shaking his head. "Thinks he has a better head for business, always has."

Mother patted his hand. "Don't get yourself all worked up now."

Daddy closed his eyes.

"We ought to be going, then," said Mother after a moment. "You need your rest and we've stayed long enough."

His eyes flew open. "Stay, please."

"We'll be back later," Mother told him. "Try to sleep." She leaned down and kissed him on his forehead. Elizabeth and then Joan said good-bye and each gave him a peck on his cheek.

When it was her turn, Frankie leaned in close, but Daddy gripped her hand. "Stay here for a minute," he whispered.

Frankie stood alongside Daddy's bed while he held on to her. All manner of things went through her head about why he wanted her to stay. None of them good.

Daddy cleared his throat. "You go on ahead, Mildred. Princess, Joan, go on with your mother, would you please? I want to have a word with Frankie."

Mother looked like she wanted to stay as well, but she must have seen something in Daddy's eye that changed her mind. She collected the two girls and ushered them out into the hall.

55

ONCE THEY WERE GONE, Daddy let go of Frankie's hand. "Frankie," he said.

"I'm sorry I left the restaurant," said Frankie. "I'm sorry you had to come looking for me. And I'm sorry this happened to you, Daddy." The words collected in her throat in a pile of letters and she could barely get them out.

"Nonsense," said Daddy, patting her knee. "I'm the one who's sorry. I shouldn't have yelled at you in the kitchen. I let my frustration about Biggs get the best of me, and you just happened to be there to bear the brunt of it. You all right?"

Frankie wiped her nose and nodded.

"Good," said Daddy, lowering his voice and glancing at the door. "Now, with all that behind us, this is what I wanted to tell you. Mr. Travers came to see me at the restaurant. He's a council member on the chamber . . ."

"With Mr. Price?" said Frankie.

Daddy nodded. "But he and I go way back. He showed me something that Mr. Price has been circulating through town." Daddy tried to sit up but winced again. "I think it's in the pocket of my shirt somewhere in here, wherever they put it."

"About boycotting the restaurant," said Frankie.

Daddy raised his eyebrows. "You've seen it, then?"

Frankie nodded. "They're all over."

Daddy's face fell. "When people are afraid, or made to feel afraid, they will believe anything."

She looked away.

"You don't think those things about me," he asked, "do you?"

Frankie could answer him truthfully. "No, Daddy."

Whether he believed her or not, she couldn't quite tell.

"I *am* German," he said gently. "An American German. And I am proud of that. As *you* should be yourself. This is your heritage. But that does not mean I am proud of what is happening right now in Germany and other countries in Europe under Hitler's rule. No, sir. For that I am ashamed. But that is not me, and I can't help where my mother and father were born or where I am from any more than I can help the color of my skin or eyes." Then one side of his mouth turned up in a smile. "Well, *eye*, anyway."

Frankie grinned.

"And I don't think it's fair to make judgments about me, or anyone for that matter, based on the things we can't help," he said. "Do you?"

"No," said Frankie.

"No," he said in agreement. "That's right."

"So what Mr. Stannum gave Mr. Price," said Frankie, "what was it?"

"Stannum?" said Daddy. "Stannum was the one?"

"I'm sorry," she said. "I could've stopped him; I should've, but I didn't know . . ."

"Travers told me that Mr. Price was bragging about having gotten to someone. I never in my life figured it would be Stannum." He put his hand over his chest and took in a long, jagged breath.

Frankie panicked. "Daddy, are you all right?"

He closed his eyes for a moment and then opened them. "I saw him at the square. He was there in the crowd when I went down. He kept telling me he was sorry. Over and over he said it. I didn't know what he meant." He took a deep breath to slow his heart. "I thought I was dreaming."

"I couldn't see what he found," said Frankie. "Not too good, anyway. But even if I could've, I wouldn't have been able to tell what it said. It was in German."

Daddy nodded. "It must have been something I got from the union. A representative came by a week or so ago and asked about using the banquet room for an upcoming meeting."

"What's the union?"

"The German Beneficial Union," said Daddy. "They help American Germans with things like insurance policies."

"That's it?"

"Frankie," said Daddy. "I need you to do something for me. It's very important, and you're the only one that I can ask."

If Daddy said anything else after that, she didn't hear it, because *you're the only one* repeated in her head at least a dozen times. Daddy needed her help—not Elizabeth's, not Joan's, but hers. This was a monumental day for Number Threes everywhere.

"Yes." Because it didn't matter what he would ask of her; Frankie was up for the job.

Daddy squeezed both of Frankie's arms. "Your mother won't want to keep the restaurant after I'm gone."

"Gone?" she repeated, shaking her head. "Please, oh please, don't say that."

"Listen now, Frankie. You can't let her sell it." He coughed and squeezed her arms tighter. "Promise me."

"Are you all right?" asked Frankie. "Maybe I should get the nurse."

He stopped coughing. "No, don't do that. I'm all right. Just a spell. Now, promise me you won't let her."

"Why?" said Frankie.

Daddy lifted his arm and clawed at the curtain beside him. He managed to take hold of a piece between his knuckles. Tugging a couple of times, he pulled the curtain back an inch or so, enough to let some light shine through. Then, taxed from the effort and unable to do more, he dropped his hand. "Because when I depart this world, I want to leave something behind that people remember. Something that people will talk about for years to come. Not just for me, but for your mother, for your sisters, for you." He closed his eyes. "I want it to matter that I lived."

Frankie nodded. He did matter, of course he did, but she of all people understood what it was like to feel like you didn't.

"Listen to me, Frankie," said Daddy, his voice fading. "If my brother has anything to do with it, well, that will be the end. We never did see things the same way, especially when it came to matters of business." He rolled the top of his bedsheet in his hands and twisted. "Now, I know this restaurant can be something special, if only your mother will give it a chance."

"But how?" asked Frankie.

Daddy shook his head. "That will be up to you. She's as stubborn as you are, you know."

"But why me?" she asked. Mother would be much more likely to do what Elizabeth or Joan asked of her. She would listen to them.

The corner of Daddy's mouth turned up. "Because," he said simply, "you, my dear girl, are the only one, I think, who can."

56

THREE WEEKS LATER, HERMANN Baum came home from the hospital. Mind your heart, now, because I do not want to raise your hopes only to have them dashed. Hermann came home, not because his health was improving or there was the possibility of his recovery. No, I'm afraid that was not the case.

Hermann, you see, had put all of his savings and business investments into the restaurant, and with it closed—*which is how it remained*—well, the Baums could not afford for him to stay in the hospital any longer.

Alas, money was running out.

And so was Hermann's time.

57

WHEN DADDY CAME HOME, he was confined to his bed and did nothing much but sleep. His weak heart was not strong enough for him to be up and about, so Mother and the girls made sure he remained as still as possible so that his heart wouldn't have to work hard and wear itself out. Bismarck, too, looked after Daddy, staying at the foot of his bed and barking whenever Daddy needed something—a drink of water, a clean bedpan, an extra blanket.

The human heart beats about 100,000 times in one day, pumping about six quarts of blood through the body and sending it a total of 12,000 miles. Did you know? That's a lot of work for even a healthy heart, but for a sick one . . . my goodness. What a toll it takes.

Most of the restaurant staff came by to see him at least a few times each week. Mr. Washington and Amy came almost every day and brought the mail from the restaurant. Mother was a stickler about visits, though, allowing the people to stay only ten minutes and not a second more. She instructed Frankie to sit by the door with Daddy's pocket watch and give a holler when the time was up.

Frankie didn't mind that job. She got to be in charge of a schedule, and when nobody was visiting, she got to spend time with Daddy. For the first few days, he quizzed her about the restaurant almost daily, asking her if she'd thought of a way to persuade Mother to keep the restaurant after he passed. He talked about his dying as if he were simply going away on another business trip, and not as if it were something permanent.

The truth was, though, she didn't have any idea how to persuade Mother to hang on to the restaurant. And the longer Mother was away from it—she'd refused to go back to the building since the night Daddy got sick—the easier it was for her, it seemed, to forget about the place. Frankie did try to talk to Mother about it a couple of times, but Mother's response each time was, "I wish we'd never opened that infernal place."

Well, what do you say to that?

Frankie didn't know. And she didn't know how she could keep her promise to Daddy.

After the first week or so, Daddy stopped asking about the restaurant and Frankie's plan to convince Mother. She didn't know if he had given up on her, or decided to forget the whole thing. Frankie didn't bring it up, either, because for one thing, it meant they would talk about him dying. And talking about that made it real. As long as Daddy was here, they could go on like this forever—him being a permanent fixture in the apartment, and her snuggling up beside him in bed and listening to his stories.

"I know about Victoria," Frankie said one afternoon. "I'm sorry about her and her baby. Your baby."

Daddy flinched at the sound of her name, and Frankie immediately wanted to unsay it. "Thank you, honey girl. It was a long time ago."

"Grandma Engel said it was a boy," said Frankie. "The baby, I mean."

Daddy nodded.

Frankie hesitated, but there was something she had been wondering about, and she needed to ask. "Did you want another boy? After you married Mother?"

"What?" he said. "Well, yes, I suppose so. But I was just happy to have any baby, boy or girl."

"But you have three girls," said Frankie. "Didn't you hope one of us would be a boy?"

"Frankie," he said.

"I was your last chance," she said. "I'm the one with a boy's name. Did you want me to be . . . something else?"

"Is that what you think?" whispered Daddy.

Frankie shrugged and then told him that it was.

"I'll tell you this," he said, patting her hand. "Never even crossed my mind."

58

MR. STANNUM SAT AT the desk in his small apartment and removed the framed photograph from his leather satchel. He took a drink from a brown flask he kept in his top drawer and stared at the worn picture of his brother in uniform. Tommy had their mother's eyes and carefree smile, their father's generous heart. He was all that was good in the world, and he died much too young, and at the hands of the Germans.

Mr. Stannum pulled the slip of paper from his pocket with the words *WHERE IS YOUR HEART?* and placed it on the desk beside the photograph.

Where was it, indeed? he wondered. The truth was, he didn't know. After Tommy, he was afraid he'd lost it for good.

59

SPEAKING OF NOT KNOWING things, Frankie didn't know much about Uncle Reinhart, Daddy's older brother, who arrived by train from California the following week. He took a room at the Dagmar Hotel instead of staying with the Baums, even though Mother offered him a bed. Frankie was just as glad that he declined, figuring that the bed being offered to him would likely be hers and Joan's. And to tell the truth, Mother seemed relieved not to have a houseguest.

Uncle Reinhart was quiet and serious and did not suffer well the whimsies of children or those whom he thought behaved like children. He was clean-shaven and wore round glasses perched at the end of his nose, which required him to tilt his head back in such a way that he looked down on everyone, even if they had the advantage of height. Although Reinhart was older than Hermann, he never married, and was no more interested in sharing his life than sharing a ribeye steak with a hungry dog.

He showed up at the Baums' one afternoon while Mother and Elizabeth were at Grandma Engel's and Joan was in the kitchen cleaning up after lunch. Joan brought him to Daddy's bedroom, where Frankie was sitting on a chair outside his door, swinging Daddy's pocket watch and attempting to put Bismarck, who was in front of her on the floor, into a mesmeric trance. "Hello," said Frankie, laying the watch in a pile on her lap.

"Greetings, little girl," said Uncle Reinhart. Stepping over Bismarck, he nodded at Frankie and went right past her into Daddy's room without saying anything else. He closed the door behind him before Frankie had a chance to say that Daddy was taking a nap or tell him that visits were restricted to ten minutes.

Frankie checked the timepiece and leaned her ear against the door, watching as each minute ticked by. Things inside were fairly quiet and cordial at first, but after about five minutes, Reinhart began to talk about the restaurant. "Don't be any more of a fool, Hermann," he said. "Get rid of the place before it takes down everything you have. You are in over your head here, man. And you can't even see it."

"Reinhart, please." Daddy's voice was hoarse. "This is not your decision to make. You don't understand me and I expect you may never."

"I certainly don't. That's one thing we can agree on, brother. You know nothing about running a restaurant and you see no problem with hanging your family's financial security on a childish whim. What's more, you've never been cut out for business. How many times have I said that to you over the years? You take too many risks."

"What do you want?" asked Daddy. "Why are you here?"

"I'm here to try to keep your family afloat. Let me handle your business affairs, why don't you? I can sort this mess out so that Mildred and your girls won't have to be burdened by your mistakes after you're gone."

Frankie gasped.

"Just like old times," Daddy said with a deep sigh. "You've never been one to mince words."

"Someone has to tell you the way things are," he said. "And for Pete's sake, it's time you come to your senses. Frankly, it's past time."

It was exactly that, thought Frankie. She opened the door and held up the pocket watch. "Time's up."

"Thank you, Frankie," said Daddy. "Your uncle here was just telling me that I should come to my senses. And you know, I think he may be right."

Reinhart adjusted the glasses on the end of his nose and looked down on his brother. "Is that so?"

"Yes, indeed," said Daddy. "I think I will have some lemon water with saltines instead of my usual afternoon iced tea and wafers, Frankie. That makes a good deal of sense to me, what do you think about it?"

Frankie grinned. "I think so, too. Lemon water is much better for a day like today. I'll get that for you now."

"Thank you, my dear," said Daddy, sinking back into his pillow. "You can show my brother out on the way. Thank you for stopping by, Reinhart. I hope you have found your room at the Dagmar suitable? Nothing like those fancy California hotels, I'd wager, but we do all right here for a small town."

Reinhart turned his back and followed Frankie into the hall. "Good day, Hermann."

"It is indeed," called Daddy, straining his voice to be heard.

Uncle Reinhart didn't return the next day, or the day after that. But at the end of the week, he came back with Mr. Dawes from the bank. As usual, Frankie waited outside Daddy's room with her ear to the door and counted down.

"What are you doing?" said Elizabeth, coming out of the bathroom, startling Frankie so that she nearly fell off her chair.

Frankie showed her the watch. "Keeping time like Mother asked."

"You were eavesdropping," said Elizabeth, "and don't say you weren't. Did Mother ask you to do that as well? Who's in there?"

"Uncle Reinhart and Mr. Dawes from the bank," said Frankie, leaning her ear against the door.

"Mr. Dawes from the bank?" said Elizabeth, scooting close to the door. "What does he want with Daddy?"

"I don't know," whispered Frankie. "I haven't been able to hear anything from all your talking."

Elizabeth elbowed her in the arm.

"What are you two doing?" said Joan from the other end of the hallway.

"Hush!" said Frankie and Elizabeth at the same time.

Joan tiptoed to them. "What's going on in there?"

"Uncle Reinhart and a man from the bank are meeting with Daddy," said Elizabeth, as if she were the proprietor of this information and hadn't just heard it secondhand from Frankie.

Frankie rolled her eyes. "Mr. Dawes is his name."

Joan wriggled herself between Elizabeth and Frankie at the door.

"Ow, you just stepped on my toe," Elizabeth said to Joan.

"Sorry," said Joan, giggling. "There's not much room." Then after a few moments, "I don't hear anything. Do you hear anything?"

Frankie shook her head. She checked the pocket watch and

waited until the second hand got to the twelve. "Ten minutes on the dot." Then she opened the door.

Mr. Dawes was sitting in a chair beside Daddy with a folder of papers in his lap. Reinhart stood next to him with his hands clasped behind his back. "You're paying your employees even though the restaurant isn't open, Hermann. You can't continue to do that," Reinhart said. "It isn't wise, and you can't afford it."

Daddy ignored Reinhart and addressed Mr. Dawes. "They are depending on me, Jack."

"I understand, but you have no business right now," said Mr. Dawes. "And unless you open your doors, your next payment will be late as well. If you're not going to open, you'll have to try to sell, or default on your loan. I'm sorry."

"Exactly what I have been trying to tell him," said Reinhart. "Though you shouldn't even consider opening. Selling, that's the ticket."

Frankie cleared her throat.

Mr. Dawes, Reinhart, and Daddy looked at Frankie, Joan, and Elizabeth as they stood in the doorway. "My timekeeper," said Daddy, smiling. "That's Frankie, and my other two daughters, Joan and Elizabeth."

Mr. Dawes bowed his head. "A pleasure to meet you, young ladies."

Daddy nodded. "Thank you for coming by, Jack. I'll be in touch." He glanced at his brother. "Reinhart, I didn't think I'd be seeing you again so soon."

Reinhart pursed his lips. "Good-bye."

Mr. Dawes laid a piece of paper on the bedside table. "Take care, Hermann."

Elizabeth showed Mr. Dawes and Reinhart to the door. "Joan," said Daddy, "I think it's just about time for my medicine. Could you get me a glass of water?"

"Sure, Daddy," said Joan. She took the empty glass from his bedside table and headed for the kitchen.

Daddy kept his eye on Frankie, studying her. "Are you in trouble?" asked Frankie.

He considered that question and answered with one of his own. "What does your mother say?"

Frankie shrugged. "That she wishes there was no restaurant. And that even if you did open the restaurant, nobody would come."

"You'll find a way," he said.

"How?"

Joan returned then with a glass of water, and both girls helped lift him forward so he could swallow his medicine. Afterward, he took a shallow breath and coughed.

"Daddy?" said Frankie.

"I'm just going to rest now," he said. "I'm tired." He closed his eyes and, after a few minutes, drifted off to sleep.

Joan left to tend to chores, but Frankie stayed close. She watched the rise and fall of Daddy's chest and listened at the wheeze of his breath, waiting for the next one to come. Finally she'd been given a responsibility worthy of a Number One, a chance to prove herself, and yet she didn't know how.

She picked up the paper that Mr. Dawes had left for Daddy. It was full of numbers and columns, and none of it made sense. Underneath that was a stack of envelopes, unopened and addressed to Daddy.

She read them all.

ALSATIA CLUB
141 WEST WASHINGTON STREET
HAGERSTOWN, MARYLAND

August 4, 1939

Mr. Hermann A. Baum
Baum's Restaurant
N. Jonathan Street
Hagerstown, Md.

Dear Hermann:

We wish to take this means of expressing to you that we feel the recent rumors of espionage, in which you were reported to be involved, are absolutely false and unwarranted.

It is very unfortunate that the rumors in question were circulated since there appears to be no foundation whatsoever for the same. In our opinion you are entirely exonerated of any part in these so-called German Spy reports.

To you as an Alsatian and a Citizen of this Community we want you to know that the Alsatia Club, as a real American Organization, is behind you 100% and have our wholehearted support.

Very sincerely yours,
ALSATIA CLUB, INC.,

Rex D. Gaver

REX D. GAVER CHR. BOARD
OF GOVERNORS

FRATERNAL ORDER OF EAGLES
HAGERSTOWN'S LEADING FRATERNITY
HAGERSTOWN AERIE NO. 694
AERIE HOME:
49 SOUTH POTOMAC STREET
HAGERSTOWN, MARYLAND
PAY YOUR DUES TO
SECRETARY
JOHN R. KERR
HAGERSTOWN, MD., *R.D.5*

August 6, 1939

Mr. Hermann Baum,
Hagerstown, Md.

Dear Sir and Brother:

We wish to express our confidence in you as a member of Aerie
694, Fraternal Order of Eagles, and as a fellow American.

We are sure that you have furthered at all times the patriotic,
the humanitarian and the fraternal teachings of our order and that
you have tried steadfastly to make your home and your business
house the abiding place of thoughts and acts that are wholesome
and righteous.

We are sure you have given and will continue to give our
country the devoted loyalty of a patriot.

You have always been alive with the spirit of liberty, a stalwart
of truth, the possessor of a keen sense of justice and a firm believer
of equality.

Thusly we express our confidence in you as a member of our fraternity and as a citizen of our great Democracy, the United States of America.

Fraternally yours,

John R. Kerr

John R. Kerr

Secretary Aerie 694

Fraternal Order of Eagles

August 13, 1939

Brother Hermann A. Baum
N. Jonathan Street
Hagerstown, Md.

Dear Brother Baum:

At the regular weekly meeting of Hagerstown Lodge No.378, B.P.O. Elks, held this evening, the Lodge unanimously instructed the Secretary to write to you and express its unqualified confidence and faith in your patriotism and citizenship.

We deplore and condemn the malicious gossip being circulated throughout this community in the past several weeks and express our deepest regret that you should be made the target for such gossip.

Be assured that we, as your brothers in the Order of Elks, will do all that is humanly possible to right this wrong.

Sincerely and fraternally,
Exalted Ruler
John E. Travers

August 17, 1939

Mr. Hermann Baum
Baum's Restaurant
Hagerstown, Md.

Dear Mr. Baum:

It has come to our attention that a rumor has been circulated
that our local post of The American Legion has been boycotting
your establishment because of your purported relationship with the
German Beneficial Union.

This letter in no way commits our post as to our opinion or
attitude in reference to the merits of the German Beneficial Union,
but we are convinced that you have become an innocent victim.

On behalf of The American Legion, I take this opportunity to
assure you that the report of our boycott is in error and you will
be favored with our future business whenever the opportunity
presents itself.

Yours very truly,
Commander
Paul H. Smit

60

FRANKIE STUFFED THE LETTERS down the neck of her dress and set off to find Joan. She found her on the side porch, putting the laundry into Mother's wringer washer. "What are you doing?" Frankie asked.

"Mother told Katie she wouldn't be needing her help around here, what with Daddy in a bad way and not working," said Joan. She poured in the powdered soap. "Do you know how to work this thing?"

Frankie shook her head. "Never mind that. Look at these." She pulled the letters from her dress and shoved them at Joan. They sat on the edge of the porch, and Frankie waited, swinging her legs, while Joan read each one.

When Joan finished, she tucked the letters back into their envelopes and laid them on the porch next to her. "It seems this is too late."

"No," said Frankie. "It isn't too late if Mother wants to open up the restaurant again. That's what Daddy wants."

"Mother doesn't want anything to do with that place," said Joan. "You've heard her."

"But we have to change her mind," said Frankie.

"I don't understand you, Frankie," said Joan. "If Mother opens the restaurant, you'll have to work there. We all will." She got to her feet and went back to the washer. She closed the lid. "I thought you hated working there?"

Frankie looked up at the sky. "I thought so, too."

•   •   •

Daddy was still sleeping when Mother returned from the market that afternoon. "How is your father?" Mother asked as she finished putting away the bag of groceries.

"Same," answered Frankie. "Tired."

Mother filled a glass of water from the spigot and took a few sips. "Where's Joan?"

"Feeding Dixie."

Elizabeth folded the grocery bag and slid it into the cabinet under the sink. "Mother, do you need anything else?"

"Check the clothes on the line, would you, Princess?" said Mother. "They ought to be dry by now."

Elizabeth slipped out the kitchen door and headed for the backyard.

"Anybody come by today, Frankie?" Mother asked.

"Just Mr. Dawes from the bank," said Frankie. "And Uncle Reinhart."

"Mr. Dawes?" said Mother. "He came here?"

Frankie nodded. "But I sent them on their way after ten minutes, don't worry."

"What did he want?" asked Mother.

"He wanted to talk to Daddy about the restaurant," said Frankie. "He thinks we should make it open for business."

Mother's mouth tightened. "He said that, did he? Well, that's very easy for him to say. And what did your uncle have to say about that? Does he think the same?"

Frankie shook her head. "Uncle Reinhart thinks Daddy should sell the place."

"Well, I never thought I'd say this, but I'm with Reinhart." Then Mother narrowed her eyes. "Frances Marie, how many times have I warned you about eavesdropping? You're not to be listening in on conversations that don't concern you, understand?"

Frankie said that yes, she did.

"Good," said Mother. "Now, what else was said?"

"That's all, pretty much." Frankie didn't want to tell Mother the part about Daddy still paying the employees even though the restaurant was closed. What would happen to Amy and Mr. Washington and Seaweed if Mother made him stop?

Mother leaned against the sink basin and brought her hand to her head. "Why did all of this have to happen? This is punishment for something, all this bad luck." She looked up at the kitchen ceiling. "What in the world are we going to do now?"

"We could open the restaurant," Frankie offered.

"Let me tell you something—if we opened that restaurant, we'd have nothing but a bunch of empty chairs. There we'd be, watching the people walk right on by our door, seeing their faces and knowing they think Hermann's in cahoots with Hitler."

Frankie fingered the letters she had stashed in her dress. "But not everybody thinks that." She pulled out the letters. "Look."

"What are those?" said Mother, eyeing the envelopes. "This is your father's mail. Frances Baum, you have no business reading these."

"But they are from people who think he is innocent," said Frankie.

"He *is* innocent!" shouted Mother.

Frankie nodded. "I know that. But now we know that other people know that, too." She swallowed. "So maybe the restaurant will be all right if we open."

There was fear in Mother's eyes. Enough that she didn't say another word. She just took the letters and headed down the hall to check on Daddy.

61

IN THE EARLY AFTERNOON of the twenty-fifth day of August, Aunt Edith came downstairs from her apartment with freshly painted lips and eyebrows the shape of horseshoes. Ava and Martha followed, in their Sunday dresses. Only, it wasn't Sunday.

"Girls," called Aunt Edith, marching through the Baums' living room. "Girls!"

Mother and Elizabeth were at the dining table sorting through Daddy's medical bills, and Frankie and Joan were in bed with Daddy, taking turns reading the day's newspaper articles to him. "I think you're needed out there," Daddy told them.

"What for?" asked Frankie.

"Why don't you go see," said Daddy, grinning. "I'm all right. Go on, I've got Bismarck to look after me."

Frankie and Joan looked at each other and then took off down the hall. When they got to the dining room, Aunt Edith's red lips were in a smile, and as Ava and Martha stood on either side of her, Aunt Edith had her hands covering their mouths. Ava and Martha were wiggling to get loose, but the three of them stuck close together like they were trying to hide a whale behind their backs.

"What's going on?" asked Joan.

Mother smiled and said, "Go get dressed, girls. Aunt Edith is taking you to see a picture."

"Really?' said Elizabeth. "Which one?"

Aunt Edith said, "Well . . ."

Before she could get any more words out, Ava knocked her rear end into Aunt Edith's thigh, setting her off balance and causing her hand to lose its grip over Ava's mouth. "We're going to see *The Wizard of Oz*," announced Ava, victorious.

"No fair!" shouted Martha, when her mouth was free. "We were all going to tell them together! And now you ruined it!"

"*The Wizard of Oz!*" Frankie and Joan shouted together, jumping up and down.

Then Frankie stopped. "But what about Daddy?" she asked.

"It was his idea," said Mother. "Don't worry, I'll stay here with him. You can tell me all about it when you get back."

The girls got dressed in a hurry and returned to the dining room before Aunt Edith had a chance to finish a glass of iced tea. "Let's go," said Frankie. "Can we sit in the front row? I want to get as close as I can to Oz."

The cinema was only a few blocks from the Baums' apartment, and the six of them set out walking, with Joan and Frankie racing Ava for the lead. The farther they got, though, the slower Frankie's steps were. She fell behind Ava, Joan, and Elizabeth, and then kept pace with Aunt Edith and Martha, even when Joan turned around and bet her she could beat her and Ava in a race.

"What's the matter, Frankie?" asked Aunt Edith.

Frankie shrugged. "I guess I'm not used to being away."

Aunt Edith squeezed Frankie's shoulder. "That's why your father thought this would be good for you. Being cooped up in that apartment for weeks upon end, that's no good for anybody. And don't you worry, now; your mother is home with him."

It was an odd thing, Aunt Edith telling Frankie not to worry, when Aunt Edith worried more than anyone—except Mother, of course. But her reassurance seemed to work, at least for now, as Frankie put aside her troubles as best she could and got her legs into a run to catch up with the others.

As the cinema came into sight, Ava pulled ahead of Joan at the last minute and was the first to get to the movie poster that was hanging in the front window. "See," Ava said, pointing, "here it is!"

When Frankie caught up, she couldn't take her eyes off of Judy Garland as Dorothy. "'Metro-Goldwyn-Mayer's Technicolor Triumph,'" Frankie read from the poster. "What does that mean?"

"It means the picture is in color," said Elizabeth. "Not black and white."

Frankie's heart raced. "Come on, let's go inside."

Aunt Edith paid for their tickets and they made their way down the stairs into the dark theater. Frankie found six seats together in the front row. "Just think," whispered Joan to Frankie, "we'll be this close to Judy Garland."

Frankie nodded, then looked behind her to see how many others were there to see the picture show. All around her the seats were filling up, but a young girl and her brother sitting in the colored section at the back of the theater caught her eye. The top of the boy's head barely stuck out above the seat in front of him, and when he complained, the girl lifted him onto her lap. As the little boy squirmed and craned his neck to see, Frankie thought about Seaweed. *What you see out of those green eyes of yours ain't nothing like what I see. And what you see ain't nothing like it is.* She was able to sit in the front row and as close to the picture as a person could get, when that little girl and her brother couldn't, when they didn't even have a choice in the matter.

This was how the world was, she knew, for she had seen it every day. But she had hardly given it much thought before now, to tell the truth. Yet, the way Daddy was treated because of what people believed him to be set her mind thinking about how colored people were treated. All unfairly, and all because of what people believed them to be.

What a frightening thing for her to realize, that what some people believed could be so cruel, and could be so wrong. What a world this was.

The lights dimmed and Frankie turned around to face the screen. The newsreel started up, but there was no relief there from the world's problems. There was talk of war and, of course, of Germans. "Nazi Germany and the Soviet Union surprised the world by forming an alliance and signing a nonaggression pact on August twenty-third," read the news bulletin, "whereby both countries agreed to take no military action against each other for the next ten years." Then President Roosevelt talked about these troubled times, and how democracy must be a positive force in order to maintain liberty against aggression abroad. Troubled times indeed, thought Frankie. The president seemed to be talking directly to her.

When the newsreel ended and the picture finally began, the words *The Wizard of Oz* appeared on the screen. Everyone in the theater cheered. Frankie looked for Judy Garland's name and for L. Frank Baum's, too, and when she saw them both, she elbowed Joan in the side.

"There you are," whispered Joan.

The dull, gray Kansas sky was on the screen for some time. In fact, everything in Kansas was gray, it seemed, not unlike Hagerstown. Frankie knocked knees with Elizabeth beside her. "I thought you said this picture was supposed to be in color." Elizabeth shrugged and then told her to be quiet.

A while later, after the cyclone lifted the house along with Dorothy and Toto and carried it away, Frankie whispered, "This is not what happens in the book. And that awful lady Miss Gulch was not in the story."

"Shh," said Joan.

Judy Garland or not, Frankie was having some doubts about this picture already. But when Dorothy opened the door to Oz, well, Frankie's mouth fell open. The colors, oh my, oh my, those colors took all the words away.

Except for these last ones from Frankie, which she whispered to Joan: "I bet that's what it felt like when you got to Aunt Dottie's."

62

FRANKIE'S HEAD WAS IN the sky on the walk home. Never before had she been taken to such a magnificent place.

She couldn't wait to tell Mother and Daddy all about it, especially Daddy. She dreamed that maybe he could see it for himself one day. She didn't know how, but she hoped.

They were just a block and a half away from the apartment, all of them singing "Somewhere Over the Rainbow"—Aunt Edith the loudest, incidentally—when they saw the ambulance speed past them with lights flashing and siren screaming. And Frankie knew— she knew, just as strongly as she knew Daddy wasn't a spy—that he was in that ambulance, and that he was already gone.

63

NEWS OF DADDY'S DEATH spread quickly through town. By the next morning, Mother and the girls were receiving flowers and visitors at the apartment. Aunt Dottie occupied herself in the kitchen by making custard. Uncle Reinhart sat quietly at Daddy's desk, sorting through papers. Mr. Washington, Amy, Julie, and Seaweed brought platters of food, and Grandma Engel and Aunt Edith helped arrange them on the dining room table. "My goodness," said Aunt Edith, "this is too much. You shouldn't have gone to so much trouble. We'll never eat all this."

"Nonsense," said Grandma Engel. "At a time like this, there are two things you can't have too much of. Company and food."

"It would've spoiled soon anyhow," said Mr. Washington. "Just sittin' there in the freezers at the restaurant, goin' to waste."

"Good thinking," said Grandma Engel.

"It Amy's idea," said Seaweed.

Amy smiled as she placed a basket of dinner rolls on the table. "There be a lot more there, too. This just all we could carry."

"Smart girl," said Grandma Engel. "But let me ask you this. Did you bring anything from the bar?"

"Mother, please."

"Get off your high horse, Edith. I wasn't thinking of me," said

Grandma Engel. "For mercy's sakes, I was thinking of Mildred. The girl is a mess."

Grandma Engel was right. It was as if Mother's skeleton had disintegrated the moment Daddy died, leaving her in a boneless lump in the living room chair. Sure, she put on a brave face for those who stopped by to pay their respects, but when they left, she fell into tiny pieces that had to be scooped up and reassembled.

Frankie understood all too well. She, too, thought that at any moment, she might dissolve into a puddle on the floor. Yesterday, she had a father. But this morning when she woke up, she didn't. And what's worse was that every minute after this one, every month, every year of her life to come, she wouldn't. That left such an emptiness in her heart that she felt as though someone had hollowed her out like a gourd.

Death may be little more than lifting off in a flying machine and traveling to another world, but what of those who are left behind?

64

THEY SAY THAT FUNERALS are for the living, and that very well may be true. But Hermann Baum's funeral? Well, that was strictly for him.

Three days following his death, there was a service at St. John's Lutheran Church. Mother wanted an open casket, and could not be persuaded otherwise by anyone, including Frankie and Joan, who had never in their lives seen a dead body before and did not want to start with their beloved father. Mother may not have been able to lift a water glass without her hand trembling, but on this matter, she was steady as a steel beam.

Elizabeth and Joan each had Mother's arm as they climbed the concrete steps to the door of the church. Frankie followed behind. Even the petticoat she was made to wear, miserable as it was and which plagued her severely, was no match for her grief.

It took all three of them to get Mother up the stairs. Frankie had both hands on Mother's back, just above her rear end, pushing, as Joan and Elizabeth lifted and pulled at Mother's arms. They made it to the top, somehow, and Elizabeth opened the door. Standing there, just inside, was someone who gave Frankie's heart a jolt: Mr. Stannum.

"Mrs. Baum," he said, holding his hat over his heart, "I, uh, I'm sorry, I just wanted to pay my respects." He shifted on his feet and mopped his forehead with a handkerchief.

Mother stiffened. "I'm surprised to see you here, Mr. Stannum," she said after a long pause. "After what you've done to my husband."

He swallowed. Shame the size of a cantaloupe, it was that big. "Yes, well, I suppose then you heard what I done," he said softly.

Mother and all three girls looked him in the eye but said nothing.

Mr. Stannum's knees buckled. "All right, then. Let me just get this out. I wanted to tell you something. I need to."

Mother waited. Frankie stepped in front of her. She didn't know what he was going to say, but with Daddy gone, she wanted to get between Mother and whatever it was.

"I was wrong about Mr. Baum." He pressed his lips together, and his mouth disappeared behind his silver mustache.

"Yes, indeed," said Mother.

"I made a mistake, but I didn't mean any harm to come to him, honest," he said. "Or to you or anyone. The strange thing is, I thought I was doing right, for the country, for my brother." He shook his head. "But I guess I knew as soon as I gave over that paper to Mr. Price that I wasn't. And I want to make things right."

Frankie wondered how on earth he planned to do that with Daddy gone.

How indeed.

Mother just shook her head. "Out of my way, Mr. Stannum. We are burying my Hermann today." She started on.

But Mr. Stannum did not get out of the way. "Wait, please." He tapped his fingers together in a steady, rhythmic beat. Then he looked directly at Frankie. "I lost something a long time ago, and I'm aiming to get it back."

Frankie watched his fingers and knew he had found her note, and perhaps his heart as well.

"I went to everyone I know," said Mr. Stannum. "Everyone that Mr. Baum had dealings with at the restaurant, his Elk lodge, the Eagles. Frankie, that's why you seen me in your daddy's office that time. I was looking for names of people he knew, anybody, so I could tell them what I done. Tell them that your daddy wasn't what they said." He balled his handkerchief in his fist.

Right away Frankie thought of the letters on Daddy's bedside table. So, Mr. Stannum had a hand in that?

"Is that so?" said Mother, after a long silence.

He took Mother's hand. "I know it don't make up, but it was all I could think to do." Then he let her go and slid his hat back on his head. "That's what I wanted to get off my chest. I'll go now." He started past them toward the door.

Elizabeth and Joan were in tears. "Come on, girls," said Mother, heading for the sanctuary.

"Mother," Frankie whispered. After all Mr. Stannum did to undo what he had done, it didn't feel right just leaving him here at the steps of their church. "Mother," she said again.

"Where are you going, Mr. Stannum?" Mother slowed her steps.

Mr. Stannum stopped. "I beg your pardon."

Mother turned. "You're going the wrong way, aren't you? The service is this way."

He blinked. Then, after a long moment, nodded. "Yes, ma'am." And he followed.

The girls got Mother to the sanctuary, where half the town, it seemed, was waiting. Mother gasped. "Look at all these people," said Joan.

"I wish Daddy were here to see this," said Elizabeth.

Frankie smiled. "I'd like to have seen his face." And then just before she realized what she had said, she saw his face, along with the top half of his body, in a casket by the altar. All at once the air seemed to leave her body and she thought she might float high up to the painted ceiling or bust through the stained glass and not stop until the sky sent her back in tiny pieces. She reached for Joan's hand so she wouldn't lift off, but she was pulled away by Amy in a hug and could breathe again.

"My girl," said Amy, "it ain't right. This never should've happened to your daddy. He was a good one." Her voice was loud, louder than you were supposed to be in church, and it carried across the room and bounced off the windows. People turned around to see, but Amy didn't seem to notice. She kept right on talking about Daddy and how sorry she was as she hugged Mother, then Elizabeth, and then Joan. Amy's mother and father were there, too, in the last pew, along with Katie, Seaweed, and Mr. Washington and their families. They all stood and offered their respects to Mother in the aisle.

Seaweed came over to Frankie. "Don't you worry none about our deal," he said with half a grin. "I'm lettin' you out."

Frankie made a face, but before she could get out a clever reply, Seaweed's grin disappeared. He nodded at Mr. Stannum, lurking in the doorway. "What he doin' here?"

Mr. Stannum stepped forward then and extended his hand to

Seaweed, to Amy, and to Mr. Washington. "I'm sorry," he said to them. For Daddy, for how he treated them, or for something else, they weren't exactly sure, but they shook his hand nonetheless.

The girls took Mother by the arms to their regular pew up front. Elizabeth went to slide in beside Mother, but Frankie stopped her. "Let's leave that space open," she said, staring at the worn polish where Daddy always sat.

Elizabeth nodded and when she sat, she took Frankie's hand in hers and gave a squeeze. Frankie gave one in return.

Daddy's casket was in front of the altar, covered in sprays of white lilies. His head was resting on a pillow, and his eyes were closed. If you squinted hard enough, you might convince yourself that he was just sleeping and would sit up at any moment and wonder why all of these people were staring at him. Frankie tried that for a while, but then found that, when wanting to imagine he was still alive, looking anywhere but at him lying there was much easier.

Grandma Engel, Aunt Edith, Uncle Hal, and Ava and Martha were in the pew behind them. Just as Miss Fisk took her seat at the pipe organ and started playing some somber tune, Frankie turned to look at Ava and Martha, expecting to see Ava's fingers up her nose or her eyeballs crossed, but instead, she just stared at the ceiling, her eyes red from crying.

Aunt Dottie was there, too, wearing a black, high-crowned hat with a diminutive veil that hung just past her eyes. Uncle Reinhart in a light seersucker suit and bow tie sat next to her, his face in his usual grimace. Only then, after seeing them together, side by side, did this occur to Frankie: Daddy was a Number Three.

Aunt Dottie leaned forward and squeezed Frankie's shoulder.

"You've gotten to be so grown up since the last time I saw you." Frankie smiled politely and then rubbed her shoulder, for Aunt Dottie had a grip like King Kong.

Miss Fisk played the final chord, and the tallest pipes from the organ bellowed such sadness that it left Frankie with a dull ache in her chest. Then Reverend Martin stood at his pulpit and read verses from the Bible that were supposed to help make everyone feel better about Daddy dying, knowing that he was going to a better place.

Let not your hearts be troubled.
So we are always of good courage.
Death is swallowed up in victory.

But Frankie knew there had been no victory for Daddy. She hadn't been able to keep her promise to him before he died. So where was the victory in that?

After Reverend Martin finished, he invited the family to come to the casket one last time before going to the graveside. Miss Fisk played short, low chords that sounded like some sort of death march as the three girls helped Mother get to her feet. They pulled her slowly, very slowly, toward the altar. Frankie kept her eyes on her feet so she wouldn't have to look at Daddy. From a distance was one thing, but seeing him up close was something else entirely. Mother must have felt the same way, because as they got closer to him, she started to moan.

Moaning, Frankie was fairly certain, was not allowed in church, and had it been Frankie doing that moaning, Mother would have cracked her on the behind until she stopped. But perhaps when you have lost your love you forget about church rules, or decide they aren't so important after all. In either case, Mother got louder and louder, and the girls tried to get her to stop, telling her everything would be all right, but she kept on. Frankie and Joan looked at Elizabeth to do something. This was much worse than the itchy petticoats, and honestly, a little embarrassing.

"Mother, please stop," whispered Elizabeth finally.

But that only made her moan more.

"It's all right," said Joan, patting her arm and trying to soothe her.

Frankie looked at all of the people in the pews, watching them shift in their seats wide-eyed. "Shhh," said Frankie. "Please be quiet. Please."

Then Reverend Martin gave it a go. He took Mother's hands and said a prayer—or shouted one is more like it, for he had to shout in order to be heard over Mother. Then he blessed Daddy in the casket and closed the lid.

Mother yelled, "Hermann!" and flung her body over the casket.

Frankie and Joan looked at each other and then quickly grabbed her arms and pulled her back. "For goodness' sakes, Mother," said Elizabeth, turning red. Frankie and Joan tried to drag her out the side door near the pulpit, but as they did, Mother fainted.

"Not again," said Grandma Engel from her seat.

Reverend Martin, who was quite experienced with Mother fainting, calmly knelt down and tended to her, while announcing, "Services will be continued at the gravesite, and afterward we hope you will come to the Baums' apartment at 33 East Antietam Street for a reception."

Perhaps Daddy intervened from wherever he ended up, because

as everyone began to stand up to leave—except for Mother, of course, who was still sprawled on the floor unconscious—Frankie got an idea.

Death is swallowed in victory.

She stepped over Mother and made an announcement of her own. "Hold on, everybody," she shouted. "There has been a change. The reception will be held at Baum's Restaurant on Jonathan Street. Everybody is welcome."

Elizabeth and Joan looked at Frankie with their mouths open.

"Really?" said Joan.

"What are you doing?" said Elizabeth.

Frankie stood firm. "What Daddy would have done."

65

FRITZ DROVE MOTHER, GRANDMA Engel, and the girls from the gravesite to Baum's Restaurant. Mother spoke not a word the entire way, but it wasn't clear to anyone whether her quiet demeanor had more to do with a widow's grief, a side effect of the fainting, or the fact that her youngest child had taken it upon herself to move the funeral reception to the one place Mother had been trying to avoid.

It was the latter, most likely.

Dear old Fritz tried to smooth things over with Mother on the drive. "You know, Mildred, there was no way all those people could've fit in that apartment anyway. Like sardines in a tin can, that's what it would've been like. The restaurant, though, there's plenty of room there. Plenty of room." He winked at Frankie in the rearview mirror.

"And there's plenty of food, too," said Frankie. "Just like Mr. Washington said."

"It does make good sense, Millie," said Reinhart, sitting next to Fritz in the front seat. "Using up the food now will mean fewer things to clean out when you sell the place."

But Mother was stubborn as a mule, and so she maintained her position and held her tongue for the rest of the ride.

At least the moaning had stopped.

As soon as Fritz pulled the car to the curb and turned off the motor, Frankie sprang into action. "Elizabeth," she said as they climbed out of the car, "you make sure the tables are set, and Joanie, you can help with the drinks. I'll get started in the kitchen. Mr. Washington, Amy, and Seaweed should be along soon to help." Without realizing it, she was giving orders like a Number One, and for some reason nobody, including Elizabeth, thought to question it.

"I'll man the door," said Grandma Engel, "and make sure everyone gets a seat. That means you, too, Millie." She led Mother inside by the hand and eased her into a chair at a table close to the door.

Uncle Hal and Aunt Edith filled water glasses while Aunt Dottie tended the bar with Mr. Dench. Uncle Reinhart wandered through the restaurant, unsure of how to be helpful. This was his first time inside the restaurant, and as he went from room to room looking, his eyes were as big as candy suckers. The tables in the main dining room filled up right quick, and Grandma Engel had to put some people in the banquet room. When that room was full, she seated people at the bar. Most of the family of the kitchen staff helped cook the food and stayed in the kitchen to eat.

Amy showed Peaches how to peel potatoes, while Mr. Washington and Seaweed cooked the meat. Even Mr. Stannum showed up to help. He just walked into the kitchen and, without saying a word to anyone, pulled on an apron and got to work cleaning dishes. Dishes, I tell you!

Things were humming along, you could say, until a gentleman poked his head into the kitchen and asked for a word with Mrs. Baum. He spoke with an accent, and Frankie couldn't make out some of what he said, including his name, if he even gave it.

"Mildred Baum?" asked Frankie. "Is that what you said?"

The man nodded. "Yes, is she here? I wish to speak with her."

"About what?" asked Frankie.

The man shifted an envelope from one hand to the other. "I'm from the German Beneficial Union, and I have an insurance matter to discuss with her. On behalf of Hermann Baum."

Frankie wiped her hands on her apron and led him into the dining room and to the table where mother was sitting and nursing a drink. She bent down and whispered in her ear. "Mother, this man is here from the German Beneficial Union. About Daddy."

Mother's puffy eyes had worry in them. She got up from her chair and walked with the man to the far corner of the room, where there wasn't as much noise. Frankie went along. "What is it?" Mother asked, sounding alarmed.

"I came to know Hermann Baum only a short time ago, but I wanted to share my condolences with you and your family," the man said. "The German Beneficial Union, madam, seeks to provide financial security and brotherhood to its members, and I was pleased that your husband joined the union a few months ago, and even took out an insurance policy." He handed the envelope to Mother. "I hope you will find this to help you continue the restaurant, perhaps?"

"Well," said Mother, "I don't know about that."

"Oh, really?" said the man. "Well, I hope you change your mind." He looked about the room. "A charming place, you have here. In any case, it was a pleasure meeting you, and I'm so very sorry for your loss."

"Would you like to stay and fix yourself a plate?" she asked.

"How nice of you. But I must get back to work." He nodded at

Mother. "Good day, Mrs. Baum." And then at Frankie, "Good day, young lady."

Frankie watched him weave through the crowd and out the front door. "What is it?" she asked Mother, eyeing the envelope.

Mother opened the envelope and read the letter tucked inside. She brought her hand to her mouth.

"What does it say?" said Frankie.

Mother read the letter again, then folded it and slid it back inside the envelope. "Your father, it seems, still is looking after us," she said. "Still looking after me." Then something caught her eye by the door.

Frankie followed her gaze and noticed Mr. Price on the sidewalk, peering in through the open door. "Just what does he think he's doing here?" said Mother. With a sudden surge of courage, she strode toward him. Frankie followed close behind.

"Good afternoon," said Mr. Price, taking a step backward when he saw Mother coming toward him. He blew smoke from his fat cigar.

"Hardly," said Mother, remaining in the doorway.

"Yes, well, I just happened to be walking by and saw the place full of people." He cleared his throat. "I'm very sorry to have learned of your husband's death."

"Thank you," said Mother.

Mr. Price peered around Mother to get a look at who was in the restaurant. "I understand you aren't going to reopen the business. Pity, after all the work and, I imagine, money you put into this place."

"Mr. Price," said Mother, "I don't know where you get your information, but it seems once again you are miles from the truth."

"Pardon?"

"I said, just how do you know we aren't opening the restaurant?"

Mr. Price flicked his cigar, and ashes fell to the sidewalk. "Is that your intention?"

Frankie, who was lingering behind Mother, grabbed her arm. "You can do it," said Frankie. "We can make it into just what Daddy dreamed of."

"Dreams," said Mr. Price. "It takes more than dreams to run a business. That's a child's point of view."

Frankie scowled at him.

Mother took a step toward Mr. Price so that her face was only inches away. She coughed at his smelly cigar and then pulled the thing from his mouth. After that, she did something that Frankie could hardly believe: she tossed it onto the street behind him.

"Let me set you straight," she said. "You know nothing about my girl, and you obviously know nothing about the Baums."

Frankie could not watch. Usually she was on the other end of Mother's scolding, and no matter that Mr. Price was getting his deserved comeuppance, Mother's delivery still made her cringe. "What we do with our restaurant business," said Mother, "is none of your business." Mother put her arm around Frankie's shoulder. "Now, we'd invite you in, but we aren't the sort of people you approve of, and quite frankly, we feel the same way about you."

Mr. Price, for once, had nothing to say. And when you have nothing to say, and no cigar to toke, the only thing you can do is move on. Which is exactly what he did.

Little did Mr. Price know that he would soon have to get used to moving on. In a surprising upset in the mayoral election that took place several weeks later, Mr. Price was handily defeated by his opponent, George Robertson. The *Daily Mail* called it a "crushing blow" and featured a cartoon on the front page with George Robertson as Mickey's Mechanical Man pummeling Mr. Price as the giant gorilla, the Kongo Killer. Victory came at last.

After Mr. Price disappeared down the street, Frankie looked up at the tiny piece of sky that was visible from the doorway. Then she stepped out onto the sidewalk, then onto the street, still gazing up, until she could see more.

"What are you looking at?" asked Mother, coming to her side.

In the middle of the street they stood, with their faces to the sky, as if seeing it for the first time and never dreaming it was so wide.

66

AND THAT, MY FRIEND, was that.

Oh, but what of the package that Aunt Dottie had been hiding in her pie safe? You haven't forgotten about that, have you?

Relax, and put your feet up. Frankie and Joan hadn't forgotten about it, either. And neither had Aunt Dottie. When Fritz arrived to bring Aunt Dottie and Joan to Hagerstown after Daddy got sick, Aunt Dottie grabbed the package from the pie safe and stuffed it into her pocketbook. She was just as curious about its contents as Frankie and Joan, so after the reception was over and after the last guest had retired, she brought it out.

"Hermann, rest his soul, asked me to hold on to this for a while," said Aunt Dottie, placing the package on a dining table in front of Mother, Elizabeth, Joan, and Frankie.

"What could it be?" said Mother, staring at the return address.

"All I know," said Aunt Dottie, looking at Frankie, "is that he was planning on surprising you for your birthday."

"*My* birthday?" said Frankie. "But it's a month away."

"It's all the way from Germany?" said Elizabeth.

"So this was the box Daddy was talking about?" said Frankie.

"What do you mean?" said Mother.

"I heard him talking to Fritz about taking a box out of town to be safe," said Frankie. "Why would he need to do that for a birthday present?"

Mother wrung her hands. "Maybe he was worried that someone would get the wrong idea about him."

Aunt Dottie reached for Mother's arm. "That may be, Millie. It doesn't take much for people to get the wrong idea. But he did tell me he couldn't keep it at your apartment or the restaurant because he knew of Frankie's penchant for spying," said Aunt Dottie with a wink. "Hermann didn't trust you, my dear. He knew your snooping habits. And he didn't want you to find it before it was time."

Frankie shook her head. All this time, it was Daddy who thought *she* was a spy.

They all stared at the box, but no one made a move to open it. Not even Frankie.

Grandma Engel was watching from the bar. "For Pete's sake, open the damn thing." She sighed. "You people."

"Go on, Frances," said Mother.

Joan pushed the box gently in Frankie's direction.

Frankie took in a breath and then cracked her knuckles to limber up her fingers. She pulled the package to her and, very carefully, began tearing the brown paper wrapping. A plain white box was underneath. She paused and then opened the lid.

Crumpled newspaper, in German, was all she saw.

"What is it?" said Joan.

Frankie shook her head. Then she pulled out the newspaper and handed it to Joan. And there, at the bottom of the box under all that paper, was a small velvet bag. Frankie lifted it out, feeling something hard inside. She pulled open the drawstring and emptied the bag into her hand.

She held in her palm a small silver-filigree brooch, in the shape of a girl's shoe.

Grandma Engel made her way over to the table. "Well?"

Mother picked it up and turned it over, admiring the metalwork. "It's beautiful."

"May I?" asked Aunt Dottie, reaching for the pin. She ran her finger over the slipper's pointed toe. "I can't say for certain if this was hers or not, but our mother had a brooch just like this one. She used to say it brought her luck."

"Really?" said Frankie. "Luck?"

Aunt Dottie called to her brother, who was sitting at the bar with his back toward them. "Reinhart, come over here and take a look at this." She added, "And be social for once."

Reinhart sat down beside Aunt Dottie and took the brooch in his hand. "I remember this."

Aunt Dottie nodded. "When our mother and father first came to this country, fleeing the Great War, they left a house and many belongings behind, thinking that one day they would return. But they made a life here, and after Hermann was born, going back was something that wasn't as important to them anymore. They tried to make arrangements about their property, but they learned that much of it was looted or lost to the government, and sadly, they died before they could see it through. Since the first few years after they passed, Reinhart and Hermann and I have been trying to reclaim some of their things, but haven't had much success.

"We've been able to track down a few pieces of art, some dishes of our mother's china," said Reinhart, "but the way things are over there now, I am afraid everything else will be lost forever." He turned the brooch over in his palm. "I didn't know that Hermann had found this." He gave the brooch back to Aunt Dottie.

"That man was always full of surprises," said Grandma Engel.

Mother looked at Dottie and Reinhart. "If this belonged to your mother, then maybe it's meant to be yours."

Aunt Dottie shook her head and put the brooch back in Frankie's hand. "No, Millie. I think it's found its rightful owner."

"Reinhart?" said Mother.

He shook his head and whispered, "You should keep it."

And the funny thing is, Frankie knew that he didn't just mean keep the brooch. After spending the day at the restaurant, somehow he could finally see things the way Hermann saw them, and Frankie knew he meant that they should keep this place, too.

67

NOW, WHETHER THAT SILVER brooch really did bring luck, no one living could tell you. But I will tell you this much: business at Baum's Restaurant boomed. It really did become an eating place of wide renown, and there was barely an empty chair each night. Some even came from miles around just for Grandma Engel's stewed prunes.

I know. I find it hard to believe as well. Prunes. *Blech.*

Although Mother's nerves were still of a fragile nature, it turned out that running a restaurant was the one adventure that didn't cause her to worry. Not too much, anyway. She rarely fainted anymore, at least. She even eased up on Frankie, who, incidentally, no longer minded being in the kitchen. Joan was with her, and soon enough Frankie came to realize that Daddy was right: the kitchen was the most important part of the restaurant, its heart and soul.

Dixie took Frankie and Joan to and from the restaurant most days, and she put on a show for customers every now and then—dividing numbers or saying her prayers—in front of the restaurant, when she felt like it. When she didn't . . . well, you know. Bismarck got in on the act, too. Frankie hooked up a wagon to him and he traveled the alleys—on his own, mind you—through town to pick up potatoes or anything else the kitchen was running low on. That dog developed a special fondness for Mr. Stannum, of all people, and was by his side most days when he wasn't hitched up to his wagon or asleep in Daddy's old office. And speaking of Mr. Stannum, his heart, now that he'd found it again, was working just fine. He actually smiled once or twice, though he didn't like anyone to see, and hardly ever yelled at Amy or Mr. Washington or Seaweed, and never fired them again.

As for Seaweed, Frankie finally made good on their deal. She convinced Mother to let Seaweed and his band play two nights a week after the dinner rush. Frankie and Joan tried to get him to play something that wasn't so full of gloom, and he obliged them . . . sometimes. But mostly he stuck to the blues, and that was all right. His music took them all to a place that they knew and once shared, rekindling the memory of Daddy, and somehow by the end of the evening they felt a little better.

Been gone so long, I said you've been gone too long
Doggone, there ain't nothing to do but cry
Been worryin' so long, I said you've been worryin' too long
Well, see here, girl, there's that look again in your eye

Beyond all that, there was only one thing left to resolve: Frankie and Joan's wager. They had both forgotten about it, to tell the truth, until one evening as they were snapping beans in the kitchen. The air had turned cool and Amy opened one of the windows in the kitchen, allowing a most pleasant breeze to drift inside. Frankie just happened to be telling Joan the story of the millions of chicken feathers, and was laughing when she recounted how Daddy and Mr.

Stannum looked with feathers in their hair. Which prompted Joan to say, "You owe me ten cents."

"I do not," insisted Frankie, tossing her bowl of beans into a colander.

"Do too," said Joan. "You swore you wouldn't have any fun."

"I didn't," said Frankie, thinking back on everything that had happened over the summer. But then she ended with a grin, "Not much, anyway."

The summer was long over, but there were still days she'd wake up and forget that Daddy was gone. There was so much of him in the restaurant, sometimes she expected to see him walk into the kitchen and check on food orders. Or put his arm around her shoulder. Sometimes she swore she even heard his voice through the heat register. Heard him call her name, telling her to look at the whole sky, not just the piece she could see out her window.

"Do you see it, Frankie?"

She would answer, "I think I do, Daddy." For now it seemed to Frankie that the sky got bigger every day.

And that, let me tell you, is just what it does.

Author's Note

A *TINY PIECE OF Sky* is a work of fiction, but the Baums' story is inspired by the real-life experiences of Albert A. Beck in Hagerstown, Maryland, prior to the second World War. Albert and his wife, Mildred, built and ran Beck's Tavern and Restaurant on North Jonathan Street beginning in the late 1920s. The restaurant was billed as an "Eating Place of Wide Renown," enjoying much success and popularity until the business was sold in 1965. Albert and Mildred were my grandparents.

Beck's Restaurant had two dining rooms along with a lunch counter and bar, and as written in this novel, customers were entertained every evening by a Hammond electric organ and on many weekends by the Jack Frost Orchestra, led by George Maurice "Jack" Frost. Just as in the story, Beck's Restaurant was situated on the edge of Jonathan Street—the three blocks in Hagerstown that are an historically African American neighborhood and the site of the first African American churches, city homes, and businesses in Washington County.

Albert Beck was born in 1890 in Jefferson, Missouri, to German parents. He married Mildred Newman in 1927, and they had three daughters: Mildred, MaryAnn, and Patricia. My mother—Patricia— often told me stories about how she was teased as a young girl, in the late 1930s and early 1940s, when classmates at school discovered that her father was of German descent. I grew up hearing stories of her family's restaurant; about rumors of spying; about how *German* was a dirty word back then; about Bismarck, their dog, and Dixie, their pony. Bismarck was, in fact, a real dog—a German shepherd— who would often carry bags of potatoes and other restaurant items in his teeth from Beck's to the other restaurant Albert owned across town, The Arcade. Dixie, too, was a real pony. Although the real Dixie wasn't a former rodeo star, she could perform many tricks, including counting and saying her prayers.

Although Frankie, Joan, and Elizabeth, as well as Hermann and Mildred Baum, are inspired by real people and grounded in real world events, these characters—and all of the other characters in this novel—and their situations are products of my own imagination.

I began thinking about writing this book long ago, after my grandmother died. We were cleaning out her apartment and found letters in a drawer addressed to Albert Beck from several civic organizations about the rumors of espionage. These letters were all dated January 1938, incidentally, well before the war began in Europe. When I read them, I knew then that this was a story I needed to write. Because those letters were, for me, where the story began, I chose to include them in this book exactly as they were written.

One other piece of history included in this story is the episode of *The Shadow* that Frankie listens to with her grandmother. I did take liberties with its air date, though. That particular episode aired in December of 1938.

Albert Beck died a few years after the boycott, not a few *weeks* after, as written in this novel. But after his death, my grandmother, with the help of her three daughters, continued to run the business and watched it truly become what Albert hoped it would be—an eating place of wide renown.

Acknowledgments

For me, writing is often a long journey, through places that are sometimes pleasant and sometimes dark and terrible. It's while in those dark and terrible places that I am most grateful for the light-keepers who helped show me the way out of the woods: Patricia Beard, Heidi Potterfield, Erin Loomis, Elisabeth Dahl, Elissa Brent Weissman, Carol Lynch Williams, Cynthia Leitich Smith, Greg Leitich Smith, and Annemarie O'Brien.

Thanks to Jill Santopolo, my incomparable editor, who pointed me in the right direction, handed me the map, and made sure I didn't get lost. Thanks also to Talia Benamy and everyone else at Philomel who had a hand in shepherding this book along the way.

My agent, Sarah Davies, believed I could find my way if I told a story from my heart. Thank you, Sarah.

At the beginning of the road were Vermont College of Fine Arts faculty and students who saw early drafts of this book and gave me a pat on the head and told me to keep going, even when my feet were tired: Tim Wynne-Jones, Alan Cumyn, Ellen Howard, Gene Brenek, and Allyson Valentine-Schrier.

Thanks to Nancy Pope, curator and historian at the National Postal Museum, the Smithsonian Institution, for helping me figure out how long it would take for letters from Hagerstown to arrive in York, Pennsylvania, in 1939. Several days, as it turns out. Gratitude also goes to Dan Letchworth, copy editor supreme, for correcting all my mistakes and then some. Great snakes, you are dee-vine.

My family went on their own journey down memory lane as

I wrote this book, whether they wanted to or not, and graciously answered my many, many questions about their life in the 1930s, about my grandparents, and about that little place called Beck's: my mom, MaryAnn and Big Paul Mundey, Millie Heinbaugh, Charles Heinbaugh, and Shirley Shirey. For that, I am indebted.

And speaking of family, I would not have been able to write even one single word of this book if it weren't for the lives of Mildred and Albert A. Beck and that wonderful restaurant they ran for so many years.

Most especially, thank you to my husband, Andy, and my daughter, Opal, for love. What a journey this has turned out to be.